William McIntyre is a Scots lawyer, specialising in criminal defence. William has been instructed in many interesting and high-profile cases over the years and now turns fact into fiction with his string of legal thrillers, The Best Defence Series, featuring defence lawyer, Robbie Munro.

The books, which are stand alone or can be read in series, have been well received by many fellow professionals, on both sides of the Bar, due to their accuracy in law and procedure and Robbie's frank, if sardonic, view on the idiosyncrasies of the Scots criminal justice system.

William is married with four sons.

More in the Best Defence series:

Relatively Guilty

Sharp Practice

Killer Contract

Crime Fiction

Last Will

Present Tense

Good News, Bad News

Stitch Up

Fixed Odds

Bad Debt

Best Defence

How Come?

Duty MAN

Second in the Best Defence Series

William McIntyre

www.bestdefence.biz
wm@bestdefence.biz

Paperback ISBN 978-1-9998133-4-5

In memory of my dad. A man less like Alex Munro it is impossible to imagine. He thought this the best book in the series, perhaps because it's the shortest. I don't know, because that's the kind of man he was. He never criticised, only encouraged.

CHAPTER 1

'That was quick.' The custody sergeant stabbed my details, one-fingered, into the computer. 'Didn't expect to see you this early on a Sunday morning.'

It was true. A two-cop bop and a police assault didn't normally have me leaping nimbly out of bed in the middle of the night, but I couldn't sleep: too much on my mind and too little in my bank account.

Clipboard in hand, the sergeant climbed down from his seat and led me along a narrow corridor where shoes and belts were neatly stacked outside a row of heavy iron doors.

'Oskaras Vidmantis Salavejus,' he read slowly from the charge sheet. 'Lithuanian, apparently.' We came to a halt outside one of the doors. 'Seems he took a sudden dislike to our Inspector Fleming.' The sergeant produced a bunch of keys. 'Out for a quiet curry, Friday night, next thing he knows your client's getting torn into him.' He handed me the charge sheet. 'Speaks English, or maybe that's only when he's pished.' He unlocked the door and held it open. It started to close as I walked in. I put out a hand.

'Leave it, will you?'

'He's a jaikie, he'll not kill you.'

I was more worried about the smell killing me than the prisoner.

'Don't worry,' I said, 'I'll not let him escape.'

'Aye,' said the turnkey, 'I know how much you Legal Aid fat cats hate to see a fee run out the door.'

I stepped inside and the stench hit me. Just who was the person with the bright idea to design cells with cludgies that flushed from outside? Did some over-cautious architect foresee problems with prisoners trying to launch themselves to freedom via the plumbing system? 'Well at least pull the plug. This place is honking.'

There came the sound of running water and the custody sergeant put his head in the doorway. 'You will let me know if there's anything else.'

The door slammed shut. I kicked the plastic mattress on which the prisoner was stretched and elicited no response. I could have given him a shake, but that would have involved using a hand, so I kicked again, harder. The dishevelled figure peeled his face from the mattress. He was tall and slim with a good head of black hair and high cheekbones. He reminded me of an upper-class bounder in a second-rate period drama. He sat up, yawned, rubbed the palm of his hand from greasy forehead to square, stubbly-chin and stared at me through bleary, blood-shot eyes.

'Who are you?' he asked, with no hint of an accent.

I backed away from his zombie-breath. 'Robbie Munro - duty agent.' He took the charge sheet in shaky hands, squinted at the page, screwed it up and tossed it aside. It hit the wall, bounced twice on the shiny linoleum floor and skidded into a corner.

'I'll take that as a not guilty,' I said.

The prisoner flopped back onto the mattress. Consultation over, I picked up the ball of crumpled paper and dropped it into my jacket pocket. 'Well then... see you in court.'

I banged on the cell door. There'd been a shift-change and a new custody sergeant, young and bristling with customer service qualifications, took me back to the front desk.

'That you finished?' he asked.

'You tell me. Anyone else want the duty man?'

He went around the counter, jumped up on the high stool and consulted the screen.

'Nope. Looks like it's been dead quiet tonight.' He dismounted and snatched a set of keys from the desk. The phone bleeped and he answered. 'On second thoughts you might want to stay,' he said, replacing the receiver. 'That was a call about Mr Abercrombie.'

Was he talking about Max?

'The lawyer at the end of the High Street. Did you know him?'

He was talking about Max - and in the past tense. Cold fear distilled in the pit of my stomach. Max Abercrombie was an old friend.

The young cop must have noticed the blood drain from my face. He looked embarrassed. 'I'm sorry. I've just started my shift and it's on the screen here. I thought you'd have heard. Mr Abercrombie was murdered - Friday night. They've got someone already and they're bringing him in right now. He'll need a brief and seeing how you're the duty...'

'No.' I placed a hand on the counter to steady myself. 'I'm sorry, I can't.'

CHAPTER 2

I took my feet off the desk, ripped January from the calendar and filed it in the bin. The first Monday in February: the worst day in the week of the worst month in the year.

Rain pattered against the window. I went over and looked out at The Royal Burgh of Linlithgow. Why had I even bothered to come back?

When I'd first qualified I couldn't wait to leave the town of my birth. Clutching law degree and tatty black gown, I'd set out into the big bad world of criminal defence, and over the years had not done too badly, subsisting on Legal Aid fees and tucking away the brown envelopes. Then, hurtling into my thirties, I'd left my employment with Glasgow lawyers Caldwell & Clark, Tyrannosaurus Rex in the world of legal dinosaurs, following a difference of opinions: I wanted me to stay, they didn't.

Cast out but with a reasonable bundle in the shoe box under my bed, I'd decided it was time to take stock, prepare for the future. It was late 2007, property prices were soaring and I wanted a piece of the action.

'Bank stocks,' Stephen, my new bestest friend and IFA, had said. 'RBS. It's the bluest of chips, been around for three centuries and safe as the houses they lend on.' Apparently there was a revolution happening. China, India, Africa, the whole world was building houses, offices, hotels, and they had to borrow the money somewhere. 'In a gold rush,' opined Stephen, who preferred to be called Steff, 'you don't invest in the mines or the miners: you invest in the guys who supply the shovels.'

A year later and I was chasing after Steff with a shovel and setting fire to RBS share certificates to keep warm. I don't know why he hadn't just pointed a gun in my face; the whole financial disaster thing couldn't have come as any more of a surprise.

So I'd gone home to West Lothian and after a pretty good start found myself teetering on the brink of bankruptcy; mainly thanks to the introduction of the Procurator Fiscal fines and Police penalty notices that had taken away half of my workload along with the presumption of innocence.

Now Max had gone and got himself murdered.

I couldn't stop thinking about my friend. We'd gone to school together, studied law together and whereas I'd escaped my small town ties, he'd stayed and put a brass name plate on his door. Though we'd once been close, time had taken its toll on our friendship. Latterly, we'd kept in touch sporadically. I tried to remember - when was the last time we'd gone out for a drink? What had we talked about? Work probably and mine most likely. That was the thing about criminal law, always something interesting to talk about: crazy clients, stupid Sheriffs, amusing courtroom incidents; there weren't too many laughs in Max's world of residential conveyancing and commercial leases.

Grace-Mary came through clad in green cardigan and tartan skirt, a pair of spectacles hanging on a gold chain about her neck. She was carrying the court diary.

'You all right?' she asked, placing two fingers under my chin, raising my face for closer inspection. 'No you're not. Look at the state of you. Why don't you go home?'

I dismissed my secretary's concerns with a wave of my hand. She sighed loudly, backed off and opened the diary while I lifted my briefcase onto the desk ready to start filling it with files. A morning in court might help take my mind off Max.

Grace-Mary lifted the spectacles from her bosom and perched them on the end of a serious nose.

'Look,' she said, shoving the diary at me. 'There's only a few cited cases. Most of them are road traffic or shoplifting. It's all mince. Send Andy. It'll keep him from getting under my feet.'

'I've picked up a duty client as well,' I told her 'Some foreign guy.'

'What is it? A not guilty plea?' She knew me so well. 'Andy can take care of that.'

Andy Imray hadn't been with me for that long, just long enough for Grace-Mary to have taken him under her wing. He'd served a year of his traineeship up north with a rural practice before moving south for court experience. Now in his second year, officially admitted as a solicitor and with a restricted practising certificate burning a hole in his pocket, my assistant was keen to get into court and strut his stuff. I'd let him have a few run outs in the JP court where he couldn't do much damage but on his one or two trips to the Sheriff court he'd tended to fare less well and I had my new Firm's reputation to think about.

'I thought you wanted the desks in here re-arranged? I'll ask Andy to help you.'

'Away. Have you felt the weight of them?'

'Not lately, 'I said.

'Well they're very heavy. You don't want the boy to strain something do you?'

I'd never noticed my assistant straining himself in any other aspect of his working life. 'Andy's not ready for Sheriff Court work.'

'Oh, go on.' She looked at me beseechingly over the top of her specs. 'I caught him trying on the spare gown again yesterday. He's dying to be let loose on a jury. Do you know he's even drafted an outline for a closing speech?'

No doubt all about scales and the golden thread of justice. The only thread of justice I knew was the one the cops used to stitch people up with.

'War is sweet to those who have never tasted it,' I said.

'And don't quote me any more Homer...'

'Pindar,' I corrected my secretary; there was a first time for everything. Leaning back in my chair, I was about to hold forth on the greatest of the nine lyric poets of ancient Greece, when Andy walked in. Caucasian, male, twenty-four, five feet seven, stocky build, with wavy black hair and dark square-framed spectacles; that's what his police description would have said.

Easier to imagine a vertically compressed photo-fit of Buddy Holly. He was carrying a steaming mug.

The reception phone rang and Grace-Mary went to answer it. Andy set the mug down on the desk in front of me. 'Another day in the fight for truth and justice eh, Robbie?'

I gave him a sideways look. If truth and justice won too often I'd be out of business. I sipped and almost choked. 'Instant?' With age comes the realisation that life is too short for instant coffee.

'Unscrew your face and don't be so precious,' he retorted - a little too cheekily for the hired help I couldn't but think. In my traineeship days the next thing you'd hear after back-chatting the boss was the sound of your arse skidding to a halt on the pavement. I let it pass.

'I'm going down to Sandy's for a real coffee,' I said, tipping the contents of the mug into a pot that was the final resting-place of a desiccated umbrella plant. 'How about you, Grace-Mary?' I shouted through to reception. 'Want anything from Sandy's?' She didn't. She was like one of those desert plants, surviving only on fresh air – and, perhaps, the occasional light misting of gin.

Andy cleared his throat. 'While you're there...'

'Bacon roll, extra-crispy, plenty of brown sauce?'

He smiled. Cheeky, perhaps, but in choice of employer and matters of haute cuisine the lad definitely had taste.

CHAPTER 3

Alessandro Cabrini owned the café at the end of the block. His father and his father before him had run the place as a proper chippy, but Alessandro who'd worked behind the counter since he was knee-high to a pizza supper, had bigger and better plans for his inheritance. No sooner had title to the shop been transferred, than he'd acquired the dry cleaner's next door and knocked through to form the eating establishment that he liked to call Bistro Alessandro and everyone else in the town knew as Sandy's.

As I approached the café, a white van screeched to a halt and double-parked, engine running, on the opposite side of the road. Three men got out. I was something of a creature of habit and so I guessed they had been driving up and down the High Street, waiting for me to show.

The smallest of the trio was Jake Turpie. Pure evil distilled, poured into an oil-stained boiler suit and walking about in steel toe-capped boots. Jake owned the local scrapyard. He also owned my office premises for which he'd seen no rent recently. The fact that he was taking the trouble to seek me out did not bode well.

'Robbie!' he called, from across the street. 'A word.'

I feigned deafness and walked faster, hoping to reach the café before I was forced to acknowledge his presence.

'Hey, baw heid!' he called again, as I went to open the door.

Ignoring him and walking straight ahead into the relative safety of Sandy's café was not an option. Jake would have seen it as a sign of weakness, and the one thing you didn't show a pit-bull like Jake was fear.

I turned to face him. The two men either side were much taller, but Jake needed minders like Snow White needed another dwarf. One of the bookends, I recognised: Deek Pudney, a brute of a man who'd worked with Jake for years. The other was much younger, Deek's apprentice, tall and well-built, with a prematurely receding hairline and bad skin.

'Jake. How's it going?' I asked, like I was interested in the answer.

He frowned, which was not necessarily a bad sign. Unpleasant things happened to people when Jake smiled; or at least he smiled when he happened to do unpleasant things to people.

'I was going to ask you the same thing,' he growled, 'but business can't be good because you're late with the rent and you know how I like punctuation when it comes to matters of finance.' He meant punctuality. But one big word was as good as another to his two cauliflower-eared pals and I wasn't about to get picky with his vocabulary. 'I've never had a bolt out of you for three month.'

'Sorry about that, Jake. Give me a couple of weeks and I should have most of it.'

'No. I want it now – the lot.'

I switched smoothly into plea-in-mitigation mode. 'Come on, Jake. Things have been a bit slow. What I need is a crime wave. There's hardly been a ripple lately.' I laughed; he didn't; I tried again. 'Look, I'm doing okay. Honest. The future's bright for Munro & Co., it's just that the Legal Aid payments aren't coming through right now.' I wasn't lying. The Legal Aid cheque was late as always. End of the financial year and the annual budget had been reached. The idea that the Legal Aid bill might actually go up always took the Scottish Government by surprise like the Council gritters at the first frost of winter. Jake gestured to the van.

'Let's go, Robbie. We can talk about this back at the yard.'

Conversations with Jake about anything, but especially money, were best done in broad daylight with plenty of witnesses. Talking, Jake could do over the phone. Giving me a Molegrip manicure required a more private and personal touch.

'Can we do this some other time?' I said, trying hard to sound casual, as though I believed a friendly chat was all he had in mind. 'I've got court in half an hour. Catch you later, eh?' I made for the café door. Deek, grinning like a slashed tyre, stepped forward, blocking the way. I turned around and faced Jake again, giving him my best smile. 'Listen, Jake. Sorry about the rent. Give me two weeks and I'll square you up and maybe bung you a month in advance – how's that sound?'

He mulled that suggestion over for point five of a second. 'No, let's do this now.'

I had to remain calm. Talking was what I was supposed to be good at; defending the indefensible, though persuading a jury to find a reasonable doubt was one thing, trying to talk a very unreasonable man like Jake Turpie out of force-feeding me light bulbs, quite another. I took a deep breath. The future was looking less bright and a lot more painful by the second. Jake strode towards the van. His two henchmen took a grip of me and were ready to follow when a silhouette formed in the café door. I didn't recognise it straight away, distorted as it was by frosted glass and the passage of time. The door opened, the silhouette materialised and onto the pavement stepped Frankie McPhee: gangster, racketeer and former generous contributor to the Robbie Munro pension fund and bar bill.

'Hello Robbie,' he said, apparently oblivious to the goons either side of me. 'They said I might find you here.' I had no idea who 'they' were but I thanked them from the bottom of my heart. Frankie continued: 'I've a piece of business I'd like to run past you. Got a minute?'

'I'm not sure...' I said, looking at each of Jake's men in turn, in case Frankie hadn't noticed I had company.

'Your friends won't mind me dragging you away,' he said, with a smile that could have set a jelly.

'Come on!' yelled Jake from the middle of the road.

Deek let go my arm.

'What you doing?' asked the young apprentice, still holding my left wrist.

'I'm going.'

'What d'ye mean?'

Deek elaborated. 'I'm leaving.'

'But…'

Deek grabbed his young colleague by the collar and pulled him aside. The boy had kept a grip of my arm and I stumbled after them. 'D'ye know who that is?' By his gormless expression the youngster didn't. Deek enlightened him. 'Frankie McPhee - that's who.'

Frankie smoothed the rough edge off a fingernail.

The big lad looked from Frankie back to Deek then over to the van where his boss was beginning to lose it. 'But what about Jake?'

There were cars queuing up in the road behind the van. Jake reached in through the driver's window and hammered on the horn.

Deek let out an exasperated sigh. 'Jake who?'

The young man had the look of a Jesuit being preached heresy. His grip on me slackened.

'You pair, get him over here now!' Jake exploded at his mutinous helpers.

Deek didn't even glance in his boss's direction. Instead, he spoke to the young man whose hold on me was now so weak that I could easily have broken free. He talked slowly and quietly as though explaining to a two-year-old child that poking one's sticky little fingers through the bars of the electric fire wasn't such a good idea. 'Trust me on this, son. Just take a walk.'

Frankie held the café door open for me. The hand on my left arm fell away.

'Catch you later!' I called over to Jake. Much later I hoped.

11

CHAPTER 4

We sat down at a corner table. Sandy arrived tossing a damp cloth from one hand to the other and took our order before disappearing through the back to perform whatever arcane rites conjured up the best bacon rolls and coffee in town.

I looked Frankie up and down and didn't let myself be taken in by the dark suit, freshly-ironed white shirt and sombre tie, not even by the big leather Bible that protruded from his jacket pocket. Perhaps prison did work, but for the likes of Frankie McPhee? I doubted it. Still, I was happy enough to see my former client. Not only had he saved me, momentarily a least, from the wrath of Jake, but back in the good old, bad old days, before he'd been, as the tabloids put it, caged, Frankie had been a main tributary of my revenue stream. Whenever one of his boys was huckled I got the call, and the very fact that I was Frankie McPhee's brief was a magnet that attracted a lot of high-quality, low-life business; however, the feature that endeared Frankie most to my heart was his habit of paying fees in cash. The man shed brown envelopes like an oak tree dropped acorns in autumn and part of me, the part that worried about the overdraft and angry landlords, hoped the rumours of his rehabilitation were exaggerated.

We made small talk until Sandy returned to set before us two mugs of coffee and a plate of rolls. Andy would have to wait for his. I hadn't eaten since hearing the news about Max and my teeth were itching to sink into a bacon roll. Sandy handed me the bill and his lips tightened into a charade of a smile. I knew what was coming.

'And how will you be paying?'

I was disappointed in him: embarrassing me this way. We had an understanding: I ran up a tab and… well… actually that was about it. I was mentally dusting down the legal aid cheque story when Frankie took the bill from my hand and put it in his top pocket.

'I'll be paying - with cash – when we're finished.'

Sandy opened his mouth to speak and then thought better of it. Something about Frankie hadn't changed - he never had a lot to say but when he spoke people generally listened.

'What brings you to the Royal Burgh?' I asked, after the café owner had sounded his retreat.

'Do you remember Chic Kelly?'

Chic Kelly: another man I hadn't heard of in a while. I had acted for him on a few occasions long time past and with limited success as I recalled. Chic was someone who enjoyed the good things in life - it was just unfortunate they always seemed to belong to other people. As a housebreaker, it had to be said, he'd been a real class act. He could break into a property faster than most people could break open a packet of fags and was as quiet as a snake in slippers. The only trouble was he kept getting nicked. One minute he'd pull off an audacious break-in, the next he'd get huckled in the pub or the bookies spending the loot. But it was not because of his undoubted talent for burglary that Chic Kelly would be remembered.

'Got done for killing that judge a few years back,' Frankie said. 'Remember?'

Of course I did. Who didn't? Though it had been much more than a few years ago that Lord James Hewitt of Muthill, the then Lord Justice-Clerk, had been blown away in the drawing room of his Perthshire mansion. A reward of twenty-five thousand pounds had been put up by the Justice Minister for information leading to the conviction of the killer, but the SOCOs hadn't got all the judicial brain-matter out of the Axminster, before Chic Kelly had been nabbed trying to sell the murder weapon: the judge's antique shotgun, covered in his fingerprints and liberally sprayed with judicial blood. Chic eventually confessed to the crime and soon the new Lord Justice Clerk was waving him off on a life sentence with no hope of parole this side of the grave.

'There was some mention of it in legal circles,' I conceded.

'Well,' Frankie said, 'his boy is up for murder too.'

'Like father like son?'

'More than you think.'

'I don't recall any High Court judges being bumped-off recently,' I said, unable to resist drawing up a mental wish list of candidates.

Frankie shook his head. 'Not a judge. A solicitor.'

I didn't like the way the conversation was headed. 'You mean Max Abercrombie?'

Frankie nodded. 'Chic's an old pal and I know the boy's mum from way back. I was talking to her the other day and said I'd look out for him.'

'Nice of you.'

'He needs a lawyer.'

'Hope he finds one – a bad one.'

I got up from my seat. Frankie tugged at my arm. 'Sit. Hear me out.'

'Sandy!'

The cafe-owner came out from behind the counter and over to our table, keeping a wary eye on Frankie. I handed him my mug of coffee. 'Put that in a paper cup will you? I've got to go.'

Sandy looked down at the untouched plate of rolls. 'You want these in a bag?'

'No,' I said. 'I'm not hungry.'

Linlithgow Sheriff Court, I'd miss the old building when it closed later in the year. Outside the entrance door a plaque was fixed to the wall in remembrance of James Stuart, first Earl of Moray, illegitimate son of King James V, half-brother of Mary Queen of Scots, shot dead as he rode down Linlithgow High Street one bright morning in 1570: the first ever recorded assassination by use of a firearm.

As far as I knew, no-one else had been shot dead in Linlithgow since; that is until Max Abercrombie was gunned down in his office just a few hundred yards from that historical locus.

The rain was lashing down as, using my gown as an umbrella, I ran into the court, past the crones who lurked inside the main door, huddled around an urn, touting hot drinks in the name of charity. In the new place I suspected they'd be replaced by a vending machine inflicting even more villainous brews upon the general public.

My plan that morning was to deal with the few routine cases I had as quickly as possible, then leave and not even think about the man who sat in a cell outside Court 2 awaiting service of a murder Petition. I expected his case would call after the rest of the weekend custodies, including my new foreign friend, had been processed. I had no intention of sticking around that long.

At the top of the staircase I was met by the court's security system: a door with a number lock, the code for which any court official was happy to divulge, presumably on the basis that terrorists intent on sabotage of the criminal justice system wouldn't be cunning enough to dress smartly or carry a black gown.

I pressed the little silver buttons and walked past the shrieval chambers into the agents' library, a large square room with a long table, some chairs, some out-of-date text books and some even more out-of-date lawyers. I hung up my coat. The cold reception was nothing unusual. Linlithgow's motto: 'Be Kind To Strangers' didn't seem to apply to me as the majority of the local Criminal Bar had not taken kindly to my arriving in their midst a year or so previously. To them I'd always be unwanted competition; an increase in the number of defence agents chasing a decreasing number of Legal Aid certificates.

I had emptied my bag of files before anyone spoke.

'Robbie!' Lorna Wylie, the only female in the otherwise male-dominated criminal bar, was a sign-them-up-plead-them-out kind of a girl. 'How are you?' She came over and gave me a hug. 'I heard about Max. Didn't expect to see you today.' She put her hands on my shoulders and looked me in the eye. 'Is there anything I can do?' Her sympathy was delivered with all the sincerity of an undertaker's get-well card. I played along.

'Thanks, I'm fine.' I put on my gown while Lorna went over to check her reflection in the glass of one of the bookcase doors. Once she'd freshened-up her lippy and run a hand through her hair, she sidled over to me again. I knew the others were listening.

'You're the duty man and this guy they've arrested – Kelly - are you...?'

'No.'

'Who is?'

'No idea.'

'But it's definitely not you? You're not acting?'

'That's right.'

'Actually, that's wrong,' said a familiarly annoying voice. I turned to see Hugh Ogilvie, Procurator Fiscal standing in the doorway all teeth, no hair and holding a thin red file of papers. Ogilvie was a career prosecutor. A man on a mission. A man who liked to do things his own way – providing it was all right with his superiors at Crown Office. 'I'm calling Kelly early. The police think he might gather a crowd and they've asked me to bring the case forward. He'll be going through on Petition, Court two, just as soon as he's seen a solicitor.'

'Help yourself,' I said. 'There's a whole roomful here.'

'I'm the alternative duty agent.' Lorna stepped forward ready, willing, if not particularly able.

Ogilvie ignored her. 'He hasn't named a solicitor which means it's down to the actual duty agent.'

The duty agent scheme was set up by the Scottish Legal Aid Board and staffed by local solicitors to provide legal representation for persons in custody who had no access to a lawyer, either because they couldn't afford one or didn't know whom to contact. It operated on a weekly rota basis and could be a lot of bother for little reward. The only thing that made it all worthwhile was the occasional opportunity to pick up something juicy amidst all the drink drivers, shop-lifting junkies and wife-beaters. Under normal circumstances I'd have been delighted with a murder.

'Forget it,' I told him.

'I don't think you mean that,' said Ogilvie. 'I took the liberty of calling SLAB. They said you can't pick and choose.' He sniggered. 'I suppose that's why it's called the duty scheme. You're the duty man this week and, apparently, if you don't act you're off the list.'

I couldn't afford to come off the duty list. As a newcomer I'd been lucky to squeeze my way on in the first place. Although something of a lottery, the two or three duty weeks allocated to each solicitor per year could be a good source of new business.

'Okay,' I said, hating myself. 'But I'm just putting him through; someone else can do the full committal next week.'

'I'll be duty agent next week,' Lorna reminded us.

'Then he's all yours,' I told her.

'I really don't care,' said Ogilvie. 'Just so long as the scumbag is represented and can't go whining to the Appeal Court when he gets what's coming to him.' He did an about turn. 'Court Two in ten minutes – be there.'

17

CHAPTER 6

I met briefly with the accused in an interview room adjacent to the cell block. His name was Sean Kelly and he was nineteen years old. That was as much as I wanted to know about the person charged with murdering my friend. I didn't even want to look at him. I explained briefly what was going to happen and accepted the papers he shoved under the screen at me.

'Thanks,' he said, when I got up to leave.

I didn't reply. The only thing the wee shit had to be thankful for was the sheet of Perspex between us.

I made my way into court. The proceedings would be in private, just myself, the P.F., the Sheriff and Sheriff Clerk would be present along with a couple of court security guards either side of the prisoner and a token cop.

Any serious charge like murder always started off with a Petition from the Procurator Fiscal requesting that the accused be remanded in custody for a week while the prosecution made further enquiries. After the 'seven day lie-down', as it was known, the accused returned to court to be fully committed for trial. Bail was now permitted on a murder charge, thanks to the European Convention of Human Rights; however, if refused, the accused was remanded in custody and the Crown had eighty days in which to serve an indictment and one-hundred and forty to bring the matter to trial in the High Court.

I'd taken a seat in the well of the court opposite Hugh Ogilvie when the Sheriff came onto the bench. I didn't recognise him. Some out of town floater brought in to take the case lest there be any accusations of bias.

Almost immediately the accused was escorted into the dock and once he'd been identified, I rose to my feet.

'Mr Kelly makes no plea or declaration,' I said.

At such an early stage in proceedings the accused wasn't asked to plead guilty or not guilty. The lack of 'plea' I was referring to was any legal challenge there might be to the competency or relevancy of the charge set out in the Petition and they didn't come much more competent or relevant than a murder charge.

'I'm moving to continue for further enquiries M'Lord,' Ogilvie said.

'Any further motions?' the Sheriff enquired.

There was no point in asking for bail. Even if, by some miracle, it was granted, the PF would appeal; meaning my client, I hated to think of him as that, being be locked up in any event, awaiting a decision from the High Court. That would take the best part of a week, so I thought it simpler all round if he did a lie-down and tried for bail at the full committal hearing next week. By then he'd be someone else's problem; Lorna Wylie's problem. With her as his lawyer the lad wouldn't be going anywhere for a while.

CHAPTER 7

After court I returned to the office and found, somewhere under the awaiting pile of paperwork, a yellow-sticky from Grace-Mary. I was to return a call to Max. According to the note he'd phoned Friday afternoon, the day he was murdered. Probably to arrange a lunch or more likely to pass me some business. I must have over-looked the message amidst the usual Friday afternoon mayhem; either that or I'd just ignored it. Some friend I was.

I didn't go out the rest of the day. Occasionally, Grace-Mary came back and forth with files and telephone messages, but no clients came in and no calls were put through to me. For that whole afternoon my secretary didn't once bring up the firm's cash-flow crisis, the faulty central heating or even the leaky cistern in the toilet. She just left me alone, sitting at my desk, staring into space, thinking about Max and how you don't know what you've got 'til it's gone.

The rain clouds had cleared and a slice of new moon had risen in a star-sprinkled sky when I left the office that evening. As I started off on my walk home I became aware of a kerb-crawling car; a beat-up crate with patches of rust along the sills and a hoarse sounding exhaust. It stopped at the kerb a few yards ahead of me. The front passenger door opened. Frankie McPhee got out. He opened the back door. 'Want a hurl?'

'No thanks, I've not far to go,' I said, wondering why he was even still in the area.

'I was hoping we could talk.'

'Not if it's about the same subject as before.' I started to walk away.

Frankie stepped in front of me, blocking my path. 'I don't want to know any confidential information. Just a quick chat so I can tell the lad's mum that he's doing all right. Five minutes of your time. Is that too much to ask?' He removed his wallet. 'Call it a consultation. How much do you charge for one-twelfth of an hour?'

He was persistent, I'd give him that. I climbed into the back of the car and Frankie got in beside me. He leaned forward and slapped the driver on one of his broad shoulders. 'You know Jo-Jo don't you, Robbie?'

I knew him all right. Jo-Jo Johnstone: a good man with a machete.

The man in the driver's seat tilted his head back. 'Hello, Mr Munro.'

'Jo-Jo shared a cell with me at Shotts,' Frankie said. 'I'm running a soup kitchen now – giving something back into the community. Jo-Jo's helping out. I've not got him converted yet but let's say he's God's work in progress.'

Jo-Jo carefully adjusted the rear view mirror, indicated and, after an age, released the handbrake before moving off slowly into traffic. He drove like an old lady. Either that or his banger of a car wouldn't go any faster.

'First of all I want to say thanks,' Frankie said. 'You know for taking on Sean's case today.'

'I hate to burst your bubble,' I told him, 'but I've not changed my mind. I had to do his first appearance because I'm duty agent. I've done it and next week someone else will be taking over.'

'There's no need for that. Keep the case and I'll pay your fee,' Frankie said. 'Not legal aid - proper money.'

We'd already had this conversation. I poked the back of Jo-Jo's neck. 'Stop the car.'

He glanced over his shoulder at Frankie who nodded reluctantly. Jo-Jo mirror, signalled and manoeuvred in slow motion and pulled into the side of the road.

I seized the door handle. The door wouldn't open. 'Is the child lock on?'

'Naw, Mr Munro,' Jo-Jo said. 'It's just a wee bit stiff. You'll need to give it a dunt.'

'I'll get it,' said Frankie.

He got out of his side of the car, came around and yanked open the door.

'Thanks for the lift,' I said as I went to walk away.

Frankie grabbed my arm. 'Robbie…'

I pulled away. 'No.'

He took my arm again. 'I know Max Abercrombie was a friend of yours and I know how you must feel.'

'No, Frankie, I don't think you do.'

'The boy's innocent.'

He seemed awfully sure about that.

Frankie put an arm around my shoulders. 'Meet him. Hear what he's got to say for himself. After that, if you still don't want to take the case, I'm gone. I'll not say another word. Promise.'

I shrugged him off. 'I'm sorry, Frankie, I can't. But, believe me, there are plenty other lawyers out there who will jump at the chance.'

Fifteen quid to wear someone else's shoes, put your fingers into holes where a million unwashed digits had gone before, all in an effort to knock over some skittles that would only stand themselves up again. It was my dad's idea. He was trying to help, I knew that, but the last thing I felt like was a fun night out.

I picked up three pints from the bar, placed them on a tray beside three packets of crisps and beat a path through the crowd, the soles of the blue and white bowling shoes sticking to the green nylon carpet each step of the way. At our lane I set out the drinks on a Formica ledge that ran along the top of the velour bench seats.

'Here you are boys,' I shouted, trying to make myself heard above Steelers Wheel and 'Stuck in the Middle with You.' If they played 'Chirpy-Chirpy, Cheep-Cheep' one more time I was going to cause a scene.

'Cheers,' said Vince, a wee barrel of a man and my dad's best mate. Clad in an arbitrary assortment of clothes, he looked like he'd jumped through a wardrobe with glue on his body. He finished typing our names into the computer then picked up one of the pint tumblers and peered at it through a pair of thick lenses. 'I've such a drouth on, I'll not swallow any. My tongue will just soak it up.'

I did what I could to dispel that particular mental image and raised a glass of ale to my lips; harshly fizzy with a faint hint of washing-up liquid.

'ALEX', flashed up on the overhead scoreboard.

My dad tore open a packet of crisps and looked inside. 'Crisps – a bloody expensive way of eating a tattie.'

'All set, Dad?' I asked, taking another mouthful of bowling-alley beer. 'Think you're up to it?'

He put down the crisps, raised his bulk and the springs in the bench on which his broad frame had been resting sighed with relief. My dad was the largest man in the place. He was the largest man most places. Early-sixties, he still had a decent amount of hair although much of it lay along his top lip. He selected a bright blue bowling ball, the heaviest available, polished the top with the cuff of his shirt sleeve and then, with took two quick strides, launched the blue sphere at the ten white pins. It had scarcely left his hand than there were skittles flying everywhere. A big red digital X flashed up on the overhead scoreboard. My dad brushed an imaginary speck of fluff from the shoulder of his shirt. 'We did say a fiver a game, didn't we?' He slapped Vince on the back, almost knocking him over. 'Come on wee man, you're up. Let's see you murder them.'

Murder. That word again. I didn't want the Kelly case, and no-one could blame me. Max was my friend. I closed my eyes and saw a pistol, fire erupting from the barrel, bullets pumping into Max's body. I opened my eyes quickly. I didn't want to think about it. Not that it was easy to think at all over the sound of laughter, tumbling skittles, trundling bowling bowls and seventies pop music. When I lifted the pint glass to my lips, my hand was shaking. I had to try and relax, put Max's murder out of my mind.

Vince man strode up to the mark. Though the wee man didn't have the power of his pal and the ball seemed to take an age to reach the skittles, he obviously knew what he was doing, scattering nine pins with his first shot and going back to pick off the straggler with a well-aimed second.

'Well done, Vince,' I said, and he shrugged with all the modesty he could muster.

My dad bit into a crisp, screwed up his face and glowered accusingly at the packet. 'Cheese and onion? In a blue packet?' He examined the small print on the back, presumably on the basis that there was some kind of breach of the Advertising Standards Code going on.

My turn. I hadn't bowled since birthday parties as a boy when there used to be inflatable bumpers down the side-gutters. I jammed my fingers into the holes and, hoping they'd come out again, took a few tottering steps, summoned up all my strength and chucked the ball down the lane. It arced through the air for several feet, landed with a thud, bounced, rolled and clipped the rearmost skittle on the left-hand side. Only nine to go.

'Taking out the hard one first? Good idea,' Vince said. 'By the way, is that what they call the bouncing bomb technique?' I could hear my dad, who had obviously recovered from his crisp-induced shock, chuckling in the background. I ignored the two of them and retrieved the same ball again as it fell from the conveyor belt. Taking a moment to gather myself, I tried to focus on the remaining pins. Skittles - how difficult could it be? I ran, skidded to a halt and released. This time the ball bounced twice and rolled into the right-hand gutter. I returned to the seats where Vince had removed his specs and was contorting his arthritic fingers into goggles while humming the theme from the Dam Busters.

My dad put an arm around me and squeezed tight. 'The boy's toying with us Vince. It's kind of him really: not wanting to show up a pair of geriatrics.' He gave me another squeeze. 'Whatever you do, don't get him riled.'

After the game we repaired to the adjacent Sports Bar, though going by the number of beer bellies in evidence the place didn't seem to attract many athletes. There was a free table between the big screen video jukebox and a bunch of eejits playing pool. Not far away, a man old enough to know better was blasting space aliens with what looked like a fluorescent green .44 Magnum. I tried not to think about guns or Max and instead forced myself to listen to Vince prattle on. He was over the moon at breaking a hundred and couldn't resist having another dig.

'Forty-two, Robbie? Well done. Maybe we should have got you riled. Who knows? You might have pulled out all the stops and scored forty-three.' He laughed so hard his glasses jiggled and threatened to fall off.

My dad put down his pint and wiped the froth from his moustache. 'Give the lad a break, Vince. It's not about winning or losing...' He took another drink of his beer. 'But that's a tenner the two of you owe me.'

'That'll be right,' I scoffed. 'You've drunk your winnings. Do you know the price of a pint in here?'

The old man shrugged. 'Ach, it's enough just to know that I'm better than you at something.'

I gave his moustache a pull. 'That's it. Next time we play? I use my good arm.'

Later, we jumped a taxi back to my dad's. On the way we dropped Vince off at his local where he had high hopes of catching last orders, so it was just the two of us.

My old man's house was small and neat and tidy, in a National Service sort of a way. I pulled up a chair by the fireside, stretched out and watched Billy the budgie head-butt his mirror and make the little bell ring. The bird had never spoken a word in its life and there was a standing joke that I had advised it of its right to remain silent.

I could hear my dad in the kitchen, rummaging in cupboards for drink and knew it would be whisky, but not the good stuff. The old boy was still smarting from Christmas when I made a Whisky Mac out of a 16-year-old Lagavulin. The thought of adulterating his precious Islay single malt with ice and a splash of Crabbie's green ginger had been almost too much for him to bear.

'And don't try to fob me off with any firewater,' I shouted through to him. 'I know there's an eighteen-year-old Bruichladdich hidden away somewhere. Your birthday wasn't that long ago.'

He came back with two glasses, a bottle of blended and a small jug of water. He poured us each a dram and raised his glass. 'Here's tae us, wha's like us?'

'Damn few and they're all deid,' I replied, in time-honoured fashion.

We talked a little, but sat mainly in silence and it was only once he'd recharged our glasses that my dad raised the subject we'd skirted all evening. 'Poor Max – it's a terrible business.' The old man yawned. It was well past his bedtime. 'I remember when he used to call round for you every morning before school – you were never ready. He was a good boy and grew into a fine man. Did the legal work when I sold up and bought this place. No fuss. Just did the business. A proper lawyer doing proper legal work.' It wasn't meant as a dig, I'm sure, but in my fragile state I felt it nonetheless.

'Someone told me you were acting for the boy charged with killing him.' My dad, formerly Sergeant Alex Munro, one of Lothian & Borders' finest, had eyes and ears everywhere. I tried to butt in and put him right, but he steamed on. 'I just told them it was your job. A professional. That's what you are. Max was your friend, but you can't let that get in the way. Doesn't matter what people are saying—'

'What are people saying?'

'Ignore them. You have to be dispassionate, detached, do your duty.' He was doing his best. I knew he didn't mean a word of it. I felt tears well up. Had to be the whisky; stirring my emotions. Usually it had the opposite effect. A few drams and I was ready to strap on a claymore and head for the Border.

'Everyone needs to be defended in court. Especially on a charge like murder,' my dad chuntered on. 'I'm proud of you. There's not many people would have the sense of professional and moral courage to do what you're doing.'

I looked up at him through eyes swimming with tears. 'Dad,' I croaked. 'I'm not acting for him. I just can't do it.'

My dad took my tumbler, topped-up my drink once more and handed it back to me.

'Glad to hear it,' he said, clinking glasses. 'Here's hoping the wee bastard swings.'

CHAPTER 9

On the way to the office next morning I dropped into Sandy's for a much needed black coffee, all the while keeping a weather eye out for my irate landlord. Two of the stylists from Jay Deez Hair Salon were having breakfast. Soon, they'd return to their world of blow dries, perms and hot oil treatments. One of them, Butch Baillie, I knew from my visits to the salon. He was a big cherubic-faced man wearing a cap-sleeve T-shirt, his bare arms white and flabby. The other I'd seen only a couple of times before, a skinny wee thing, hair tied in bunches, biting chunks out of a fried-egg roll and letting the molten gold trickle down the back of her hand and onto the paper napkin tucked into the neck of her pink T-shirt.

I called over to them. 'All right Butch? How's the new girl shaping up?'

Fittingly for a man in his line of work Butch owned a great deal of hair. He wore it long and was constantly brushing wisps of it out of his face. 'Nikki's got her first tint at eleven.' He elbowed his young colleague in the ribs. 'It'll be the highlight of the day.' The girl in the pink T-shirt giggled, almost choking on her bite of roll.

'Where's the boss?' I asked.

A few weeks previously, Jacqui Dillon, the proprietor of Jay Deez had been caught three times in the space of half an hour by the same speed camera. She'd left home for work, realised she'd forgotten something, gone back for whatever it was, then set off for work again. She'd never noticed the white van at the side of the road, the one with the wee hatch in the back door through which she was being photographed by a speed camera. Nine penalty points to go along with the three already on her licence would have meant a totting-up disqualification and I'd received a distress call from her, horrified at the thought of having to put her cerise BMW Z4 in mothballs for the next six months.

The offices of the Procurator Fiscal closed at four o'clock on a Friday afternoon. I'd popped in around three fifty-five, cornered one of Hugh Ogilvie's deputes and put it to her that Jacqui's three indiscretions had all been part of the same course of driving and in terms of section 27(4) of the Road Traffic Offenders Act 1988 it wouldn't be competent to impose three sets of three penalty points consecutively. Andy had even dug up a case about it: Green –v- O'Donnell from nineteen ninety-seven, which might have been required if the depute hadn't been in such a hurry to be off and running. By three fifty-nine I'd sealed the deal that eventually saw Jacqui plead to one speeding charge resulting in three penalty points and a sixty pound fine. My finances being what they were, now was the time to squeeze out a small fee.

Using first one hand and then the other, Butch flicked back his hair, swinging his head from side to side as though he were in a hairspray ad. 'Haven't seen Her Majesty since we loused on Friday. She should have phoned if she wasn't coming in - at least that's the rules for the rest of us - but, hey, she's the boss.'

Sandy came from through the back, white towel draped over one shoulder, and leaned on the counter. I could tell by the expression on his face that the matter of my outstanding tab had reached crisis point.

I ordered a coffee and took out my mobile.

'Does that thing run on batteries or gas cylinders?' Butch's young companion squeaked.

'You're wasting your time,' Butch held up a slim metallic-pink mobile that put my clunky phone to shame. 'Mine's is bust. I've got Jacqui's. You looking for an appointment?'

I wondered. Why not? I needed a trim, and I could raise the small matter of my fee while Jacqui cut my hair.

'Why don't you swing by tomorrow afternoon?'

Sandy poured me a coffee, muttering something about people being able to find money for hair-do's and drummed his fingers impatiently on the countertop.

Butch asked. 'Two o'clock sound okay?'

Two o'clock sounded just fine.

CHAPTER **10**

Ripping through the morning mail there was no sign of a legal aid payment sheet.

Grace-Mary came in and thumped a pile of files on my desk before walking out again. Each of the files related to an upcoming trial for which the intermediate diet would be calling in court the following day. I would be expected to be ready by then to advise the Sheriff on the state of my clients' defence preparations.

I opened one or two of the files and skimmed through stacks of witness statements and copy productions. The Procurator Fiscal was bound by law to disclose the prosecution case but liked to wait until the last minute to do so. I now had to sift through it all and identify any procedural issues that required attention: challenges to admissibility, potential special defences, attacks on character, uncontroversial evidence and so on.

There was plenty there to keep me and my assistant busy for most of the day. Come to think of it, where was Andy? There was me paying him Law Society recommended rates, or very nearly, and yet he never materialised before nine each morning and come five o'clock you could practically see the small tornado of dust twisting over his chair as he battered out of the door.

At that precise moment I heard footsteps in the hall and went through to reception just in time to see my assistant traipsing in. 'What time do you call this?'

'Sorry, I'm a bit late' he said, sipping from a tall paper cup. 'Sandy's was chockers.'

He sat down and put his feet up on his desk. I knocked them off.

'Robbie's feeling a bit rough this morning,' Grace-Mary told Andy. 'I think he had a wee drink last night,' she added, conspiratorially, though she was standing only a few feet away from me. 'Here.' She presented me with some more prosecution statements hot from the printer. 'It's all right. At times like these you need to unwind a wee bit.' Her face was strangely contorted, and it slowly dawned on me that she was smiling. I wasn't used to sympathy from my secretary.

Andy snorted. 'A hangover. No wonder he's so crabbit.'

I wasn't sure if I'd heard correctly. 'Crabbit?'

'It's true,' Grace-Mary said, kindly, 'but it's nothing to worry about - you're always crabbit. As for you,' she turned on Andy. 'Never mind sitting there giving cheek to boss, there's a heap of filing needing done.'

'Do I have to?' Andy whined at me. 'I'm a trainee solicitor not some sec—'

Grace-Mary's adopted a more natural frown.

My assistant rolled his eyes and blew out in frustration. He lifted the wire basket brimming with letters and attendance notes that sat on my secretary's desk, next to the out-of-date photo of her grand daughter. These days Tracy Gribbin was a Goth: two-tone make-up, multiple body-piercings and more chains than the public lavvies. I could understand why my secretary preferred the wee girl in the picture, all ringlets and curls and hand-knitted jumper.

As Andy walked past, I picked out a slip of yellow paper from the basket.

'What's this?'

'A telephone attendance note,' replied Grace-Mary, not looking up from her typing.

'Thanks,' I said. 'I can see that. The words, 'Telephone Memo' at the top sort of give it away.' I read the note aloud. 'Chic Kelly phoned?'

Grace-Mary nodded. 'Well not him, the social worker at Glenochil phoned on his behalf.'

I yawned. My earlier caffeine boost was wearing off. 'What does he want?'

'He wants a visit and you're due in court in half an hour.'

'Maybe the prison won't provide quilted bog roll and he feels his human rights have been breached,' Andy said, retrieving the note and dropping it back into the wire basket.

'That's enough from you,' I told him. 'Nip back down to Sandy's and get me an Americano.'

Andy put down the basket and held out his hand. 'Money?'

'Tell Sandy to put it on my slate.'

'Do I have to?' Andy moaned. 'It's embarrassing.'

I glanced down at the note. Chic Kelly phoning me for a visit? It had to be about his son. Someone else labouring under the illusion that I'd act for the youth charged with killing my childhood friend. It was something I didn't want to dwell on. What I really wanted was a hair of the dog. There was a pub across the road. Linlithgow was full of them.

'Never mind,' I told Andy. 'You keep on with your secretarial duties; I'll get my own… coffee.'

'You'll not bother yourself,' said Grace-Mary, her psychic powers as ever attune. She delved into the swear box, a glass jar filled with coins and about the only solvent asset in Munro & Co. 'Here.' She dropped some coins into my assistant's outstretched hand. 'Don't be long.'

Andy was back in minutes. Presumably, Sandy's was now a lot less chockers. 'So, are you going to keep Sean Kelly's case?' he asked, handing a cardboard cup to me.

Grace-Mary was banging a letter out. 'No, he isn't,' she said, not looking away from the screen.

'Then how come the defence post-mortems in the diary?'

Grace-Mary stopped typing and gave me a look. 'Robbie, you're not?'

I took a sip of coffee. 'Someone's got to do it.'

'Then let someone else do it,' she said.

'Like who? I'm the duty agent. No-one's going to volunteer to go to an autopsy.'

'I'll go,' Andy said. 'I've never been to one before. Might be a good laugh.'

My fists clenched and I could feel the blood drain from my face. The thought of seeing Max's dissected body was bad enough but as a source of entertainment…

Grace-Mary stepped in front of Andy.

'What's the matter?' he complained. 'I said I'd go, didn't I?'

'You're going nowhere.' She put her hands on his shoulders and pushed him down into a chair. 'You're staying right here and helping me shift some filing cabinets.'

There can't be many worse ways to spend a Tuesday afternoon than watching the remains of a childhood friend being picked over like the Boxing Day turkey.

When I'd set off for the autopsy, I'd consoled myself with the thought that the sooner the defence post-mortem examination was carried out the sooner Max's body could be released for burial and laid to rest. Now that I was actually there, standing outside the mortuary in the rain, I dreaded the thought of what was to come and almost wished I'd taken up my assistant's offer. Volunteering for things didn't feature strongly on Andy's CV. Ask him to see a new client and he complained, suggest that he come in early and open the mail and he'd like as not feign injury, but mention the chance of watching some poor sod being carved-up on a slab and suddenly he was your man. I knew why: post mortems are a source of excitement to young lawyers, something to boast about in the pub to their mates. The novelty soon wears off. One or two messy autopsies down the road and your average legal-trainee starts to seriously consider a career in conveyancing.

I tried the mortuary door. It was locked. I wasn't sure why. No one was likely to escape and who in their right mind would want to break in?

I found shelter from the rain and, as I huddled in the doorway, my mind raced back to Mrs Clark's primary three class, where a seven-year-old Robbie Munro was trying to smother a balloon with a congealed mass of paper and glue in the hope that it would miraculously assemble itself into a paper-maché piggy bank. Miracles were in short supply that day and I was ready to splat the whole thing against a wall when the new boy came over, all short back and sides, puppy fat and sticky out ears. He'd somehow rescued operation piggy bank, and I'd been so pleased it didn't even matter when on Father's Day my Dad had wondered what he was supposed to do with a misshapen pink football.

After that Max and I became something of a team. We walked to school together, went to the swing-park together. Max helped me with homework, and I dealt mercilessly with the bullies out to steal his packed lunch.

Because Max's father was dead and mine very much alive and a widower, a large part of our formative years was spent trying to devise intricate and, no doubt, highly transparent schemes to throw our respective parents together in the off chance that romantic entanglement and marriage would one day ensue. By the time Max's mum eventually did remarry (a shopfitter from Bishopbriggs) we had more or less given up the whole idea for a dead loss.

I'd never been sure just who'd thought first about a career in the law, but, whoever it was, the other had also thought it an excellent idea and we'd both gone off to University where Max came to the rescue once more with his copperplate lecture notes and insight into the impenetrable mysteries of constitutional law.

A drip of cold water from the door frame precision-bombed the back of my neck, shocking me into a return to the present day and the sight of a man clad in brown overalls, green wellies and carrying an umbrella advertising a local undertaker.

'Dying to get in?' the mortuary assistant chuckled, as he dug deep in his overalls and produced a bunch of keys with which he let me out of the rain and into his sweetly pungent world of decaying flesh and pine disinfectant. 'You here for Abercrombie?' He laid a hand on my shoulder, a doleful expression on his chubby little face. 'I've bad news – he's dead.'

I wrestled the desire to rip off one of his green wellies and wrap it round his grinning chops. Eventually his laughter deteriorated into a chesty wheeze and I calmed myself, remembering why I was there and who was lying in a chilled drawer in the next room.

'I'm expecting Professor Bradley,' I said.

'I know. The Crown's been here already. You'd think one hatchet job would be enough. I'd feel sorry for the poor bugger if he wasn't dead already.'

My hands were being drawn uncontrollably towards the green wellies when onto the scene entered Detective Inspector Dougie Fleming wearing what in the opinion of Lothian and Borders Police passed for plain clothes. I didn't suppose his mother owned any bonnie baby rosettes, but I noticed he was looking even rougher than usual. His lip was split and a row of butterfly stitches held together a cut above his left eye; souvenirs, I imagined, of his scrap with my drunken Lithuanian client in the curry house. What was his name again? Salavejus? Whoever he was, he and I had a day in court with DI Fleming to look forward to.

'Good afternoon, Mr Munro,' Fleming said, like he didn't mean it. He gestured to the doorway. 'Allow me to introduce Detective Chief Inspector Lockhart.'

I was expecting an older, perhaps better-groomed, version of Dougie Fleming. What stepped into the room was a tall, athletic female in a tan raincoat. She seemed very young to have achieved such a high rank.

'Petra Lockhart.' She smiled and shook my hand. 'Hope you don't mind. The Fiscal suggested we come along and keep an eye on you.'

'Plod.' The mortuary assistant sized up Fleming. 'Saw you lurking around the hospital canteen earlier. I've never seen pies disappear like they do when you lot are around.'

'Aye, and it would take a detective to find the meat in them.' Fleming said, reaching into his pocket and taking out a pack of smokes.

'You'll need to go outside if you want to do that.' The mortuary assistant gave Fleming a scalpel slash of a smile 'It's the law.'

Fleming glanced at his senior officer. 'Ma'am?'

'If you really have to.'

On his way out, Fleming dodged the figure of Professor Edward Bradley bustling his way in. 'Robbie, how are things?' Not waiting for an answer, the pathologist tore off his overcoat, gave it a shake and draped it over a radiator. 'In a bit of a rush I'm afraid – got a suspicious death in Dumfries at five.'

If he had to be quick, I wasn't going to object. As far as I was concerned the sooner I was out of there the better.

The assistant helped the Professor into a lab coat before wheeling through a trolley draped in white. Without ceremony he whipped back the sheet to reveal the dissected body of Max Abercrombie.

'I see that the Crown team's already been here,' Prof. Bradley said. 'Don't tell me, Ken Crichton, right? Couldn't carve a roast. Anyway, here goes. Switch the tape on, Jim.'

'It is on,' said the mortuary assistant.

'Ah. Then let's get started shall we?' The Professor pulled back a section of chest skin complete with creamy layer of adipose tissue, thus affording himself access to the thoracic cavity. He held out a hand and the assistant put a probe in it. 'This is the body of a male adult...'

I couldn't watch.

'Not got the stomach for it?' Fleming gloated when he saw me stepping out of the front door to join him in the drizzle. He blew out a lungful of smoke. 'How's your dad? The Force lost a good man the day he retired.'

'So he never stops telling me.' I wasn't one to fraternise with the enemy, but even standing in the rain, inhaling Fleming's secondhand smoke, was better than witnessing the events going on inside. I'd stay there until the whole nasty business was finished and catch a word with the Professor rather than wait for his written report. 'What's with your glamorous buddy?' I asked Fleming, in an effort to talk about something other than why we were there.

'Bit tasty eh?'

'Haven't seen her around before.'

'High-flyer on loan from Fettes.'

'Slumming it?'

'Don't let the looks and the posh accent fool you.' Fleming tipped the ash off his cigarette. 'Lockhart's from East Pilton or Drylaw or somewhere scummy like that. Somewhere the weans play tig with hatchets. Her dad was a cop too, a grunt, community officer or something; at least he was until there arose the small matter of shady goings on with certain licence applications.'

'What kind of licences?' I asked, glad for a bit of gossip to take my mind off what was happening through the wall from me.

'Pubs, clubs, extended hours. Lockhart's old boy used to do the police reports for the Licensing Board. The bigger the bung the better the report. He was careless. It couldn't go unnoticed forever. Eventually, he took the honourable way out with a tow-rope and the next-door neighbour's apple tree.'

I winced. 'Ouch.'

'Didn't put Lockhart off though. She'd already joined the Force at eighteen and went on to make sergeant at twenty-three. After that it was onto Uni and a proper law degree.' He said it as though I'd snipped my degree out the back of a cornflakes box and coloured it in with some crayons.

'You seem to know a lot about her.'

'Everyone knows a lot about Petra Lockhart. She's not what you'd call publicity shy.' He took another few rapid puffs, the red-hot tip growing longer with each drag, curving downwards. 'I bend the rules and get my knuckles rapped. She breaks them and somebody gives her a bloody medal. Thinks she knows it all and doesn't mind telling the rest of us how to do our jobs.' Fleming drew hard and blew smoke down his nose. 'Probably end up making Chief Constable – stuck-up bint.'

Anyone Fleming disliked couldn't be all bad. I was just glad they had someone good on Max's case.

After a couple more puffs, Fleming pinged the half-smoked cigarette away and went back inside. I followed him as far as the corridor outside the examination room where I paced up and down until the sound of surgical implements clattering into a stainless-steel bowl told me the ordeal was almost over. I went back inside.

'That should do it,' the Professor said, ripping off a pair of bloody latex gloves and dropping them into a nearby waste bucket. The comedian in the green wellies scurried around, tidying up. Once he'd replaced the white sheet and wheeled the trolley away, he fetched the Professor's coat.

'You'll have my report in two or three days, toxicology will take longer,' said the pathologist. 'Still, I don't suppose the findings will differ much from the Crown's. Used to mentor Ken Crichton, you know. The boy would give butchery a bad name, but he's usually pretty thorough.'

I walked the Professor to his car and let him do all the talking.

'There are some superficial signs of a struggle: a few scratch marks, though really nothing much in the way of blunt trauma. Cause of death: two gunshot wounds to the thorax with associated damage to the internal structures, lungs, heart, major blood vessels, result: massive blood loss, hypovolemic shock and multiple organ failure. From the angle of the wounds and the deceased's height I'd say he was standing when he was shot. May have been bearing down on his attacker. One bullet passed through the right hand before it entered the chest so must have been fired at fairly close range. The other fragmented into two pieces, the bigger piece slicing through the left internal thoracic artery and lodging in the rear fifth thoracic vertebra.'

He placed his tool bag on the back seat of the car.

'Weapon?' I asked.

'I'd guess at a thirty-eight, something like that.'

The Professor wasn't exactly going out on a limb; the underworld was swimming in ex-military hardware. A thirty-eight was a noisy beast. Not that it would have mattered. Max's office was at the rear of an old sandstone building with walls that were feet thick. You could have let off a twenty-one-gun salute in there without disturbing the neighbours.

'Doesn't sound like a professional hit,' I said.

'No, definitely amateur-hour. To do it properly you'd go for a two-two. They're quiet and it's not hard to get hold of a pre-Dunblane target pistol. A double tap to the base of the skull, using soft nosed rounds on a low charge - no exit wounds and minimal blood spray - just a couple of slugs ricocheting around inside the skull doing maximum damage in a clean, quiet and efficient way. Of course, that's assuming you can take your victim by surprise. Otherwise you probably would need a cannon to stop someone the size of... Sorry, Robbie. Got a bit carried away there.' He placed a hand on my shoulder and squeezed gently. 'It would have been quick.' It was scant consolation. It made me feel sick to think of Max confronting his attacker, reaching out, trying to grab the gun, fighting for his life and being shot at point blank range.

The Professor lowered himself into the driver's seat of his geriatric Volvo estate. 'Robbie, why are you even here? You're too close to this.'

A strangled, 'I'm duty agent. It's my duty,' was the best I could come up with.

'Well this case is above and beyond the call. Get rid of it.' He slammed the door shut, the engine roared into life and in a moment and a cloud of exhaust he was gone.

CHAPTER 12

Jay Deez was busy. Every chair taken, every stylist hard at it with brushes, tongs, scissors and spray. I'd hardly been in the place and already one of the junior stylists had washed and conditioned my hair, massaged my scalp and was now leading me, damp towel around my shoulders, from the sink area to the styling floor. It was a far cry from the gauge three, sides, back and over the top that kept my usual barber occupied for about five minutes. My hair wasn't used to this high level of attention and I was beginning to feel decidedly uneasy when Butch appeared by my side. He sat me down, pushed some cans of hairspray, a styling comb and a pile of celebrity mags to one side and placed a cup of filter coffee on the ledge in front of me. Ferns of steam crept up the big mirror.

'What do you think of the monstrosity?' he asked, whisking away the towel and wrapping a protective gown about me, tying it securely at my neck. He tilted his head at the vast and varied array of paperweights on display in a small alcove in the corner of the salon. The three glass shelves on which the paperweights were distributed were lit from beneath by a row of spotlights recessed in the work surface. 'Jacqui had it put in the other week there. Needed somewhere to keep her collection. Suppose she had to do something. The bloody things were starting to breed.' He rubbed my wet hair between his podgy fingers and studied it thoughtfully for a moment or two, lips pursed. 'Paperweights,' he blurted, letting go my hair. 'All my fault.' Butch flicked his own hair to either side of his head. 'I should never have brought back that crystal maple leaf the year I went to Canada. Jacqui had to go one better and buy that big ugly thing.'

He was referring, I guessed, to what was the centre piece of the display: a large glass globe with a rainbow swirl and a blizzard of bubbles caught inside.

Butch brushed his hair back again with the back of each hand. 'After that it just snow-balled. Now no-one has to think about what to get the guys at Jay Deez for a present. Isn't that right girls?' he shouted at his colleagues over the noise of blasting hair-driers. Not one of them looked around from what they were doing but their heads nodded in unison. 'Nae boxes of chocs for us. Oh no, dead simple. If you want to get that lot down at Jay Deez a prezzie,' he spoke the name of the salon like a curse, 'just get them a lump of glass.' He ruffled my hair. 'Sad thing is Jacqui actually likes them.' He raised his voice again. 'And what the boss likes, the boss gets, isn't that right girls?' The same heads nodded again in some kind of Pavlovian reflex. Butch lifted up some more of my hair and looked at my reflection. 'What were you thinking?' he asked, head tilted to one side. 'Go crazy, I might give you a discount.'

'Just a trim's fine.'

Butch's fat features registered confusion, as though I'd asked for a procedure with which he was unfamiliar. 'A what?'

I took a sip of coffee. 'Jacqui not in today?'

Butch folded his arms and scowled at me in the mirror. 'Is that a problem?'

It was most certainly a problem. For one thing I was expecting a freebie and wasn't sure how well Butch would take to that suggestion, but in answer to his question I shrugged non-committally and said, 'no, not really.'

'Good.' Butch marched over to where the new girl was trying to empty a shovelful of swept hair into a stainless-steel bin and spilling most of it in the process. He placed a meaty hand on each of her shoulders and steered the girl across the floor and into place behind my chair. 'Nikki will touch up your grey bits. After that I'll do what I can. He gave my hair a disdainful flick. 'Who normally does for you? Black and Decker?' There was an obedient titter from the rest of the staff.

Butch continued. 'There's not much to work with but I'm thinking something graduated, feathered maybe, and come to think of it your colour's all wrong, doesn't match your skin tone. Have you thought about lightening up a bit?' I hadn't. 'How about Cinnamon, no, Copper? Yeah. Copper. Not all over, that would be too much, but definitely highlights – how's that sound?'

It sounded terrible. I didn't have that many grey bits and I was getting used to those I had. I didn't really fancy them being touched-up, far less coloured copper. A rising tide of helplessness threatened to engulf me. I wanted to escape, leap up, rip off the gown and make a frantic dash for the nearest barbers. I remained stuck to my seat. Was this how the holocaust victims felt? The Germans say we're only here for a shower. No need to panic. Remain dignified. Everything will be fine – probably. And that's when help arrived. Not the Red Army, but in uniform nonetheless. From my position and the angle of the mirror I could only see a pair of trousers and shoes. Dark trousers with stitched permanent creases and heavy black shoes, toes polished to a high degree. Cop trousers. Cop shoes. I remembered how my dad would use his fingers to massage the polish into the leather of his own police issue footwear then heat the toe caps over a flame before taking a duster and setting about them without mercy until they shone like ebony mirrors.

I twisted and looked over my shoulder to see D.I. Dougie Fleming and his attractive, high-flying superior whom I'd met at Max's autopsy.

'Jacqui Dillon?' Fleming enquired in a loud voice.

'Not in today,' Butch called over to him. 'Haven't seen her since Friday. The rest of us still have to work though. Isn't that right girls?' The row of heads nodded.

Lockhart noticed me and came forward. 'Mr Munro?' she said to my reddening reflection, the hint of smirk on her pretty face. 'I thought that was you. Look, I know this is not a good time, but I wonder if I could bother you—'

'You'll need to wait.' Butch flicked a strand of hair out of his face. 'I'm just about to bother him - with these.' He snipped a pair of scissors in mid-air. The young would-be tinter at his side collapsed into a fit of the giggles.

Lockhart ignored him, her eyes locked on mine in the mirror. 'It's about Max Abercrombie.' She held up her hands defensively. 'I'm not going to ask any questions about your client.' I really wished people would stop calling Sean Kelly that. 'I just thought you might be able to fill me in on a few things regarding Mr Abercrombie's personal life.'

'Wasting your time pet,' Butch said. 'Robbie spends his life telling his clients to blank the pigs - no offence - you've got no chance.'

Butch had indeed grasped the Munro and co philosophy on police interviews and, in any case, I didn't have much recent knowledge of Max's personal life. Latterly, we'd hardly seen each other. I also didn't feel too much like talking about my friend as I was still trying to come to terms with his sudden death; however, at that precise moment, the opportunity to help the police with their enquiries did hold a certain appeal. I unfastened the gown, pulled it from around my neck and twenty seconds later was trotting out of the salon with the two cops at my heels.

CHAPTER **13**

The muster room was police speak for a kitchen area with a big wooden table in the middle, some chairs, a few grey metal lockers and a sink full of dirty dishes.

I pulled up a seat and politely refused Dougie Fleming's offer of a coffee. I knew how he felt about defence agents in general and me in particular and didn't trust him not to give me a saliva cappuccino.

Lockhart took off her sweater, loosened the collar of her blouse and sat on the edge of the table. It was all very casual, her approach designed to put me at ease. It was an atmosphere that Dougie Fleming seemed keen to dispel, standing beside my chair, staring down at me.

I shouldn't have come. Yes, it had been a handy escape route from the clutches of Butch and his trainee-tinter, but I was still duty agent, if only for a few more days, and, though it pained me to think in those terms, it followed that Sean Kelly was my client. Discussing his case with the police, even if they were only seeking background information on the victim, did present something of a conflict of interest.

'How well do you know Jacqui Dillon?' Lockhart asked.

It wasn't a line of questioning I'd anticipated, and I had to think for a moment or two. I knew Jacqui like I knew a lot of the girls from the salon. They mostly lived locally and frequented Sandy's café.

'Do you usually have your hair done there?' asked Lockhart, a cute little smile on her face.

'No – not usually,' I replied.

Lockhart was about to speak when Fleming butted in. 'When did you see her last?' he demanded and received a look of mild annoyance from his senior officer.

'Have you seen Miss Dillon recently?' Lockhart asked.

I had to think about that for a moment. 'I may have seen her out and about or at the café but the last time we spoke was two or three weeks ago.'

'About a road traffic violation?' Fleming made it sound like she'd gang-banged a mini.

'I think it would be easier, Inspector,' Lockhart said, 'if only one of us asked the questions. We don't want Mr Munro to feel as though he's being interrogated.'

I doubted whether Fleming cared what I thought.

'Why the questions about Jacqui?' I asked. 'I thought you wanted information on Max.'

'We do.' Lockhart cleared her throat. 'And we'd like to know if you ever saw Mr Abercrombie and Miss Dillon out together… socially.'

'What? Like on a date?'

Fleming sighed loudly.

'Yes,' said Lockhart patiently. 'Out for dinner perhaps, or the cinema, that sort of thing.'

I laughed. Max was the most married man I knew and Irene Abercrombie definitely not the sort of woman to let any man trifle with her affections.

'No,' I said. 'That seems very unlikely to have ever happened.'

'Told you, ma'am,' Fleming said. 'Load of rubbish.'

Lockhart ignored the remark. 'It has come to our attention—'

Fleming coughed meaningfully. His senior officer conceded the point.

'It has come to my attention, that Mr Abercrombie and Miss Dillon may have been having an affair.'

'Nonsense,' I said.

Lockhart continued. 'My source doesn't think so. Seems fairly certain that there was a romantic affiliation of some sort.'

Max? Play away from home? It was almost too ridiculous to contemplate.

'Who told you about this supposed romantic affiliation and just how drunk were they at the time?' I asked.

'You'll forgive me if I protect the identity of my source.'

I'd liked to have known who it was, and why they'd let whoever it was out of the nuthouse, but I let it go.

'Whatever,' I said, 'the fact is, now you're looking for Jacqui?'

Fleming interrupted again. 'Just answer the question.'

Lockhart glared at him. 'Inspector, when I need your assistance I'll let you know.'

Fleming stomped over to the sink and helped himself to a glass of water.

'To answer your question,' Lockhart said, 'I would like very much to speak to Miss Dillon, if only so that we...' she looked over at Fleming. 'So that I can eliminate her from my enquiries.'

'And she hasn't been seen for how long?'

'Since Friday night.'

The night Max had been killed.

'Is she a suspect?' I asked.

Fleming blew out his cheeks and let loose another loud sigh.

'Inspector Fleming doesn't think so, but let's just say,' she stared meaningfully at Fleming, 'as the senior officer, in charge of this murder investigation, I'm keeping all lines of enquiry open at the present time.'

'How does this affect Sean Kelly?'

Lockhart laughed. 'You'll remember it was me who asked you here for questioning?'

'And you've established that I know nothing about Max and Jacqui having an affair. Now I'd like to know why Sean Kelly is remanded on a murder petition when there's at least one person you, as officer in charge, haven't ruled out as a possible suspect.'

It was almost surreal. That I should actually believe for one moment that Max would be involved in extra-marital relations was crazy enough, without the suggestion that my hairdresser client could have been his murderer. I put it down to my defence agent instincts kicking in on autopilot. If the cops were still actively investigating the case, why had they locked up my client? Albeit he was soon to be my ex-client.

Fleming had had enough. He slammed his glass down hard on the metal draining board.

Before he could say anything, Lockhart had lowered herself from the table and stood facing me. She was tall, only a couple of inches shorter than me, five nine or thereabouts. I don't know what perfume she was wearing but I could have stood there smelling it all day. 'Mr Munro…' She took a pace back and cleared her throat. 'There is a very strong prima facie case against Sean Kelly. He'll likely be put at the scene by two eyewitnesses who heard an argument between Mr Abercrombie and another male on the evening of the murder. You will be notified shortly of an identification parade. As yet we don't have a motive but there exists physiological evidence suggestive of a struggle between the deceased and your client. I think you'll agree that's more than enough to support initial proceedings.'

'And Jacqui?' I asked.

'Like I've already said…' She stared hard at Fleming. 'That particular avenue of enquiry remains open.'

CHAPTER **14**

I fumbled sleepily amongst the books on my bedside table, located my alarm and beat it into submission. Another restless night punctuated by dreams about Max's shooting.

I got out of the sack and tottered to the bathroom. On the way I cracked my leg off a bedpost, the shoogly one with the annoying tendency to fall off and drop to the floor with a loud clunk during moments of high passion. It was the first time it had been disturbed in a while. I was rubbing my knee when the phone rang.

'Hope I didn't interrupt your beauty sleep, Mr Munro.' The duty sergeant was bright and, I thought, unnecessarily breezy for that time of the morning. 'Inspector Fleming asked me to call, wants to do Kelly's ID parade at ten.'

I'd learned on my return to the office the previous afternoon, following my discussions with the lovely Chief Inspector Lockhart, that the Procurator Fiscal had rubber-stamped the release of Max's body. With no objection from me on behalf of the defence, it meant the funeral could now go ahead and the morning's court had been suspended until later in the day to allow local Faculty members to pay their last respects. As duty agent, I had little option other than to attend the parade, but I'd be cutting it fine for the funeral; nonetheless, as there were only two witnesses: Max's paralegal and receptionist, and as they'd be going to the funeral as well, I didn't foresee any major difficulty.

I avoided my usual early morning trip to Sandy's for a bacon roll and coffee. I wasn't feeling hungry. The mere thought of food made me feel queasy.

'What you doing here?' asked the duty sergeant when I walked into the station.

'ID parade,' I said. 'Hope you're all set. The funeral's at eleven.'

'You're going? I think the Inspector imagined you would be staying away - you acting for the accused and all.' He must have read my face. 'Anyway…' he hurried along, 'the parade's not happening here. It's a VIPER 1 up at Livingston.'

I should have known. My brain just didn't seem to be working properly. There was no way I could make the drive to Livingston, attend the parade and be back in time for Max's funeral.

'You'll have to phone Livingston and tell them to postpone the VIPER.'

'Don't think so,' said the sergeant. 'The lad's on his way from Polmont. There's an inspector and a sergeant standing by. Everything's ready.'

'Shit.'

Lockhart appeared behind the front desk. Her hair was wet. A sweat-soaked sports top clung to her slim athletic torso. 'Morning, Mr Munro. You'll need to excuse me. I've been out for a run.' She gave her head a vigorous rub with the white towel that had been slung around her neck. 'Anyway, what are you doing here? I thought you'd be up at the VIPER.'

I explained my predicament.

'Not a problem,' she said. 'Sergeant, what wheels have we got?'

The Sergeant didn't check the board on the wall that had several hooks but only one set of keys dangling. 'Zilch. Everything's out.'

'What are those for?' Lockhart pointed at the lonely keys.

'Sorry, ma'am. Those are for the Firearms Response Vehicle.'

'Perfect.' Before the man with the stripes could verbally express the look of protest on his face, Lockhart had tossed her towel at him and unhooked the keys. Grabbing my arm, she led me at speed outside and around the rear of the police station to an awaiting fluorescent yellow and blue chequered flying machine. Beautiful and decisive. I was beginning to see why she had made Chief Inspector.

CHAPTER **15**

Like everything else, identification parades had succumbed to the relentless march of technology. No longer did the accused line up beside reluctant stand-ins dragged from the high street, while nervous witnesses viewed proceedings wondering if the two-way mirror really worked. The first stage of the new Video Identity Parade Electronically Recorded procedure involved capturing a moving image of the suspect and compiling a virtual line-up using other images sourced from a database of thousands, held by West Yorkshire Police.

The witnesses weren't brought in until the second stage, VIPER 2, usually a few days later. At that time they were shown a compilation on DVD and asked to make an identification. Popcorn was optional.

Sean Kelly was wearing the standard remand kit of jeans, white trainers and an orange polo shirt embroidered with a Scottish Prison Service logo on the left breast. The Reliance security officer unlocked his handcuffs and ushered him into the room. Other than the prisoner's lank, greasy hair and an insipid complexion, he seemed well enough for someone dubbed-up twenty-three and a half hours a day and sharing toilet facilities with a psycho from Easterhouse.

When he came into the VIPER room it was the first time I'd had a really good look at the person charged with Max's murder. During our earlier brief encounter before his court appearance I'd been in no fit state to care. Now for some reason, perhaps it was Lockhart's interest in Jacqui Dillon, the AWOL hairdresser, I was curious.

'In you come, son,' said the inspector, pointing at the swivel stool that was situated in the centre of the room, fixed to the concrete floor.

The young man sat and stared around at four breeze-block walls, coated with matt white paint. Every VIPER room throughout the country was built to the same dimensions and layout.

'I'm inspector Docherty, this is sergeant McColl and I take it you know Mr Munro.' The prisoner gave me a half-baked smile. I remained tight-lipped.

After the inspector had gone through the formalities, recorded the details of all those present, noted down a description of the accused and read out loud the parade procedures, I was asked if I had any objections to the arrangements. There was one obvious one and I had the young man's prison shirt removed and replaced by a sports top from a selection of T-shirts the VIPER team kept handy for just such occasions.

Once the subject was properly attired the inspector nodded to the sergeant which was the signal for the man with the three stripes to take over. The Sergeant left his computer terminal, went over and pulled down a projector screen that stretched from ceiling to floor behind the prisoner's back. He adjusted the stool, lowering its height by spinning the seat around with the young man still sitting on it. 'Right you are Sean,' he said, switching on the halogen lighting, 'look into the camera.'

Kelly did as he was told and his face appeared on the computer monitor where there was a cross drawn in correcting fluid and the sergeant lowered the stool some more so that the subject's nose was aligned precisely with the white cross-hairs.

'Great. What I want you to do is keep looking straight into the camera and hold up this card.' He handed Kelly a white card with a long number written on it in black felt-tipped pen. 'Hold it in front of your face, count to five, then lower it. Once you've done that, keep staring straight ahead until I tell you to look to your left, then to your right and face the camera again and count to ten, not out loud, in your head.'

It always seemed such a simple enough process but I'd yet to see anyone perform it first time without a hitch. It took Kelly four goes. On his first try he turned right then left, instead of the other way around. On the second go there was too much body movement.

'Just turn your head,' said the sergeant. 'Keep your body still.' By the third attempt, Kelly had slouched and his face was too low on the screen but the fourth take was a wrap. After that the sergeant beckoned us over to the computer to view potential stand-ins. There were several pages from which we were allowed to select a shortlist of eight. Like most of my clients he complained when he didn't see any doppelgangers of himself but, once it was explained that the only criteria for an ID parade stand-in were gender, age and similar colouring, he chose fairly well.

The virtual parade was to be viewed by two witnesses. The sergeant decided he'd make two separate compilations with all eight stand-ins and the subject in different positions on each. Kelly looked to me for guidance. I suggested he not go first or last; other than that it was down to him. He asked to be placed second and sixth. Then it was time for him to go.

'Will I see you at court on Monday, Mr Munro?' he asked.

Why didn't I just say no? Was I beginning to have second thoughts about Sean Kelly? Such as why would a young lad like him march into a solicitor's office and gun down the proprietor in cold blood? As insane as it seemed to me that Max might be having an affair, wasn't it more likely that he'd been killed during some sort of moment of high emotion with his paramour? Why else had Jacqui vanished? The investigating police officer clearly hadn't ruled it out.

'I don't think so,' I replied.

'You think I killed Mr Abercrombie —'

'Remember where you are, son,' said the inspector. 'If you want to speak to your lawyer we can arrange an interview room.'

'You do - you think I killed him.'

I didn't know what to think. Deciding such things as guilt or innocence were other people's responsibilities. I didn't answer his question; I just stood there and watched as the young man was handcuffed and led away.

CHAPTER 16

Another butt-clenching drive later and I was back in Linlithgow, where Lockhart parked the car at the rear of the police station. As officer in charge of the murder investigation, she wanted to attend Max's graveside and hurried off to shower and change into uniform. Fast though the trip had been, all flashing blue lights and wailing sirens, it had gone eleven o'clock. I didn't want to draw attention to myself by walking into church late, so I set off on foot for the cemetery. Even walking I'd arrive well before the funeral cortege.

On the High Street the weather was cold and windy. I pulled up the collar of my raincoat and set off on foot, thinking about Max and the good old days. Outside a paper shop a sandwich board declared 'Local Lawyer Gunned Down'. The very thought of the funeral was making me feel sick. I wasn't hungry but I needed food, something inside me to take away the cold empty feeling.

The heavens opened as I came out of Sandy's carrying a bacon roll in a brown paper bag. I took shelter in the alleyway at the side of the café and by the time I had finished my roll the sudden cloud burst had reduced to a drizzle. I was wiping my hands on the paper bag when a dog ran from the backyard of the shop and down the alleyway, almost bowling me over. It was a skinny mutt with lop-sided ears and a half-chewed tail. I must have disturbed it while it was raking for food because I could see a wheelie-bin lying on its side, contents strewn across the ground.

The dog loped out of the alley and onto the street. As I watched it go, I saw a dirty-white Astra van come to an abrupt halt at the side of the road and a large man wearing a pair of overalls and black ski-mask jump out. The smoky after-taste of fried-bacon quickly went stale. I dropped the paper bag and before it had hit the ground at my feet, the man in the mask had charged down the alley, grabbed me by my throat and was trying to lift me off the ground. He lowered his masked face level with my face. The knitted mouth was sewn shut, even the eyes holes were stitched so tightly that it couldn't have been easy to see out. If he'd said nothing, I think I would still have guessed who he was but when he spoke the voice was unmistakable.

'Mr Turpie wants his money or he wants something broken.'

Deek Pudney. The mask wasn't to conceal his identity from me, merely a precaution in case he was seen running into the alley. The van I was sure would very soon be burned out on some waste ground or crushed at Jake Turpie's scrapyard. It was my fervent hope I wouldn't be in it when it was. I kicked out and caught Deek high on the shin and it was enough for him to let me go. I backed off, treading in rubbish scattered by the dog, Deek lumbering after me.

'Nothing personal, Mr Munro. Just doing what I'm told.'

Maybe, but Deek Pudney was a man who enjoyed his job. Fists clenched, I was readying myself, the Light Brigade set to charge the Cossack artillery, when I saw someone enter the close entrance behind him. 'Chief Inspector!'

I could sense a wide grin forming under the mask. 'Don't give me that,' Deek growled. He advanced until a tap on his shoulder brought him to a sudden halt and turned to see Petra Lockhart, rigged out in full dress uniform. Dougie Fleming and two beat officers stood behind her armed with CS spray canisters.

'Inspector Fleming,' Lockhart said, 'arrest this man. Book him for parking on a double yellow for starters. After that you can use your imagination. I've heard it can be quite vivid at times.'

Deek stood dumfounded as Fleming strode forward and ripped off his mask. The big man was soon handcuffed.

Lockhart gestured me to come forward. 'You'll need to get a move on if you don't want to be late for the funeral. Can I offer you a lift?'

What a woman. She'd rescued me for the second time that morning. I walked down the alley towards her, smiling, squeezing past my assailant and grinding a heel into one of his big fat feet on the way.

CHAPTER 17

'In the sure and certain hope of resurrection...'

Cold and dreich. A fitting day for a funeral. An impatient north wind whipped the minister's robes and riffled the pages of his Bible.

Irene Abercrombie stood by the graveside, her children either side. I hadn't seen the kids for quite a while. They'd grown. Once I'd been Uncle Robbie, an always-present at family occasions. Over the years, the get-togethers had become fewer and fewer until birthdays and Christmases were only cards on the mantelpiece. When had that happened? Where had the years gone? In recent times, my contact with the Abercrombie family had been restricted to professional dealings with Max, usually conducted by telephone. I'd punt my non-criminal clients his way and now and again he'd refer me a local businessman facing road traffic or domestic violence charges. Once in a blue moon we'd grab lunch but, usually, I'd be rushing off to court before the sticky-toffee pudding arrived.

'Earth to earth, ashes to ashes, dust to dust,' intoned the man in the back-to-front collar. He closed the Bible, bent over and scooped up a handful of dirt letting it filter slowly through his fingers and into the hole in the ground. I shuffled forward with the other mourners who were filing past the open grave to pay their last respects. Staring six feet down at a polished lacquered box with shiny bronze nameplate already partially obscured by clods of dirt, for a moment I was lost in my memories, alone with my grief. A swift shove in the back brought me rudely to my senses. I tried to keep my balance but stumbled, sprawling across a mound of earth that was camouflaged by a sheet of bright green plastic turf.

I looked up at the figure in black standing over me and into the contemptuous stare of Irene Abercrombie whose lace veil was raised to reveal a tear-stained face. 'Get away from here, you blood-sucker,' she spat at me. 'You were supposed to be his friend, but you can't turn down a fee, can you? Legal Aid rates – fifty quid an hour - that's the price of your friendship.' I clambered to my feet as Max's widow kicked dirt in my face. Other mourners gathered around, one or two of them mumbled something vaguely apologetic that I didn't quite catch and led her away to a waiting car, leaving me wet and muddy and ashamed.

Soon the crowd had dispersed and a line of traffic snaked its way through the narrow cemetery roads. Two gravediggers emerged from the shelter of a nearby cypress tree, doffed their caps to the deceased and lifted their tools. I stayed, watching them work; the crunching and clanging of spades and Irene Abercrombie's words ringing in my ears.

I should have told her. Told Irene how I'd been forced to act for Sean Kelly, that he'd soon have another lawyer. With Lorna Wylie acting in his defence, at least Max's widow could be assured of a conviction. And there lay the problem: I had a doubt. Not a reasonable one, not yet, but a doubt nonetheless and until I was satisfied as to the boy's guilt I would never rest; for if, as Frankie seemed convinced, the young man was truly innocent then someone else was guilty. I really had to keep acting. What better place to be than on the inside, speaking to witnesses, examining the Crown productions, assessing all the evidence, making up my own mind? Surely that was better than leaving it up to fifteen people on a jury to consider some half-baked defence cobbled together by Lorna Wylie?

The sound of footsteps caused me to turn and meet the stocky yet dapper figure of Gordon Devine, senior partner of Glasgow city centre firm, Hewitt Kirkwood & Devine. 'Gorgeous' Gordon was wealthy, brash and flamboyant; a man palatable only in small doses. He was wearing a black Crombie coat over his trademark dark suit with wide chalk pinstripes.

His face was tanned and moisturised, his improbably jet-black hair swept back.

'Bit morbid, isn't it?' he said. 'The murderer's brief at the graveside?' Devine blinked his eyes a few times. It was a habit of his. He seemed to never blink and then just when you thought he had some kind of snake eyes he'd blink several times in quick succession as though trying to make up for lost blinks.

I brushed mud from my coat. 'Max was a friend. What's your excuse? Things a bit slow? Trying to rustle up some executry work?'

Devine stopped blinking. 'Law Society business.' The smile on his lips was as smooth as the felt collar of his coat, the look in his eyes as cold as the dirt piling up on Max's coffin. 'We like to show face at these type of events - lend support.' He made it sound like a charity cheese and wine. 'Heard you'd gone back to your roots,' he went on in his oily voice. 'How are things shaping up out in the sticks?'

Before I could answer, a royal blue Bentley slid to a halt nearby. Devine stooped and pinged a dod of muck from the hem of my raincoat. 'Anyway, about this murder. If you feel you have to bail out, conflict of interest and all that.'

'It's legal aid.'

Devine feigned a hurt expression. 'I don't mind the occasional spot of legal aid.' First I'd heard of it. Devine's manicurist probably charged more than LA rates. 'Pro bono and all that,' he said.

'Pro bono for you is what I call making a living.'

'Whatever. Pass me the papers and I'll take a shufty.'

It was tempting. I could withdraw from acting and Sean Kelly could still get himself some very decent legal representation – but I wouldn't be in control.

'Thanks,' I said. 'Let me think about it.'

'How'd it go?' Grace-Mary asked when I got into the office next morning. I showed her the dirty smear down one side of my raincoat that no amount of scrubbing had managed to shift.

'Oh,' she said. 'That well.' Andy didn't acknowledge my presence. He was sitting hunched over his desk, reconciling a pile of precognitions with an indictment witness list, using a felt-tipped pen to mark off those who'd been precognosced.

'How goes it?' I asked. Andy didn't look up. He lifted a statement, checked the name and ticked it off. 'Hard at it, I see.' Andy sighed and picked up another precognition, pen poised. He swatted my hand away when I tried to ruffle his hair. 'Preparation - boring but very important,' I said. 'You know, court work can be tedious too. It's not all liar, liar pants on fire.'

Grace-Mary peered at me over the top of her glasses, brow furrowed, lips pursed in mild disapproval.

'You've a First Diet this morning,' she said.

First Diets were the same as intermediate diets but where the case was more serious and being dealt with by way of solemn rather than summary procedure.

I'd almost forgotten the case of Her Majesty's Advocate against Oskaras Salavejus. I could have done with a trial, and the fee that came with it, but the case was crying out for a plea of guilty and that was exactly what I'd been going to recommend to my client - until I'd learned from the Clerk's office that Sheriff Brechin was down to deal with First Diets that day. The plan now was to bump the case on to trial and hope for a more lenient sentencer at that stage.

'Have you seen the file anywhere?' I wrenched open the bottom drawer of the filing cabinet. It hadn't been oiled in a while and screeched horribly. I was searching under 'S' when I heard Grace-Mary cough meaningfully.

Andy closed the file he was working on and held it out to me.

'Andy's been preparing that case for days now,' Grace-Mary said in a highly rehearsed tone. 'Been down to the Bombay Balti and precked the witnesses himself. I'm sure he must know it inside out.'

I caught a glimpse of my reflection in the mirror near the door. There was quite a lot of grey in my hair. I'd never really given it much thought before but at this rate I'd be white before I was forty. Another loud cough from Grace-Mary. 'I'm sure Andy could handle a wee first diet.'

Andy held out the Salavejus file to me. I took it and studied it, conscious of Grace-Mary's stare and that Andy had momentarily raised himself from his marinade of self-pity and was now casting an optimistic eye in my direction. I gave him the file back. 'All right. But stick to the script. It's a straightforward plea of not guilty. Got that? Not guilty, continue to trial and that's it. Okay?' Andy nodded vigorously. 'And if Sheriff Brechin starts banging on about discounts for early pleas - ignore him. A discounted sentence from Brechin is like a swingeing sentence from anyone else. Clear?' Andy was still nodding.

'Good,' Grace-Mary said. 'That means you'll have plenty time to return some calls, Robbie.' She peeled a yellow Post-it note from the frame of my computer monitor and stuck it onto the back of my hand. 'Some newspaper guy - posh and very persistent - wants to speak to you, wouldn't say what about.' She stuck another note on top. 'Oh, and Mr Turpie called too. Says it's urgent.' As the vindictive features of Jake Turpie flashed before my eyes, Grace-Mary slapped another yellow sticky onto the back of my hand. 'Glenochil. Chic Kelly's prison social worker phoned again. Says Mr Kelly's wondering when to expect you.'

I screwed up the note and hurled it in the bin. 'I'm not going. He'll only want to find out what's happening to Sean —'

'Oh, it's Sean now?' she said. 'That's not what you were calling him the other day there. The swear box thought it had won the lottery.'

I let that pass.

Grace-Mary wasn't finished. Arms folded she drummed a bicep with her fingers. 'Well? Have I to phone back and say that the boy's new lawyer can go see him?'

'Yes... maybe... no... I don't know.'

'Well while you're thinking it about it...' She handed me a carrier bag containing an assortment of tools, screwdrivers, spanners, a hammer and such like. 'The cistern in the loo is still leaking and driving me crazy. Then there's the squeaky drawers on that ancient filing cabinet that you refuse to replace.' She sat down at the reception desk. 'Afterwards, if you ask nicely, I might give you a hand moving the furniture around in here. It was a bit heavy for Andy and I still say you're not making good use of the space in here.'

The main perk of self-employment is being your own boss.

Grace-Mary put earphones on and began to type. 'Now clear off, I'm busy.'

It's good to be in control.

CHAPTER **19**

There was quite a crowd outside Linlithgow Sheriff Court, Monday morning. Max's death had caused a stir in the quiet town of Linlithgow. Although there was some crime locally, most of the serious stuff came from elsewhere. The Sheriff Court at Linlithgow had jurisdiction purely due to historical reasons, the town having been appointed a Royal Burgh as far back as the twelfth century. That was why after centuries the administration of justice was soon to be transferred nine miles to the south and the sprawling new town of Livingston.

As I neared the court I recognised the faces of a number of those present: the Provost, Max's bank manager, his accountant, a few neighbours and several old school friends. Not exactly a group of angry townsfolk, there wasn't a pitchfork in sight, but the gathering was a show of civic disapproval by a town that had lost not only a well-liked lawyer but one of their own.

I weaved a path amidst the throng and stepped over the chain bordering the Court car park. There were a few cat calls shouted in my direction, but they were drowned out by the sound of a Reliance Security van turning off the High Street onto the service road between the courthouse and the County Buildings. The big white vehicle, a row of tinted windows along each flank, turned and came to a halt when met by the congregation blocking its path. Boos and jeers rang out. One ill-informed man in the crowd broke ranks, ran up to the slow-moving van, banging his fists on the back doors, screaming, 'Peedo!' In response, four constables and a couple of traffic wardens sauntered out from the nearby police station and ushered the onlookers to one side of the road, where without much difficulty they were held at bay until the white van could move off again to the rear of the courthouse.

I walked on into the court. My earlier than usual arrival that morning was with a view to intercepting the new duty agent, Lorna Wylie, before she got her hooks into Sean Kelly. I'd had a restless weekend and a sleepless Sunday night. If I let Lorna Wylie take over the case, she would go through the motions, rack up the legal aid fees, but would the correct person be convicted? The thought of an innocent young man going to prison while the real culprit went untraced was one I wasn't prepared to contemplate further. I was a notoriously poor judge of character, but, even taking Jacqui's mysterious disappearance out of the equation, no matter how hard I tried I could not conjure up a mental image of Sean Kelly gunning down my old friend in cold blood. For one thing, what possible motive could he have had? Surely he would have to have been put up to it by someone else and there was no point catching a fly if the hornet went free. I had to continue acting. Find out the truth. When the jury came back with a verdict, I had to know in my heart of hearts that justice had been done, not so much for the accused as for Max.

The only occupant of the agents' robing room when I walked in was a newspaper on legs. The newspaper lowered and I saw one of the older members of the local Faculty, now retired. I didn't know his first name. I assumed he had one, but no-one ever called him by it. He was always Mr Stirling a crusty old guy who dropped into court now and again and spent his time in the robing room, reading the newspaper, gossiping, drinking cups of tea that other people bought him and berating the Scottish Government, irrespective of which political party happened to be in power. I liked him.

'I hear you're out of the case, Munro,' he said. 'Quite right, Max Abercrombie was a good lad, a safe pair of hands. If you're like me you'll be glad to see that little shit downstairs jailed for the rest of his natural.' He snorted. 'Except thanks to those in charge of our so-called criminal justice system he'll probably say, 'oops, sorry', do twelve years and get out on one of those tag things.' He raised his newspaper again. 'Just be grateful that with Barbie the bubblehead for his lawyer, he ain't walking away from this.'

Moments later Lorna Wylie rushed into the room and over to one of the big sash and case windows She had on a steel grey suit, white silk blouse with a black velvet cross-over neck-piece, held in place by a diamond stud. She looked out at the scene below in the courtyard then turned to me, her face aglow beneath the layers of make-up.

'Do you see that crowd?' she asked, breathlessly. 'I'm waiting for the cameras to arrive before I make an appearance.' She glanced down at herself, smoothed her hands over her thin frame and held them out at her sides.

'How do I look? Those TV cameras put pounds on you.' She looked at me. 'What's wrong?' she asked. 'Is my lipstick smudged? Since they put those ultra-violet light bulbs in the toilets to stop the junkies finding a vein, making-up in the ladies is a no-go - unless you want to come out looking like Coco the Clown's big sister.'

'No, you're fine,' I assured her. There was no easy way of saying it. 'Lorna, I want to keep acting for Sean Kelly.'

'Forget it.' Lorna took a press-powder compact from her handbag and checked her lippy in the mirror just in case I'd been lying. She smacked her lips together. 'He's mine.'

'Why don't we ask him who he wants?' I suggested.

'Nope.' Lorna snapped the compact shut and took another glance out of the window. 'I've checked with the cells. Reliance says you're no longer acting and as he hasn't asked for anyone else they've got him down on the sheet as one for the duty agent. Which means me. You've had your chance.' She smiled smugly, climbed into her crisply starched court gown and flounced out of the room.

CHAPTER 20

Most of those sitting at the long trestle tables were giving their undivided attention to the bowls of soup and hunks of bread being laid out in front of them. I pulled up a seat at the end of a row of jaikies, junkies and a German tourist who'd been rolled on Rose Street and couldn't remember who he was, where he was or who'd won the war.

Frankie McPhee came out of the kitchen carrying an enormous pot between two paisley-patterned oven gloves. He placed it on a steel trolley and commenced to dish out steaming ladles of broth. When he caught sight of me, he trundled over with the trolley. 'What brings you through to Auld Reekie?' he asked.

'Sean Kelly. I've been thinking and I might be prepared to give him the benefit of the doubt – for the moment.'

Frankie looked pleased. 'Let me finish dishing up and we'll talk.' He poured me out a ladle of soup. 'Try this. It's my mother's recipe.'

I took a taste and wondered how the man had survived childhood. Frankie and his ladle moved off. I set down my spoon.

'You not wantin' yours?' asked the man sitting next to me.

I wasn't sure which smelled worse, him or the soup. I raised my hands. He pulled the bowl over and got stuck in - years of Special Brew and Dettol cocktails could do that to your tastebuds.

I went through to the kitchen. It was well equipped with a huge gas hob and oven, rows of shiny cooking utensils, pots and pans hanging along the walls and one immense vegetable rack holding heaps of potatoes, carrots and turnips. Over at the table in the middle of the room someone was stacking bowls: Big Jo-

Jo Johnstone. I guessed no-one ever complained about the service.

Soon, Frankie came in and parked his soup trolley. Without a word he led me through a fire exit, and we walked together in the grounds of the old church, through a graveyard overgrown with brambles and purple terrors where a dilapidated stob and wire fence marked an uncertain boundary. Beyond lay an area of waste ground stretching as far as the Edinburgh to Glasgow railway line. We stopped and looked back.

'I'm going to knock the place flat,' Frankie said, breathing clouds of white into the cold night air.

'I wouldn't have thought you'd be into knocking down churches,' I said.

'The Church is the people, not the building. These old Victorian monstrosities would put anyone off Christianity.'

He did have a point. The moment I'd walked into the place I'd been reminded of end of term services, boring sermons, outdated hymns and getting a clip round the earhole for crunching POLO mints. 'And after you've demolished it?'

'I'll build a new place. Bright and welcoming. Fill it with art and music. Make it a public attraction open twenty-four/seven. People will want to come in just to look around, be part of it, and all will be welcome.' Frankie was warming to his theme. 'There'll be a hostel for the homeless, drug and alcohol counselling, sports facilities, healing rooms. I'll bring Christ to the community.'

'It all sounds very commendable. Very expensive.'

'The Lord will provide.'

'You seem very sure about that.'

'Knock and it shall be opened unto you, seek and you shall find, ask and it shall be given unto you —'

'Especially if you have a stocking over your head and a sawn-off in your hand.'

Frankie gave me a weary smile. 'I made a lot of money in my previous life and I've still some of it left.'

'I suppose it helps having never paid tax,' I said. 'Whatever happened to 'render unto Caesar'?'

Frankie's look of discomfort lasted only for a moment. 'Caesar would only spend it on another war.' He kicked a loose stone into the undergrowth. 'Sean Kelly. Why the change of mind?'

'I haven't changed my mind. I'm just not so sure now.'

'And what are you going to do about it?'

'I want to meet with him, hear his side of things.'

'I'm glad. But why are you telling me? Is it about money?'

'I'm no longer acting for Sean so I can't book an agent's visit to see him. I was wondering if you were going to see him anytime soon. I might tag along.'

A light rain had started to fall. Strands of hair stuck to Frankie's forehead and he slicked them back with his hand. 'I've an evening visit booked for tomorrow at seven fifteen. We'll need to check in by seven at the latest. If you like, I'll meet you at your office around half six.'

'I'm not promising anything...'

'I know that,' he said, 'but, believe me, you're doing the right thing.'

CHAPTER 21

HM Prison Polmont became a Young Offenders' Institution as part of the 1983 prison reforms but the locals still refer to it with fondness as 'The Borstal'. It's the biggest prison in Scotland, housing the vast majority of young prisoners, and was where Sean Kelly awaited trial for the murder of Max Abercrombie.

'So,' I said, as I drove down the steep hill through the village of Maddiston. 'Sean Kelly's mum - an old flame?'

Frankie screwed up his face. 'More of a burnt-out cinder, really. Of course, I know Betty's husband from the old days. Chic worked for me now and again. What a thief, by the way. He could steal the sugar out of your tea. There was nobody like him.'

'No-one like him for getting caught afterwards, either.'

Frankie could only agree. 'Aye, it was a nightmare trying to keep him off the bevvy and out of the bookies. Anyway, when I bumped into Betty and heard about Sean I said I'd do what I could to help out.'

In days gone by, a 'help out' would have involved paying the Crown witnesses a visit. Frankie was sheer magic at that. One word from him and, hey presto, instant amnesia.

Intimidation was Frankie's stock in trade. In the beginning, his main sources of income had been money-lending, the occasional spot of armed robbery and, chiefly, a portfolio of clients, mainly pubs and clubs, to whom he provided a protection service. Some establishments were happy to pay to have Frankie show face, his very presence letting the punters know it wasn't a place to be getting rowdy or anti-social with the management. Others were not so keen, but they all paid. It was simply a commercial outlay, like plate glass cover or life insurance. In fact, it was both. Later, Frankie acquired a number of drinking establishments of his own, many at knockdown prices. He could have delegated the running of these businesses to others and enjoyed the good life. He didn't and it was his hands-on approach to business that was to prove Frankie's downfall; that and the CCTV that caught him extracting payment from the nose of a late-payer.

The video evidence was so good that when his case came to court it hadn't been much of a trial, more of a movie premiere with the Sheriff a disgruntled critic. Duly convicted, Frankie checked into Barlinnie for a three-month vacation courtesy of the Queen. It was a stay in jail that with remission should have lasted six weeks; instead he'd served six years.

I brought the car to a halt at a set of traffic lights and took a sideways glance at the man sitting next to me. His strong facial features had softened over the years, but I wasn't convinced that prison had changed any more than his outward appearance. I asked him about his time inside and his face lit up as he recounted the gospel according to Saint Francis of Saughton.

It had been the end of another day. Another twenty-four hours chalked on the prison wall of life. Frankie lay on his bunk, bereft of cigarette papers and choking for a smoke. That was when he'd noticed the little New Testament lying in the corner of the cell. It had a red, fake-leather cover, tattered and worn, and, by the number of missing pages, Frankie wasn't the first guest to have run out of Rizlas.

Frankie tore out a page and laid on a pinch of tobacco. Then it happened, or so he said. Conversion. Not exactly a blinding light on the road to Damascus though just as effective. The page he had ripped out contained John 3 verse 16, a passage even I knew, vaguely. Frankie reminded me:

'For God so loved the world that he gave his only son that whomsoever believes in him shall not perish but have everlasting life. Me! That night I read what was left of that wee book and in the morning I awoke a new creation.'

I'd heard the rest of the story six years previously. Frankie's newfound faith had been greeted by the other inmates with due respect. He was Frankie McPhee after all and had to have an angle; it was just that no one could figure out what it was.

Enter Danny Gilzean, a big fat man with a florid face that proclaimed a fondness for the wine of Scotland. Prison was his second home and frequent incarcerations let his wife's bruises heal and her bones knit.

Gilzean checked into Barlinnie on an unpaid fine the week Frankie was due to finish his short stay. Through sheer ignorance of who he was dealing with and intrigued by Frankie's alleged spiritual transformation, the fat man subjected Frankie to a torrent of abuse and blasphemy as part of his own brand of inquisition.

One day, following what was diplomatically referred to in court as 'a frank exchange of views', Gilzean struck Frankie across the side of the face. The fat man, it seemed, had gleaned a knowledge of scripture from somewhere. 'Now let's see you turn the other cheek.'

Gilzean's fatal mistake was to grossly over-estimate Frankie's theological depth.

Frankie turned to me and smiled sadly. 'Turn the other cheek? I had no idea what the man was talking about.'

The New Testament in the pocket of Frankie's prison trousers began at John's Gospel Chapter 3. The Sermon on the Mount, the beatitudes along with half an ounce of Golden Virginia, had gone up in holy smoke long before.

There was a punch, Gilzean's head hit the ground like a meteorite and one less place was set for dinner that night. Around the same time a couple of distillery workers were laid off and an unhealthy wife became a healthy widow.

And that's where I came in. The Crown, as it did in all but the most clear-cut of cases, offered a plea of culpable homicide leaving Frankie with two choices: take the deal or toss a coin with the jury. Heads it's an acquittal, tails it's a mandatory life sentence. Frankie took the deal and was handed down a nine-year sentence, six with full remission. It was better than life but a bit steep given the mitigating circumstances. I suspected the judge had received a word from the Lord – the Lord Advocate.

'I always said you should have taken it to trial and pled self-defence.'

Frankie shook his head. 'I pled guilty because I was disgusted with myself. I'd been a Christian for barely a month and I had taken the life of another human being.'

I supposed Danny Gilzean could be classified as a human being – if the term were applied loosely enough.

I took a left turn and drove down a long, winding driveway, traversing a mountain range of speed bumps towards the splendid new façade of YOI. Prison building: one of Scotland's few boom industries.

'They say it's all flat screen TV's and X-Boxes,' Frankie said. 'Easy time.' He took his eyes off the great white building at the end of the road. 'Trust me there's no such a thing.'

'And why should it be?' I asked. 'You think it's easy for Irene Abercrombie and her kids.'

'The boy's innocent.'

'So you keep saying.' I parked the car. 'But I'd like to look into his eyes and have him tell me that himself.'

CHAPTER 22

The door to the visit room opened and a prison officer installed Sean Kelly in a chair with his back to the far wall. Scottish Prison Service guidelines stated that all visitors must occupy the seats nearest the door, presumably in case the guests were in need of a sharp exit. I didn't think we were in much danger from young Sean. Perhaps Max Abercrombie had thought the same.

We should have been meeting in the open visit area but the screw who took us through recognised me and, assuming I was there on official business, let us use one of the agents' rooms across the way.

The prisoner stared at me and then at Frankie. 'What's he doing here?'

Frankie set his big black Bible on the table and took a paper bag from his pocket. Strictly speaking it was a breach of Her Majesty's Prison regulations to give items, even pan-drops, to prisoners, but if that was the extent of Frankie's offending these days, I was confident the Queen wouldn't make a fuss. He held out the bag and gave it a shake. The young man took one. Frankie shook it again.

'Have another - for Ron.'

'Who?'

'He means later-Ron,' I said. 'It's like a joke only not as funny.'

The young man's face threatened to crease, the muscles in his face fighting for control as though if he smiled he'd burst into tears. He helped himself to another sweet.

'Sean,' Frankie said, 'you're charged with murder and you need a lawyer.'

'I've got a lawyer. Miss Wylie.'

'Yes, but you need a good lawyer. You need Robbie Munro.'

'Yeah? Well he doesn't want me. At least Miss Wylie wants to help.'

I pulled the bag of sweets across the table. 'You can have Miss Wylie.' I took a pan-drop and popped it into my mouth. 'In fact, if you killed Max Abercrombie, I'd rather you stuck with her. But if you're innocent - I'll see to it that you're acquitted and I'll nail the real culprit or die trying.'

'Listen to the man, Sean,' Frankie said. 'Robbie Munro never let me down.'

It was good of him to say so. Although I'd acted for many of his associates or henchman, call them what you will, I'd only represented Frankie on a handful of occasions and two of those had resulted in conviction and his only two prison sentences.

The prisoner returned his gaze again to Frankie's big black Bible. 'I suppose if Mr McPhee says you're okay…'

I leaned across the table at the prisoner. 'Before we go any further, I have to hear from your own lips that you didn't do this thing.' It was something I'd never asked a client before. Normally, guilt or innocence didn't come into it; such matters were for the jury. I was far more interested in sniffing out reasonable doubts, but then I'd never before had a client charged with killing a friend of mine.

The prisoner said nothing. He just sat there, head bowed, staring at Frankie's Bible and sucking his sweet.

'Okay, for a kick-off why don't you tell me where you were on the evening of the murder.' Nothing. 'Did you know Max Abercrombie? Did you have business with him?' Not a cheep.

Frankie leaned forward, hands clasped, knuckles white. 'Listen, Sean, you've got to talk to Mr Munro. Help him to help you.'

The prisoner thought things over for a moment or two. 'Robbie Munro, Lorna Wylie. What's the difference? The cops have nothing on me. No-one can prove I killed anyone, so why do I even need a lawyer?'

Frankie leapt to his feet and both hands on the tabletop leaned across at the prisoner. 'Wise up, son. Believe me, if the cops say you're het, you're het - and if you don't face up to that pretty pronto you're going to spend the best years of your life eating sausage and beans with a plastic fork.'

He was right. People thought the police investigated a case until they found the culprit. In reality they found a culprit and prepared a case around him. Detective Chief Inspector Petra Lockhart might be keeping an open mind about the investigation: Dougie Fleming had designated Sean Kelly as the murderer and wouldn't be going out of his way in the search for other possible suspects. Much easier for him to cut the cloth that he had to the right size than go looking for new material.

Sean Kelly stood and walked past us to the door. Frankie put a hand on the boy's shoulder and spun him around. 'Sean, you need someone to help you fight this charge and the best fighter I know is Robbie Munro. Now why don't you sit down and answer his questions?'

He pulled away from Frankie. 'What can he do? What can anyone do?' The young man pulled up his shirt. The side of his body was covered in thin lacerations, one or two of which were held together by butterfly strips. 'My first shower in a week. I was that desperate for a wash I never saw the razorblade in the soap. I told the prison doctor what happened and now I'm a grass and everyone wants a piece of me.' He stared down at his feet.

'Please, Sean,' Frankie said. 'Sit down and talk.'

The prisoner paused for a moment, his hand on the doorknob. He was on the verge of tears and I felt something I hadn't expected: sympathy. What was it about the boy? No matter how hard I tried I still couldn't picture him with a gun in his hand, far less pulling the trigger.

'Let me be clear,' I said. 'I don't really care what happens to you. Max Abercrombie was my friend and if you murdered him then, frankly, I'd like to cut you up myself.' I went over and stood face to face with the prisoner. 'But tell me you're innocent and I promise to get you out of here.'

The prisoner turned to Frankie. 'Thanks for coming, Mr McPhee. Tell my mum I'm doing fine.' He opened the door and was about to step into the corridor where a prison officer was waiting. At the last moment he turned and looked me straight in the eye. 'It wasn't me,' he said and left.

I watched him go. Was Sean Kelly a chip off the old block? Appearance-wise he didn't resemble his father and he was intelligent, polite, and well-spoken; attributes one did not readily associate with Kelly senior. I wanted to believe him, but it could have been he'd inherited some of his father's other characteristics. As I recalled, Chic Kelly had been a thief and an excellent liar.

CHAPTER 23

'Word travels fast,' Grace-Mary said, looking out of my office window.

Having only just returned from court that Wednesday morning, I was hoping to take a look at a few files and prepare for the following day's intermediate diets before having to go back to court for the custodies at two.

I left the desk and joined my secretary at the window from where there was a good view down the length of the High Street. Beyond the Cross Well and up the hill from the direction of the Sheriff Court strode a familiarly large figure. Even at a distance I could see the jutted jaw, lowered brow and imagined a moustache bristling with indignation. My meeting with Sean Kelly had taken place only the night before. The mandate to Lorna Wylie breaking the news that I now had instructions to act for the murder-accused was still in a wire basket waiting to go out with the afternoon post. I'd expected my dad to pay me a visit. I hadn't expected it to be quite this soon.

'Tell him I'm out,' I instructed Grace-Mary.

'Tell him yourself,' she said, leaving the room and taking with her a small stack of invoices that had inconveniently arrived in the morning's mail. She closed the door behind her. Three minutes later it opened again.

'It's your dad,' Grace-Mary said, quite unnecessarily since the old man was already filling the doorway. She ducked out of the room again.

'What do you think you're playing at?' The old man loomed over me, his face crimson. 'Not even you could live with yourself if you got that murdering wee slime-ball off the hook.'

'I think Sean Kelly may be innocent,' I said, trying to convince myself as much as my dad. 'Max was shot twice in the chest at point blank range. Does that sound like the work of a nineteen-year-old whose only previous conviction is for peeing up a close?'

My dad straightened and held up his hands in mock surrender. 'Sorry, my fault, I forgot - your clients are always innocent.'

'They are,' I said, lighting the blue touch paper and refusing to retire to a safe distance. 'At least until proven otherwise.'

He gave a loud snort and sat down. 'Well, that shouldn't take long. Not with Petra Lockhart in charge.'

'You know her?'

'I know of her. Fine cop. D'ye not mind that case with the Edinburgh councillors a few years back?'

A few years back to my dad could mean anytime during the past decade.

'Remind me,' I said.

'Lockhart got a tip-off about dodgy dealings in the planning department and tried for a warrant. The Sheriff said no chance, not on the basis of a source that Lockhart refused to reveal. Despite that, the bold girl breenged ahead, crashed through the door of the chairman of the sub-committee on the eve of a public enquiry and discovered brown envelopes galore. The Crown managed to justify her actions on the grounds of urgent necessity. Three City councillors got four years each and one Sheriff got a free transfer to the Shetlands or somewhere with nothing to judge but sheepdog trials. It was a hell of a gamble and if it hadn't worked, I'll tell you, she'd have been drummed right out of the Brownies. Took a lot of courage. I heard she made D.C.I. on the strength of that collar alone.'

Sounded like the Lockhart I knew. A woman of action who saw what needed doing and got it done.

'Then there was that paedophile ring, just last year – '

'Okay,' I said, 'point taken.' My dad was making it sound like the woman could leap tall buildings at a single bound. 'I'm happy they've put someone good onto Max's case. I want the killer caught as much as everyone else. I just want to be sure they get the right person.'

'Oh, they've got the right person. Have no fears on that score. They're piecing together quite a nice little case on young master Kelly.' My dad was warming to his subject. 'From what I hear, he's put at the scene by at least two witnesses.'

I already knew about the witnesses. It had been almost close of business on the Friday evening in question when Max's receptionist and a paralegal saw someone fitting Sean's description come into the office. He'd gone into see Max and later, as they were leaving for the night, the two members of staff had heard a commotion. According to their police statements they hadn't thought much of it at the time. At six foot three, sixteen stones and a former amateur boxer, an obstreperous youth was nothing with which Max couldn't cope.

'And there's forensics as well.'

'What have they got?'

'DNA. Fingerprints. The full works is what I heard. I have it from a reliable source that they found a fragment of your client's skin under one of Abercrombie's fingernails.' He smirked cruelly. 'He even had his name in the appointment diary. Dumb or what?'

I looked at my father. He always liked to be one step ahead.

'I wish you worked for me, Dad. I could do with all the inside information that always seems to come your way.'

'Not a chance.' He was unable to keep the note of triumph from his voice and, his temper receding, I tried to change the subject. 'Would you like a wee half?' I asked. That usually worked.

He hesitated, ran a finger across his moustache and sat down. 'What have you got?'

'Macallan.'

'Eighteen?'

'Ten-year-old.'

'Suppose it'll have to do.'

I fetched the bottle and nipped through to the kitchen, returning with two glasses. By that time my dad's complexion had taken on a more natural hue. So far, so good. I poured us each a drink and he grudgingly clinked his tumbler with mine. Would it be too obvious if I tried to get his mind off Sean Kelly by steering the discussion around to football, his favourite topic of conversation?

Grace-Mary popped her head in the door.

'Sorry to interrupt,' she said, not looking it. 'But Mr McPhee phoned again. He was asking about Sean Kelly's case and to see if you've booked a visit with his dad in Glenochil yet.'

Damage done, my secretary withdrew.

The old man looked at me. 'Mr McPhee?'

'Yes,' I said casually, 'Frankie McPhee.'

He laughed, saw I wasn't joining in and gave me the look: the one I'd first seen as a fourteen-year-old, caught sneaking out to the school disco with four tins of his McEwan's Export up my jumper. That had been the same night I'd drunk a whole bottle of grenadine believing it to be alcoholic, thrown-up and gone crying to him in a panic thinking I was vomiting blood. His eyes narrowed and his moustache turned down at the edges. 'No. Do not tell me you've taken up with Frankie McPhee.'

'Give the man a break, Dad.'

'I'd give him a break all right.'

'He's got an interest in Sean Kelly's case and wants to know what's going on. I don't actually tell him anything confidential. He's just concerned.'

'He's a killer.'

'One who's served his time.'

'Served his time?' My dad was on his feet again, once more leaning over the desk at me. 'He should be serving a dozen life sentences.'

'Then maybe you and the rest of the boys in blue should have caught him more often.' The words were out before I could catch them. I winced. John Barleycorn was a poor advocate.

My dad knocked back his drink and slammed down the empty tumbler. 'And maybe you shouldn't have pulled every stroke in the book to get him and his gang off.' I settled back for the onslaught. 'I've never understood you - defending scum like Frankie McPhee.'

'Dad, it's my job. What you can't thole is that while your career was spent locking people up, I make my money setting them free.'

He replenished his glass and threw the drink back down his throat. 'Taking up with a man like that. The man who killed your own mother.'

Here we go, I thought.

My mother had been a schoolteacher in the small mining town of Bo'ness on the Firth of Forth. There had been a pupil in her class, a bright lad by the name of Francis McPhee. He came from a broken home; most people were of the opinion he'd broken it. He was what my dad used to call 'a juvenile delinquent' and set for a life down the pit or, more likely, in prison. Mrs Munro had other ideas. She took an interest in the boy. She tutored him, brought him home after school to study. For a short time, he became one of the family.

I was a baby and sound asleep the night the police called to say that Frankie had been arrested for some minor misdemeanour. He was going to be questioned and they wanted a responsible adult present. His own mum was out, and probably drunk, and so Frankie had asked for his teacher. A car was sent and my mum set off without saying good-bye to her husband, who was in bed after coming off a late shift and whose opinion of Frankie would later be confirmed. At a tight corner on a wet night the driver lost control. Back then there was no ABS, no crumple zones, just a ton of steel doing sixty. The car hit a tree. Walls fall down on impact. Hit a wall and you're in with a chance. Hit a tree and there's no give. She died instantly.

I liked to think I could remember her. I kept their wedding picture on my desk, but in reality that's all she was: a pretty wee woman standing next to my dad in a black and white photograph. A woman who had died a very long time ago.

'It wasn't his fault and, anyway, Frankie's changed,' I said.

My dad splashed some more whisky into his glass. 'Men like that don't change.'

'Maybe not but I can't be picky about who my clients are. Not in my line of business.'

'Business?' He was really letting rip now. 'A run-down Legal Aid bucket shop for junkies and hoors, more like.' The record was on the turntable and it was getting a good old whirl. 'You could have been something. When you first qualified they were all after you, all the big firms.'

I took his glass and poured the contents back into the bottle. 'I was with a big firm – remember – Caldwell & Clark?'

'Aye, and you threw it all away.'

'They stopped doing Legal Aid work. I understood the reason, I just didn't agree with it.'

'Legal Aid,' he scoffed. 'If you'd stayed where you were you'd be in line for senior partner one day and doing proper legal work for proper people, decent people.'

Alex Munro was a proud man. I wasn't about to tell him that his own failing health was one reason I had returned to my hometown. My dad had raised me; always busy with his work, never too busy for me or my brother, Malcolm. Malky had moved down south and we rarely saw him. My dad had always been there for me and now I would be there for him. For the sake of both our blood pressures I should have kept quiet, but I didn't. 'Decent people? You mean rich people and to hell with the rest.'

'If I find out McPhee's up to anything I'll bring the law down on him like a ton of bricks and...' he jabbed a finger at me, 'anyone else associated with him.'

'Give it a rest,' I came back at him. 'You're not a cop anymore so you can stop acting like one. You're retired. Learn to live with it - I know I'm trying to.'

He got up out of his chair. 'Once a cop,' he said, 'always a cop.' He riffled the bristles of his moustache with a finger. 'Just remember: if you flee with the craws, you get shot with them.'

Conversation over. 'I'll phone you a taxi,' I said, wishing I'd kept my mouth shut.

'Don't bother, I'll walk.'

There was no use arguing. I followed him to the door. 'Okay if I come by and see you tomorrow?'

'I'll be busy the morn.'

There was no talking to the big bear. He'd be fine tomorrow. He was like that. Heat up, cool down. No wonder the doctors despaired. By the time we'd gone down the stairs, through the close and onto the pavement his temper was already on the ebb.

'Thanks for the drink.'

'You're welcome,' I told him. 'But take it easy when you get home. Remember you've had your whisky ration for today.'

'Don't worry about me,' he said, taking a hold of my arm as I turned to leave him. 'If Frankie McPhee's got his hooks in, it's you who'd better be bloody careful.' And, with that parting word of advice, ex-police sergeant Alex Munro set off down the High Street like he was back pounding the beat.

CHAPTER 24

The weeks rolled by. I owed Jake Turpie another month's rent, still didn't have the money to pay him and was surprised that I hadn't heard further on that score: my landlord being something of a stickler when it came to credit control.

On this particular Thursday morning, however, as I awaited admittance to the cells at the Sheriff Court, my main concern was not my landlord but rather the fate of my client Oskaras Vidmantis Salavejus. I still wasn't sure about him. Yes, he was an alky, yes, he seemed to like causing public disturbances and yes he was not averse to a spot of rough and tumble with officers of the law. The question was: did he have the potential to be one of my dripping roasts - a regular source of income in an uncertain world? I wasn't going to find the answer to that with him lying in jail. I needed Salavejus out and about, getting drunk, getting into more bother and getting caught - legal aid certificates didn't grow on trees.

Unfortunately for both of us, Salavejus was of no fixed abode and so ineligible for bail. Apparently, he was no longer welcome at his previous address and the social work had drawn a blank at finding him a place to stay: hard enough to find accommodation for a single male, far less one with a funny name and a drink problem.

The turnkey dragged himself away from the mental rigors of the Sun crossword and unlocked the door to my client's cell. I walked in to meet four walls coated in yellow gloss paint, smeared with stains of uncertain provenance and covered in graffiti. According to the legend scraped deep into the wall, 'Young Skid fae Bo'ness' had been there, as had others less skilled in stone masonry.

I sat down beside Salavejus on the only piece of furniture: a wooden bench pocked with cigarette burns. The prisoner had scrubbed up nicely. By the looks of things his time on remand in Saughton Prison had been well spent for he was a whole lot cleaner, better fed and sober.

'I want to plead guilty,' he said.

I wasn't about to disagree, especially now that I'd been informed who'd be presiding. It paid to know your local Bench and the important thing to know about Sheriff Lawrence Dalrymple was that he liked to finish the day's business as quickly as possible. The chance of a lunch-time finish at Nuremberg and Larry Dalrymple would have given Hermann Göring probation.

'Glad to hear it,' I said. 'You cop a plea. I say how sorry you are, the Sheriff goes home early and next week some old dear has her garden dug by the latest recruit to the community service team. Everyone's a winner.'

Upstairs in courtroom one the Procurator Fiscal, Hugh Ogilvie, leafed through his case file. The very sight of Ogilvie in a court room was a rare occurrence. Generally speaking, he preferred to let his army of deputes fight it out in the trenches while he stayed in the office, engaging in hand-to-hand combat with the paperwork and massaging the conviction statistics. By his presence across the table from me I knew he could smell an easy victory. I took a seat on the opposite side of the table from him.

'You're late,' he said.

I loved it when he fed me one-liners. 'And you're a tube - but I'll try and be early tomorrow.'

Apart from being fun, winding up the PF was all part of the job. Sometimes it knocked them off their stride, helped even up the scales. After all the prosecutor came to court with a thoroughly prepared, no-expense-spared case. Not only that but most Crown witnesses were cops, whose feats of memory were envied by elephants and who attended courses at Tulliallan to learn how to handle smart Alec lawyers. With odds like that the average legal aid, fixed-fee defence needed every little bit of help it could get.

Although Ogilvie didn't look up from his file of papers, the corner of his left eye twitched. I was heartened to know my remark had hit home but today I didn't need to get the PF riled. I wasn't going to trial. Not with a pig of a case and a soft sentencer like Sheriff Dalrymple on the bench. I'd get things wrapped up quickly, go back to the office and catch up on some work. I might even have time for a haircut, though I'd be giving Jay Deez a body-swerve.

From behind me I heard the sound of clumping boots as Salavejus was brought from the cells to take his seat in the dock. The golden rule of the presumption of innocence never seemed much of an advantage when the law also insisted that the accused sit in the dock between two security officers.

'Let's go,' said the Sheriff Clerk. He waved to the Bar Officer who in turn went off to entice the Sheriff from his chambers.

A murmur of anticipation ran through the rows of unempanelled jurors. I glanced over at them. What a system: tried by people too stupid to dodge jury service. Scots legal procedure no longer permitted the defence to challenge prospective jurors unless there was a good cause. In those fondly remembered not so long-ago days, the defence had been allowed three freebies, which meant ditching the teachers and anyone called Reginald. Not anymore. In these enlightened times we had to take what we got and, as the list of assize no longer revealed the occupations of those to be balloted, theoretically an accused could be on trial for bank robbery and have sitting in judgement fifteen tellers from the Bank that likes to say, 'Guilty.'

'Next time you're late I'm having you done for contempt,' said the PF who had obviously been working on his snappy rejoinders.

'Shuggy, why don't you put a sock in it and I'll have us out of here in ten—'

'All rise!' bellowed the Bar Officer glad to be exercising vocal chords that in another life had welcomed new recruits to the parade ground.

The Sheriff came in and everyone stood.

'Brechin?' I accused the clerk. 'Where's Larry the Lamb?'

The clerk's face wrinkled sympathetically. 'Sorry. Sheriff Dalrymple phoned in. His grand daughter's got a piano recital.'

Sheriff Brechin laid out a big blue notebook and placed his fountain pen on top. The judicial appointment system is a mystery to many, but I was entirely familiar with Albert Brechin's route to the bench. It had started with a spell in the Army, then off to the Bar where he was best known for his availability. A move to the prosecution service looked on at one point when an old chum of his landed the post of Lord Advocate, but the last thing the Crown Office needed was a legal lard head like Bert Brechin solving the prison over-crowding crisis with streams of botched prosecutions. For an Edinburgh Academy F.P. and card-carrying New Labourite there had been nowhere to go but up.

The Sheriff opened his notebook. 'Sheriff Clerk?'

The Clerk put fresh tapes into the machine and switched it on. 'Call the diet, Her Majesty's Advocate against Oskaras Vidmantis Salavejus.' The clerk winked at me and said in a low voice. 'Been practising that all morning.' The accused stood up. 'Are you Oskaras Salavejus?'

Oskaras confirmed that he was.

'Who appears?' enquired the Sheriff, vaguely.

I got to my feet. 'That would be me, M'Lord.'

'Mr Munro, how does your client plead?'

The words stuck in my throat. I couldn't plead guilty - not now. Talk about a big hitter? Brechin was the Babe Ruth of sentencing. With him sentencing, a charge of breach of the peace would have been bad enough, but assaulting a police officer – a detective inspector? Brechin would dish out the severest of tonkings for an offence of that nature. I wasn't playing into his hands. It's a bad plan that can't be changed. Who'd said that –

Tacitus or Publilius – some guy in a toga and probably not with this particular scenario in mind, but I decided that the man in the dock could take his chances with a jury.

'Mr Salavejus pleads not guilty,' I said and resumed my seat.

The accused called out to me from the dock. I heard him but didn't turn around.

The Sheriff looked down at me. 'Mr Munro, I think your client would like a word with you.'

'No, my Lord,' I said firmly. 'He wouldn't.

CHAPTER 25

According to the two charges on the indictment, a breach of the peace and an allegedly unprovoked attack on Detective Inspector Dougie Fleming had taken place a few weeks before, within the Bombay Balti restaurant on Linlithgow High Street, handily placed not far from the police station.

On the first day of the trial the Crown had set the scene by calling a waiter and a couple who had been sitting at a nearby table. My attempts at cross-examination had scarcely made a dent in the Crown case thus far. Now we were into day two and the PF was delving into the meat of things. Books of photographs were produced showing Fleming's injuries: the cut over his left eye, which the Crown maintained amounted to permanent disfigurement - though in my opinion any alteration to Fleming's facial features could only be an improvement - a fat lip and some tenderised ribs. It was nothing controversial and I'd agreed all the medical evidence in advance. Better to let the clerk read out a joint minute of admissions than have a police surgeon go into graphic detail in the witness box.

The alleged victim was to be the prosecution's final witness. It was always best to end on a high note and Hugh Ogilvie knew that this witness could be relied on to make a rammy sound like Ragnarok.

Detective Inspector Douglas Fleming entered the witness box, raised his right hand and took the oath in a loud solemn voice. He bowed to the Sheriff, nodded to the PF, smiled at the jury and was led through his evidence, spouting his version of events in a well-rehearsed manner.

'I leapt to my feet advising the accused that he was under arrest,' he said, when at last Ogilvie had brought him to the relevant part of the incident.

'And do you see that person in court?' asked the P.F.

'Yes, sir, that's him there.' Fleming pointed straight at Salavejus.

'Are you pointing to the man in the dock?' asked Ogilvie, as though clarification were required.

'Yes, sir, the man seated between the two officers.'

The two Reliance officers, either side of the accused, stiffened and sat up straight as the eyes of the jury turned in their direction.

'Thank-you inspector, please go on.'

'In my haste to apprehend the accused, my foot caught the leg of the chair, causing me to stumble. The accused took advantage of this. He proceeded to seize me, head-butt me and punch me about the body.'

'Seize me, head-butt me, punch me about the body,' the Sheriff repeated loudly in case the jury were hard of hearings. With great care he jotted down this important piece of evidence. When he'd finished he looked up and smiled at the witness. 'And your assailant, you say he is the man in the dock?'

Fleming pointed once more directly at the accused. 'That's him, M'Lord.'

'And you were in uniform, Inspector?' the PF asked.

'That's correct, sir. I'd been giving a lecture at Tulliallan on interview techniques.'

I'd bet he had. Teaching the new recruits how to note down statements in pencil and have them signed in ink. Fleming was one of the few local cops who'd refused to go with the new electronic notebooks.

'So there would have been no doubt in anyone's mind that you were a police officer.'

'None whatsoever.'

'Thank you, I have no more questions, Inspector,' said the deeply gratified PF.

'Yes, thank you Detective Inspector Fleming,' the Sheriff chimed. 'I'm sure the ladies and gentlemen will find that evidence most helpful when it comes time for their deliberations.' Then, almost as an afterthought, 'Do you have any questions for this witness Mr Munro?'

The Crown was ready to close its case and I'd not yet had so much as a sniff of a defence. There was nothing for it; I'd have to go fishing. I'd also have to be very careful. One wrong question and either Fleming or the Sheriff would be straight in with their size twelves causing even more damage to my client's already battered prospects of an acquittal.

I rose to my feet. 'Yes, M'Lord. I'd like to clarify one or two points for the jury.'

'Very well, but it all seems perfectly clear to me,' said the Sheriff.

I began. 'Inspector Fleming - you enjoy Indian food?'

True to form Fleming wasn't giving an inch. 'I enjoy a range of cuisine, Mr Munro.'

'On this culinary occasion you dined at the Bombay Balti. Tell me, were you dining alone?'

'No, I was accompanied by my wife who at the time of the incident was elsewhere.'

'Indisposed, Inspector?' prompted the Sheriff.

'Powdering her nose, M'Lord.'

I interrupted the friendly banter between Sheriff and witness. 'What did you have to eat?' I was feeling my way gently, searching for an opening.

He thought about it. 'Chicken tikka madras with fried rice, as I recall, Sir.'

The Sheriff shuffled his papers impatiently.

'And it was while you dined on those succulent chunks of barbecued chicken that you noticed my client?'

'It was impossible not to.' Fleming looked to the jury and made his position clear. 'He came in roaring and singing.'

'Joining in with the piped music, you mean?'

'No, I don't. I mean roaring and singing.'

'You're not a music lover?'

'I can assure you, Mr Munro, your client is not Frank Sinatra. Not even Robbie Williams.'

One or two of the jurors smirked and for a moment I thought the PF was going to roll in the aisle. Even the normally mirthless Sheriff Brechin threatened to crack a smile. 'What's wrong Mr Munro?' he enquired. 'The Inspector not singing from your hymn sheet?' Only the Sheriff found the remark funny. He cleared his throat. 'Is this line of questioning leading anywhere?'

I hoped so and ploughed on. 'Surely, Inspector, you are not a man to be annoyed by some singing.'

'I wouldn't call it singing. I'd call it shouting and disturbing the peace.'

The cardinal rule of cross-examination, so they say, is never to ask a question to which you don't already know the answer; however, the people who dole out such pearls of wisdom spend a lot of time writing books and not much in court speiring awkward witnesses. In practice, those actually carrying out cross-examination have frequently to take a gamble, especially when the defence case is not so much weak as it is helpless.

'Shouting what exactly?' I was opening the door for Fleming in the hope that he'd play up the breach of the peace and take the spotlight off the more serious charge of assault. Juries love to reach a compromise; it gets them home sooner. I'd be more than happy if they thought the whole thing was nothing but a drunken stramash, came back with a guilty on the breach and let the assault slide into the hazy realm of not proven.

Fleming sighed. 'I don't recall exactly. It was just shouting.'

'Is it not your job to remember what people shout - so you can tell us all about it afterwards in court?'

Fleming looked at the ceiling.

'Inspector?' the Sheriff asked, when the witness showed no sign of answering. 'Answer Mr Munro's questions and maybe he'll stop asking them.'

'He was shouting at me. I don't know what, something about... about me and his girlfriend. As I think I've said - he was very drunk.'

'And do you know the accused's girlfriend?' I asked.

'I didn't know who the accused was, how would I know his girlfriend?'

'And I take it the accused's behaviour, the singing, the shouting, the public disturbance, it caused you concern, Inspector,' the Sheriff intervened. 'No doubt you and any reasonable person would have been alarmed by his actions?'

I was about to object when Fleming latched on seamlessly to the Sheriff's outrageous leading.

'Indeed, I was alarmed, M'Lord. I nearly choked.'

And there it was. That adminicle of evidence that comes along in every trial. Occasionally it erupts onto the scene like a rampaging bull. More often than not it creeps in on tip-toes and if unnoticed tip-toes right out again. It was my job to notice it. I moved closer and leaned both hands on the witness box.

'And so, Detective Inspector, it's at this point that you leap up and shout - in the middle of this busy restaurant?'

'I'd had enough of his behaviour and advised the accused to get out or be arrested.'

I laid it on thick. 'You stood up and shouted at him over the heads of the other diners?'

Fleming sensed the change in my questioning, though as yet he didn't know where I was going. I only had a rough idea myself.

'He was only a few feet away.'

I slapped on some more. 'Your mouth, full of chicken tikka and basmati rice?'

'I...told you... I was eating... at the time.'

'You were annoyed?'

'Annoyed? Yes, for the other diners more than anything else.'

'Angry?'

'Well...'

'At being disturbed? At being alarmed by this man?'

'I...'

'Clearly distressed?'

'I don't... probably...yes.'

'Red in the face?'

'Perhaps, slightly.' said the inspector, his face ablaze.

'And staggering about?'

'As I've already said, I stumbled over the leg of my chair…'

'And that's the moment my client seized hold of you?'

'Yes. And he head-butted me.'

'An accidental clash of heads surely?'

'Not at all.'

'And he punched you I think, Inspector,' said the Sheriff, checking his notes.

'Yes,' said Fleming.

I stepped in again.

'In summary then, you nearly choked, you were on your feet, red in the face and Mr Salavejus came over and seized you.'

'He butted me. He punched —'

'Yes, thank you for clearing that up for us Inspector.' I returned to my seat, hoping I'd done enough. It wasn't going to get any better.

'Clearing what up, Mr Munro?' exclaimed the Sheriff, playing to the crowd. 'I'm afraid, I'm none the wiser!'

I couldn't resist. 'Perhaps not M'Lord, but, one hopes, better informed.'

CHAPTER 26

There was no way I was going to let Oskaras Salavejus go anywhere near the witness box. Hugh Ogilvie's style of cross-examination might have been more bludgeon than rapier, still I wasn't having my client mess up what little progress had been made. The Crown case finished early afternoon and it being Friday the court adjourned for the day. The jury was released with the usual admonition not to discuss the case with anyone and to return fresh on Monday morning for closing speeches.

I went back to the office to check how things were going only to be informed by Andy that Grace-Mary had dislodged a filling on a piece of treacle toffee and had left early to go to the dentist. I realised he had his coat on.

'Where do you think you're going?' I asked.

'I'm not going anywhere,' he said, taking off his coat. 'I've been. To Abercrombie & Co's – remember you asked me to go?'

It was true. I'd seen copies of statements the police had taken from the staff there but wanted to know more about the last few days of Max's life and any unusual goings on. 'Find out anything useful?'

'Nothing new I'm afraid. The Law Society has sent someone in to wind up the business and he doesn't know anything. The conveyancing paralegal is still off work with shock or nervous debility or something and Mr Abercrombie didn't have a secretary as such; everything there is computerised, voice recognition, the lot. But I did get this from the receptionist.' He handed me a thick sheaf of A4 stapled in the corner. 'It's a print-out of his diary. I don't know if it will be of any interest.'

I took the papers through to my room where Grace-Mary had left some urgent mail on the desk. There was a batch of Crown productions for the Kelly case including a forensic report. I scanned it quickly. The marks and biological material found on Max were consistent with him having been in recent physical contact with Sean and vice versa. My dad had told me as much weeks ago. Now I had the evidence in black and white before me.

'While I was there Mr Abercrombie's receptionist told me that they'd been up at Livingston police station for the VIPER two a while back,' Robbie said.

It must have been during Lorna Wylie's short-lived involvement in the case. I'd yet to receive the identification parade report. 'And?'

'Her and the paralegal watched the DVD and were both confident that they'd picked out the person who they say was Mr Abercrombie last appointment the day he was killed.'

Eyewitnesses, now forensics as well. It was time for me to clarify a few details with my client. His defence of 'it wisnae me' just wasn't going to cut it.

CHAPTER 27

I took a form from the reception desk and filled it in with the: prisoner's name and number as well as my own details. Visits to Polmont Young Offender's Institution finished at four-fifteen prompt and the screws started getting twitchy at a quarter to. By four o'clock on a Friday there was more chance of getting on a 747 with a bump in your hijab. 'You're too late,' said a prison officer. He had short ginger hair and the strain on the trouser button that sat about a foot below the tip of his black clip-on tie suggested a man who knew how to unwrap a pie supper. He was standing a few yards away leaning an arm against the frame of the walk-through metal detector in such a way as to show off the damp patch under his oxter.

I glanced up at the clock: five past four. I slid the form across the counter to the female receptionist who looked at the piece of paper in silent disbelief.

'I said you're too late.' The screw came over and grabbed the form.

I grabbed it back and gave it once more to the receptionist. 'I'll not be long.'

The screw snatched the form out of the receptionist's hand. 'I know - because you're not going in.'

I thought about asking nicely but it had been a long day and I couldn't be bothered grovelling to some fat-arsed screw with a personal hygiene problem, just because he was trying to get off on a flier for the weekend. I took out my mobile telephone and punched in a number, like I was punching his face.

A few feet away, the phone at the reception desk bleeped. The receptionist hesitated then answered.

'The Deputy Governor, please,' I said.

The receptionist looked from the phone to me to the screw.

Ginger threw the form at the receptionist and turned on his heel. I cancelled the call and followed him upstairs to the visit rooms.

'You've five minutes,' he said, after I'd stowed my mobile in one of the lockers.

'Ten,' I said. 'Your clock's fast.'

Five minutes later, Sean Kelly trudged into the cubicle and sat down. The dark rings around his eyes testified to another sleepless night.

'I'm here to talk about this.' I unfurled my copy of the forensic report. 'Do you know what it is?'

Sean thumbed through the pages. 'DNA? He glowered at me defiantly. 'What do you want me to say? I've already told you; I never killed that man.'

Through the glass in the door, I could see the screw sitting on the table at the end of the corridor, Humpty Dumpty in uniform, swinging his legs and watching the clock.

'Did you ever meet him?' The prisoner returned his gaze to the tabletop. 'Well?' No answer. 'Have you ever been to his office? Talk to me Sean.'

'All right. Yes – I've been there,' he said at last.

Now we were getting somewhere.

'When?'

'The night he was killed.'

'Why?'

Sean shifted uncomfortably in his seat. 'Last time I visited my dad we had a bit of a barney. He was getting on at me 'cos I'd packed in my college course.'

'And?'

'He said I was a waster. That I didn't know how lucky I was.'

'And?'

'I said some things.'

'Like?'

'Like he wasn't exactly a great role-model.'

That had to qualify for understatement of the year. 'Is this story going somewhere, Sean?'

'I'm trying to tell you. The last time I saw my dad we were arguing and he tells me he's always tried to do his best for me and my mum. I told him that getting locked up for life hadn't really been a big help to us and then from nowhere he comes out and tells me he's innocent.'

A person in jail maintaining their innocence? How not very unusual. 'Sean, people talk a lot of crap when they're trying to win an argument. You should hear me in court.'

'Mr Munro, before that day I'd visited my dad twice a month, every month, since I can remember. That whole time he never once talked about his case.'

'What did you normally talk about?'

'I dunno. The usual stuff: football, my mum, the doos.'

'Pigeons?'

'Aye, my dad's a fancier, me too. They were always around when I was growing up. We had some right crackers. I've got this one just now—'

I held up a hand and cut him off. It was the first sign of passion I'd seen from the boy, though, locked up in that place, I didn't think that pigeons would be the birds he'd be missing the most.

'We've not much time,' I told him. 'I need to know why you went to see Mr Abercrombie.'

'Because I believed my dad. Why would he lie?' Because he was good at stealing and lying and not much else, was the obvious answer. I let the boy continue. 'He told me he was dying and that he wanted to leave us some money. He was pretty doped-up and didn't go into detail, but he was going on about a reward and how he'd hidden something, and I was to find it and take it to you.'

'Why me?'

'He said you'd know what to do. I was to tell you to get a good deal for me and my mum any way you could. My dad liked you. Said that you were all right. That you'd do anything for money.'

I felt that was a bit unfair – obviously, it would depend on how much money we were talking about. 'Take what to me?'

'A package.'

'What has this got to do with Max Abercrombie?'

'I didn't know who you were or where you were. My dad told me to try an outfit in Glasgow.'

'Caldwell & Craig?'

'Yeah, I think that was them, but they said you'd left and moved to Linlithgow so I looked up the Yellow pages and when I couldn't find you, I thought I'd ask about.'

Abercrombie & Co. Had Max been killed because I couldn't afford to advertise and he came first in the phone book?

'Keep going,' I said.

'I went to see Mr Abercrombie. He was very nice. Told me not to worry. He said that you and him were friends and he'd pass the package on to you.'

Why hadn't Max simply directed him to my office? It was only the other end of the High Street. Had his nose been bothering him perhaps? Or was he suspicious, trying to protect me?

The young man continued. 'He wanted to know what was in the package. I told him I didn't know and that it was private. He opened it, looked inside. I tried to stop him. I grabbed the bag—'

'Bag?'

'The stuff was in a bag and he grabbed it and there was a bit of a struggle. The next thing he's opening the fire escape with my head and I'm out in the side alley. He told me not to go see you and that I should take the bag to the police.'

'Mr Abercrombie was found dead in his office the next morning,' I said.

'We argued. He horsed me. My feet never touched.'

'They have a fragment of your skin under one of Mr Abercrombie's fingernails.'

'I struggled a bit. That's all. Honest.'

'What's in it?'

The prisoner shifted again in his seat.

I repeated the question. 'What's in the bag?'

'I don't know.'

'You really trying to tell me you never looked?'

'Mr Munro, as far as I know, only my dad and Mr Abercrombie have seen inside that bag.'

The screw slid off the desk and waddled down the corridor towards us. I had to work fast.

'Where is it?'

Sean looked at the tabletop.

The screw tapped on the glass window in the door.

I seized Sean by the front of his shirt. 'Where is it? Where's the bag?'

The prisoner's mouth was set in a determined line. I hauled him across the table.

'Hey!' yelled the screw.

He tried to open the door, but I pushed it shut with my foot. 'Tell me!' I roared at Sean.

On the other side of the door, a fat face threatened to explode. Sean pulled free of my grip. The screw barged in. 'Right Kelly, stay there!' He grabbed the prisoner, pushed him and held him against the wall with one hand. 'And as for you,' he said to me, jerking a thumb at the open door. 'Your time's up.'

CHAPTER 28

H.M. Prison Glenochil squatted in the shadow of the Ochil Hills, near Tullibody, Clackmannanshire and held mainly category B and C prisoners who knew that the joys of open prison or freedom on an electronic tag were only a few months of good behaviour away.

Following my frustrating meeting with Sean Kelly I suddenly placed a great deal more importance on the frequent calls that had been made to my office by his father.

I parked in a visitor's bay and trudged the long walk to the front gate, cursing every falling raindrop. What a way to spend a Saturday morning. If I'd wanted to work my weekend there was a mountain of unanswered mail on my desk and plenty of upcoming trials to prepare for. The one thing I could have done without was yet another prison trip. I spent too much time in the slammer as it was. Count up all the hours I'd spent on prison visits and I reckoned it was equivalent to a sentence for string of housebreakings or a reasonably serious assault.

At reception, I flashed my Law Society I.D. card, walked through the metal detector and waited as my briefcase trundled through the X-ray machine and along the conveyor belt towards me. A prison officer appeared swinging a bunch of keys attached to his belt by a chain, each link a year served. 'Agent for Kelly?'

He led me through a series of doors, upstairs to a small windowless room inside which there was a wobbly table, two shoogly chairs and the faint aroma of stale urine. On one of the chairs sat an old man. It was many years since I'd clapped eyes on Chic Kelly and I hardly recognised him. The Chic I remembered had never been what you'd call fat, but he'd been well built. The person sitting across the table from me was emaciated. The skin at his throat hung in loose folds and sparse, spiky hair stuck out from his head at all angles. A washed-out red polo shirt and pair of faded denims, both several sizes too large, only served to complete the illusion of a scarecrow with no fashion sense. He stared at the wall as though in a trance and didn't seem to notice that I'd entered the room.

The door slammed shut. I went over and offered him my hand. 'Been a long time,' I said. The prisoner didn't budge at first and then after a moment or two his eyes drifted in my direction. He stared hard at me but said nothing. 'Robbie Munro, I'm here to see you,' I said, rather stating the obvious.

He seemed to be in pain and took several deep breaths before he spoke. 'About time,' he said, each word a struggle. 'Have you seen Sean?'

I'd been granted a half-hour slot and was grateful for that at short notice on a Saturday. There was no time to waste. I was there to ask questions not answer them.

'Yes, I have. What's in the package?'

'What do you mean? I thought you said Sean had been to see you?'

'Sean took it to the wrong lawyer by mistake. Now he'll not tell me where it is.'

The prisoner's eyes lost focus for a moment. There was a lengthy pause before he replied. 'You mean you've not got it?' he gasped at last. His body stiffened. His hands clenched and unclenched, his face tightened into a grimace.

I wondered whether I should get help. Slowly his body relaxed. He sat back and wiped a hand across his mouth. 'Where's the package? Where's Sean?'

Had nobody told him?

I don't know where the package is. Sean won't say. He took it to another lawyer and now that lawyer is dead.'

'The cops. Have you been to the cops? Have you done a deal? What about the newspaper?'

'Chic,' I said. 'Sean's been charged with murdering the lawyer. Don't you know that? He's on remand. There'll be no deal and it's all over the papers.'

Maybe I could have broken the news more gently.

With unexpected speed, the prisoner jumped to his feet, knocking over his chair in the process. He lunged for me. I leaned back, placed a foot on the edge of the table and shoved. The table hit Chic at thigh level, not hard but it didn't need to. He fell.

The door burst open. The screw marched in and looked accusingly at me. 'What's going on?'

I shrugged. 'Ask him.'

'It's all right,' Chic said, wheezing, fighting for breath. 'Just an accident… I'm okay.' The screw gave me a long sideways look and then between us we helped the prisoner back onto his feet and into his chair.

'Sorry about that,' Chic said, once the prison officer had left us alone again. He sounded more coherent now. Maybe the surge of adrenalin had cut through whatever drugs he was on. 'I can't handle it anymore.' He gave a bitter little laugh 'Then again, I'll not need to. Not with the time I've got left.' He took a few deep wheezy breaths. 'You wouldn't believe the dope they've got me on. There's junkies in here would kill you for it.'

'The package you asked Sean to deliver didn't reach me,' I told him, moving things swiftly along before he decided to take another little turn to himself. 'Tell me what it is, where it is and what I'm supposed to do with it.' Under normal circumstances I'd have a couple of additional questions along the lines of, 'how do I get paid, how much and when?' but these were nothing like normal circumstances.

'I don't know where it is. I told Sean to hide it somewhere safe. It was years ago. He was just a laddie at the time. I told him he was never to look in it and that I didn't want to know where it was.'

Okay, so only Sean knew the whereabouts of the package and he wasn't prepared to divulge its location. 'Tell me what's in it.'

Chic bowed his head, put a hand on the table to brace himself and for a moment I thought he was going to fly for me again. He didn't. He held his breath, squeezed shut his eyes and bit his bottom lip. 'You know why I'm in here,' he panted, coming out of the seizure. 'For killing that judge?' He looked me straight in the eye, just as his son had at our first meeting in Polmont YOI. 'Well,' he gasped, still gripping the table edge, 'it wasn't me.'

Oh, no, I thought. Here we go. There was a legal presumption that a person found in possession of recently stolen property was the thief. Lord Hewitt of Muthill had been blown away by a stolen shotgun - his own extremely valuable antique shotgun. The same shotgun, in fact, that Chic Kelly, housebreaker extraordinaire, was found trying to flog the next day. As I recalled, he'd pled guilty.

Chic was a man, old before his time, dying a painful death in prison. I humoured him. 'Who was it then, Chic? Who killed the judge if it wasn't you?'

Chic took a few deep breaths and sat back in his chair. He stared across the table at me, the whites of his eyes yellow, the rims red raw.

'Frankie,' he said. 'He gave me the bag. He thinks I destroyed it, but I didn't. Frankie McPhee killed the judge and what's in that bag will prove it.

CHAPTER **29**

Cairnpapple Hill, the site of an ancient burial ground, lies in the Bathgate Hills not far from the pretty village of Torphichen to the south of Linlithgow. It is the highest point in West Lothian offering on a good day, or so it is said, a line of sight that stretches across the width of Scotland from the Bass Rock in the east to the Isle of Arran in the west. The countryside around is desolate, the wind blows incessantly and the few trees that draw sustenance from the rocky soil are thin and spindly.

Jacqui Dillon's body was found in an area of scrub heather and blaeberry not half a mile from the Neolithic cemetery. A body doesn't last long exposed to the elements and the proprietor of Jay Deez Salon would have gone undiscovered had it not been for a troop of orienteering Boy Scouts that, well off-route, literally stumbled across her. Corpse discovery: there was probably a badge for it.

When Jacqui hadn't come into work for a day or two the staff had found it slightly worrying and later her prolonged absence from the salon was a cause for concern. Now that she was definitely not coming back, the girls didn't know what to do. They didn't even know if the boss had next of kin. Butch thought there might be an aunt in Ayrshire but Jacqui's life outside of the shop was largely a mystery.

I learned of her death late Sunday afternoon. The police were looking for someone to identify the body and had phoned around the girls from the salon who unanimously nominated Butch. He wanted me to go with him.

At the morgue, we were met by two uniformed officers. One, a female sergeant, stepped forward and introduced herself. It couldn't have been an easy job preparing friends and relatives for the shock of seeing a loved one in a state of advanced decomposition, but I could tell she had done this sort of thing many times before. She spoke unhurriedly, calmly, her tone formal yet sympathetic. Pretty soon she had put Butch at ease and when satisfied that the hairdresser was ready for the ordeal, a discrete nod to her young male colleague was enough to have him disappear out of a side door.

Moments later there came the soft squeak of rubber wheels on tiled floor, and I felt Butch tense as a metal trolley disturbed the vertical plastic strips that hung across the wide doorway of the examination room. He took one of my hands in his sweaty grip and squeezed, cracking my knuckles.

The female officer spoke again, this time explaining in her firm but gentle way that due to trauma, decomposition, environmental factors and interference from what she described as 'natural agencies', Jacqui's facial features might not be recognisable. Again she nodded to her male colleague who slowly pulled back the white sheet. Cause of death wasn't much of a puzzler. The bullet had gone in at the left temple and exited the lower jaw taking much flesh, tooth and bone with it.

At the sight of his dead employer, Butch's mouth went slack. He wobbled for a moment, expelled air like a weather balloon with a slow puncture and collapsed in a heap, despite the young constable's best efforts to catch him. The policewoman gave me a wry look.

While we were manoeuvring the fallen hairdresser into a recovery position, the trolley was put in reverse and trundled out of sight. When Butch eventually came round, we were taken to a small waiting room and plied with sweet tea and some rather soft Bourbon creams; however, even duly refreshed, the big man was a wild horses job and could not be cajoled into a return trip to the examination room. Time marched on. The policewoman looked at me. 'Did you know the deceased?'

The trolley was wheeled through again.

The identification procedure was pretty much a formality. Jacqui had been found fully clothed, still wearing her jewellery and with a credit card in the front pocket of her jeans. The various items had already been shown to some of the girls at the salon who had confirmed them as belonging to the boss, but, before the body could be released for burial, the authorities required corroboration by way of the deceased's physical identification. Dental checks of what teeth were left intact would take time and fingerprint comparisons hadn't been possible due to the effect of 'natural agencies'- the small furry kind with big teeth and long tails. That's where I came in.

Mercifully, most of what was left of Jacqui remained covered by a sheet and I was shown a selection of potentially distinguishing features of which I recognised the tattoo of black and white Scottie dogs at the top of her right arm, the mole on her top lip and a small scar at the corner of her right eye, or socket as it now was.

It was well after six when I dropped off the traumatised Butch. I was fairly shaken-up myself. I hadn't truly seen the hairdresser as a gun-wielding assassin, but her disappearance had shed a shadow of doubt over Sean Kelly's guilt and been the reason I'd felt justified in representing him. Now it transpired that Jacqui had also been shot dead, and her body dumped where clearly no-one ever expected it to be found. I would have ditched the Kelly boy's case there and then had it not been for the ramblings of his father which, together with Frankie McPhee's arrival at my office only days after Max's murder, had presented me with a new, if not yet reasonable, doubt. I needed to think seriously about what to do next, but right at that moment I had an even more pressing matter to attend to.

As I returned home that Sunday evening I stopped off at the office to pick up the Salavejus file. I had my closing speech to make in the morning and although I knew the line I was going to take, it wouldn't do any harm to refresh my memory on the evidence given that I was going to have to ask the jury to ignore most of it. My mobile phone rang when I was walking up the stairs. It was my dad.'

'Robbie? Where are you?'

'The office.'

'On a Sunday?'

''fraid so. You know how it is for us bucket-shop proprietors. We can't be taking time off like proper lawyers who do work for decent clients.'

There was silence on the other end of the line.

I laughed. 'What do you want?'

'Oh, nothing,' he said, airily. 'I've not eaten yet and I was just wondering if you'd be dropping by for your tea.'

My dad was sitting at the kitchen table when I arrived at his place half an hour later. There were plates, forks and knives and a bottle of brown sauce laid out and he had a kitchen-roll bib tucked into the neck of his shirt.

'Did you remember the pickled egg?' he asked as I set down before him a bottle of Barr's Irn Bru and a warm newspaper parcel. As if I'd be allowed to forget.

After we'd eaten, I washed and put away the dishes while the old man made us a cup of tea.

'How's the case going?' he asked.

I didn't think Max's death was a subject we should discuss just when relations between us were improving. 'Is that why you asked me round? To talk about my work? I thought it was just an excuse for a free fish supper.'

I followed him through to the sitting room where he plumped himself into his usual armchair and pulled the local newspaper from the side of the cushion.

'I was reading about it in the paper.'

'I think we should leave Max's case out of it for tonight.' That's how I still saw it. It wasn't Sean Kelly's case it was all about Max and finding out who'd killed him.'

'Not Max - the soldier you're representing.'

'Soldier?'

He gave me his, I'm-one-step-ahead-as-usual, look and handed me the newspaper.

War Hero Stands Trial for Cop Assault proclaimed a small headline on page seven, part of the weekly court roundup.

Oskaras Vidmantis Salavejus, Lithuanian-born former Captain in the Royal Anglian Regiment, assaulted a high-ranking police officer, a court heard. Salavejus seized Detective Inspector Douglas Fleming (36) – they had to be kidding: thirty-six, was that all? - while he dined at a local restaurant and struck him on the head and body to his injury. Salavejus (33) who was awarded the Conspicuous Gallantry Cross during service in Afghanistan denies the charge. The trial continues before Sheriff Albert Brechin, Robbie Monroe defending.

Pity they hadn't spelt my name right – as usual - all Marilyn's fault. I folded the newspaper and gave it back.

'Thought you should know. The guy's obviously done out of the park but... well, if you pled him guilty... you know what Bert Brechin's like with soldiers,' my dad said.

It hadn't escaped me that the only time Sheriff Brechin ever showed any sign of leniency was when dispensing justice to soldiers, serving or veterans.

He handed me the newspaper again. 'You can keep it if you like,' he said.

I knew it was my dad's attempt at a peace offering.

'If you think it will be of any use to you.'

Oskaras Salavejus: hero to zero. He was an officer, if no longer a gentleman. 'You know what, Dad? I think it just might.'

CHAPTER 30

Monday morning. I sat thumbing noisily through the Criminal
Procedure (Scotland) Act 1995; a piece of legislation subject to
the frequent whimsy of the Scottish Government. It used to fit
in my pocket. These days I could hardly lift it off the table. When
the PF reached what he no doubt regarded as the exciting climax
to his remarks, the heavy volume sort of accidentally slipped
through my fingers onto the floor and I was pleased to see that
this minor incident had diverted the attention of several
members of the jury.

Eventually, Ogilvie sat down. It was my turn. From
experience I was well aware that jurors fell into two categories:
those who didn't want to be there and those who wished they
were somewhere else. I was also sure that the attention span of
even the most diligent juror could be measured in seconds rather
than minutes and that those who had day-dreamed their way
through the evidence dared not admit it to their colleagues -
even although they'd all done the same. That's why the closing
speeches were so important. A short, sharp speech, spoken with
conviction, was often all a lazy inattentive juror needed to reach
a decision.

'Mr Munro?' said the Sheriff. I didn't move. 'Mr Munro?' I
remained motionless, deliberately building the tension, making
sure the jurors were paying attention and at the same time
readying myself to say whatever it took, just so long as when I
sat down again the masters of the facts saw neither black nor
white - only grey. 'Mr Munro, if you will.'

I waited a little longer. I could hear one or two of the jurors
fidgeting, shifting in their seats wondering if something was
wrong. When I sensed all eyes were on me, I stood and faced
them. They weren't fifteen men and women. They were fifteen

hurdles standing between me and victory. I wouldn't be long. The more the defence lawyer says, the guiltier the jury thinks his client is.

'Ladies and gentlemen,' I rubbed my brow for effect. 'I know you will not have found this an easy case to judge.'

From his vantage point in the public benches, D.I. Dougie Fleming failed to suppress a chortle. Momentarily distracted, I looked over just in time to see Andy come into court and take a seat at the back, the merest hint of a sadistic grin on his face. How pleasant it is, when the sea is high and the wind is dashing the waves about, to watch from the shore the struggles of another. Lucretius: not the cheeriest of Roman philosophers, probably why he topped himself.

I continued. 'The Crown would have you believe my client carried out a brutal, unprovoked assault on a police officer. Not a bit of it, ladies and gentlemen. What happened in the Bombay Balti was something selfless. Something courageous. Something noble.'

I turned to look at my client and all fifteen heads in the jury box turned with me. Oskaras sat slumped in the dock. I willed him to sit up and look more heroic.

'My client has served his country, served you and me, ladies and gentlemen, in the killing fields of Afghanistan and Iraq. Laid his life on the line so that others might live.' I put my hand in my pocket and produced a medal. It was my dad's Police Long Service medal, but it looked the part. 'Helping others, with no thought for himself, is second nature to Captain Oskaras Salavejus, holder of the conspicuous gallantry cross.'

'M'Lord. None of this was led in evidence.' The PF was on his feet objecting.

Sheriff Brechin for once saw things the way of the defence. 'Are you disputing the fact that the accused is a Captain or the holder of an award for gallantry, Mr Ogilvie?'

'Neither, M'Lord,' muttered the PF, sinking slowly to his seat again.

I couldn't have timed the PF's objection better. His apparent unwillingness to let the jury hear of my client's status and bravery in the field would not have gone unnoticed.

I battered on. 'You see, my client's selflessness, and sense of duty are things Detective Inspector Fleming and the Procurator Fiscal can't understand. Please don't view the events in the Bombay Balti through their jaundiced eyes. Don't accept their distorted vision of what took place. Do not bow to the Crown's demands to find my client guilty.'

One or two of the jury were now casting suspicious glances in the PF's direction. They had no idea where I was going – not yet - but no-one, Procurator Fiscal or not, was telling them what to do.

'By now,' I continued, 'you must surely know my client's true motive.' I looked at the jury, making eye contact with each of them, one by one. Fifteen blank expressions stared back at me. They were hooked. It was time to summon the mist of reasonable doubt.

'Captain Salavejus may have had a couple of drinks too many. He may, indeed, have been loud and raucous. Perhaps his singing was off-key, but - when duty called - he was there. Oh, his methods may have been crude, his efforts clumsy and misunderstood,' something caught in my throat, it was a technique that had taken many speeches to perfect, 'but, ladies and gentlemen, I can assure you, my client's actions came straight from the heart.'

CHAPTER **31**

The trial was over by mid-day. After some unusually fair directions by Sheriff Brechin the jury came back in half an hour with a not proven verdict on the assault charge and a guilty on the breach of the peace. Brechin imposed what was for him an extremely lenient thirty-day back-dated sentence, which meant that with time served Salavejus was once more free to go forth and offend. And like most clients for whom a defence lawyer achieves a really good result, he didn't wait to say thanks.

Pleased at the result, I let Andy take me for a celebratory drink. The Red Corner Bar was my dad's local, sitting sandwiched between a wine bar selling over-priced Beaujolais and a pseudo-tavern pouring pints of beer with bits in it. Personally, I'd have found either of those neighbouring drinking holes preferable to the Red Corner, but there was somebody there I wanted to see. Cutting our wake through the cigarette smoke, we made our way past the social lepers congregating outside the front door and into the pub where a couple of regulars shifted themselves an inch or two to let us in at the bar.

The barman who was standing at The Deep End, so named because of the number of older patrons who sat at that end of the bar and occasionally had trouble getting off their stools and making it to the bog in time. He was holding forth to a covey of flat-caps on the subject of some off-side goal or other and in danger of rubbing a hole in the pint glass he was drying with a grubby towel.

Andy waved at him.

'With you in a second,' the barman said, acknowledging our existence without looking in our direction.

I sat on a high-stool and studied the limited array of single malts on the top shelf, my eyes wandering down to the gantry below the optics where the synthetic smile of a scantily clad page-three girl beamed out at me from behind a few strategically placed packets of peanuts. To her side was a framed black and white photograph of a boxer, his hair slicked back, hands wrapped in white gauze. He was crouched, ready to spring and unleash the fury of his fists. The time it was taking to get served - I knew how he felt.

Eventually, the barman placed the thoroughly dry beer glass on a shelf and made his way down to what I logically assumed, and sincerely hoped, was The Shallow End. He was new, or at least I hadn't seen him before. Andy, ever the optimist, ordered two chilled bottles of Innis & Gunn and settled for two luke-warm pints of heavy. I could see him hungrily eyeing up some SPAM rolls that lay asphyxiating in cling-film on a tin tray, so I shouted up a couple of bags of dry-roasted.

The barman set down the pints and tossed the packets of nuts on the counter beside them. 'Six – twenty,' he said, holding out a hand.

'Is the boss in?' I asked and the barman grunted in confirmation. 'Tell him Robbie Munro's here - I'll be over there.' I left the empty outstretched hand and ushered Andy to a table near the fruit machine.

'And so ends the bloody business of the day,' I said, after I'd sipped the head off my pint.

'That was quite a speech.' Andy set down a half empty glass and wiped his mouth. 'First time I've heard the Heimlich manoeuvre being put forward as a defence.'

I tore open my bag of peanuts. 'Thanks. I was quite pleased with it.'

'You know,' Andy said, 'I did a lot of work on that file and I don't recall Mr Salavejus, or anyone else, saying that they thought the Inspector was choking.'

'Don't you?'

'No – I don't. Are you really telling me he told you to put forward that defence?'

I palmed a handful of peanuts.

'Well?' Andy demanded.

'Sorry?'

'The Heimlich manoeuvre.'

'What about it?'

'Were those his instructions?'

I didn't like the way the conversation was headed. Client's instructions were all very well in theory, but start going down that road in practice and I found you ended up with either a transparently implausible defence or the truth - both were usually best avoided.

Andy looked at me accusingly. 'You made it up, didn't you?' He didn't quite synchronise the words with his next pull from the pint glass and so spilled some beer down his front. 'The whole thing. It was a complete fabrication.' He dabbed at his tie with a beer mat.

'A fabrication?' Next he'd be calling the defence a tissue of lies and I might burst into tears.

'Well, it wasn't the truth.'

'Quid est veritas?' I asked. Lapsing into Latin is usually a good way to end an unwanted conversation, but Andy wasn't to be so easily put off. 'Let's leave Pontius Pilate out of this.' He ripped a corner off his bag of nuts, poured some into his mouth and chewed for a moment. 'The fact is you made it up. The entire defence, you invented it.'

'Flatterer.'

'I'm being serious, Robbie. You can't just make up a defence and then present it to a jury, like it's been handed down to you on tablets of stone - it's completely unethical.'

His voice was loud. One or two regulars turned to stare.

'Keep talking,' I said. 'I need all the publicity I can get.'

'It's not funny. You deliberately misled the court.'

'That presupposes I knew the truth of what happened,' I said.

Andy gave a hollow laugh. 'You must have done. It was obvious from the statements – they were all on the file. I know. I took them.'

I pushed my peanuts to the side. 'Tell me. Were you in the Bombay Balti on the night in question?'

'No. Of course not.'

'Then you don't actually know what happened.'

'Neither do you.'

'That's my point. Neither does the Procurator Fiscal, though it didn't stop him from charging my client with assaulting Dougie Fleming. All I did was present the jury with an alternative scenario. One that, for all I know, might have happened.'

'Yeah,' Andy said. 'In a parallel universe.' He swung back on his chair. 'Come off it, Robbie. There's no doubt that Oskaras Salavejus was as guilty as sin.'

'Oh yes there is. At least eight people on the jury had a doubt.' I studied the face of my assistant. So keen, so earnest, so much to learn.

'Andy,' I said, 'it's important you know what being a defence lawyer is all about. Boilermakers make boilers, shoemakers make shoes, bookmakers make lots of money and defence lawyers make doubts. Good defence lawyers make reasonable doubts. It's our job. It's what we do.'

Andy turned his attention to his pint, brows knitted. 'Robbie...' He looked worried. 'Criminal defence work... I don't know... I don't know if I can do what you do. I don't think I can just make stuff up.'

'You don't have to make up defences,' I said. 'Every puzzle has a solution, every crime has a defence. It's only a matter of finding it. And stop worrying about the truth so much. It can look after itself.'

Andy stared deep into the beer glass then up at me. 'And the law? What about it?'

The boy was deeply troubled. Who cared about the law? It changed all the time. The politicians couldn't leave it alone for five minutes.

'Courtwork is war,' I told him. 'And to quote Cicero: 'in times of war the law is silent'. In court, all that matters is that when the smoke clears you and your client are still standing and there aren't prison bars between you. Victory, that's the thing. It's what reputations are made of and in our business reputation is everything.'

Andy shrugged. Unconvinced. 'And justice?' he asked.

'She's blind,' I said. 'Which is handy if you want to pull a fast one.'

I would have loved to have continued the debate. Jurisprudence was my favourite subject at Uni: no right or wrong answers just plenty of waffle; however, at that moment the back-room door swung open and out walked a man on legs that were not long enough for his body.

Brendan Patterson was as short and wiry as the tufts of hair that sprouted from the neck of his shirt, his ears, his chin, everywhere, in fact, apart from the top of his head. His face was tanned and leathery, inscribed with deep creases, his nose flattened and crooked. White scar tissue stood out vividly beneath each eyebrow. One look at him and you knew he had no problem emptying the bar at closing time. 'Oh, it's you,' he said.

I stood up. 'We'll talk about this later.' I told Andy and ruffled his hair. He hated it when I did that. Which was mainly why I did it. 'I'll see you back at the office.'

Brendan's study was a complete clutter. Compared to it, my untidy office was a minimalist's paradise. There were crates of empties stacked along one wall, jostling for space with an army of mops, brushes and pails. Kegs of beer and boxes of crisps were piled high all over and in a corner lay the mortal remains of an industrial-sized deep fat fryer. Even the wall space was congested, plastered with paper-clippings and old boxing posters, mostly featuring His Truly.

Brendan went over to a small roll-top desk overflowing with paperwork. He tipped a grey cat from the only chair in the room and sat down. I leaned against a filing cabinet. Its thick brown enamel paint chipped and scored. On top was a pile of magazines: The Ring, Boxing Monthly, and so on, and balancing precariously on top of those: a black and white portable TV with a coat-hanger aerial, showing an early afternoon soap.

'Sorry, about the mess,' he said. 'I've been doing my accounts.'

'Remember and send the tax man the right set.'

Brendan furrowed his brow, slipping my dig like a weak left jab. 'And to what do I owe the pleasure of this visit?' I detected a note of suspicion in his voice. 'I don't see you in here much.'

'Just passing. How you been keeping?'

'Ach, not bad. I'm off on holiday next week. Lanzarote, all inclusive. In fact you've come at a good time.' He rummaged about the desk and from under a pile of invoices and V.A.T. returns retrieved a passport application form. 'You can sign this for me while you're here.'

All those years at law school hadn't been wasted after all.

'Got a black pen on you?'

I hadn't.

'Saw you at the funeral,' I said, as Brendan patted himself down. 'You and Max still kept in touch, then?'

He pulled open a series of drawers. 'Now and again. You know how it is. In fact we were out on the town not long before he was killed.' He found a small red bookie's pen in a bottom drawer. 'I got tickets for the St Andrews Sporting Club: Scotland/Ireland. Some handy boys on show.'

Max had boxed in his younger days. It had been his mother's idea because her son, who'd always been tall for his age and a target for bullies, needed toughening up. Max had been such a quiet, gentle soul that he'd hated the idea, but, to everyone's surprise, had grown to enjoy the sport and from the day her boy had come home with his first black-eye, Mrs Abercrombie had wished she'd never opened her mouth.

'Max was still keen?'

'On the boxing? Oh aye, he liked to know who was up-and-coming. It was a good night. The girls enjoyed themselves. We all did.'

I had met Brendan's other half, Angie O'Hara: a body from Baywatch, a face from Crimewatch. She was all matt black hair, fake tan and more cheap bling than the Argos catalogue. The sort of girl you'd find in a boxing crowd, knocking back a rum and coke and baying for blood. But Irene Abercrombie? I didn't think so. Irene's idea of a good night out would not include a scoop with the lads and being sprayed with blood from a right-cross. No, Irene was definitely more a string quartet with a Kir Royale at the interval.

'Girls?'

Brendan bent over the desk and scribbled blue ink on the back of an envelope. When he stood up straight again his face was flushed and he had a lopsided grin. 'Nothing serious. Just a bit of fun.'

'Anyone I'd know?'

Brendan flashed a smile. 'What goes on tour...'

I left that particular line of enquiry alone for the time being at any rate. 'Was he any good?'

123

'Eh?'

'Max. Boxing. Was he any good?'

'Good enough - for the amateur ranks, but, no, not good-good.' Brendan stooped to continue his search in the bottom drawer. 'At least he knew it and stuck in at the school. Not like me.'

From what I remembered of Brendan's academic abilities at primary school, getting his head punched in for a living was as good a use for it as any.

'You've done all right. Brendan Patterson, 'The Linlithgow Lion'. We were all dead proud of you. They don't give away gold medals with every ten litres of unleaded.'

'The Commonwealth Games,' Brendan scoffed. 'I beat up a Canadian, a Kiwi and some witch doctor from Bongoland who couldn't box eggs. It wasn't until I turned pro that I found out what the fight game was really all about. That's when I learned I didn't have what it took to be champ. I had the guts but not the guile.'

'You were our hero. Harry Carpenter interviewed you on telly once.'

Brendan shrugged. 'I was a journeyman. That's being polite. A tomato can is what the yanks used to call fighters like me. Someone who wouldn't stink out a fight but wouldn't trouble the contender too much. Someone who'd give the crowd what they came to see – blood.' He crouched down on his hands and knees. 'I did the right thing. Got out of the game as soon as I'd made enough money to buy this place.' He ducked his head and looked under the desk.

'Did Max say anything to you?'

Brendan surfaced. 'Like what?'

'I don't know. Did he seem all right to you? Was he worried about anything?'

'You sure you were just passing?'

'You know me, Brendan. I'm always working.'

He gave me a look that must have loosened the bowels of many an opponent. 'Well, I'm saying nothing at all that'll help

124

you. Give me five minutes alone with your client and I could save the country a lot of money.'

'It's not like that.'

'Don't tell me – he's innocent.'

Two people I never wanted to see sitting side by side on a jury were my father and Brendan Patterson.

'Until proven guilty. It's what we lawyers call the presumption of innocence.'

'Eh?'

'It's the law.'

'Innocent - everybody's always innocent.'

I understood how he felt at the loss of his friend, but his tone was a trifle self-righteous coming from someone I had defended on numerous reset charges over the years. If Brendan was any more of a fence he'd have needed a lick of creosote once a year. 'That's a judgement I don't have to make,' I told him.

'Well,' he said, 'to answer your question, I have no idea why anyone would want to kill Max. He was a pure gent.' Brendan reached under the chest of drawers and dragged out a badly chewed Bic. He drew a black line across the palm of his hand. 'We're in business.'

I decided not to press him any further about Max. I reached down and patted his shiny head. 'Don't worry. I'll not charge a fee for signing your passport.'

'That's very good of you considering you've never paid for a drink since...'

While he thought of an amusing quip, I took the pen and started to countersign the application form.

'...since the Pope was a proddy,' he came out with eventually.

I left that particular denominational conundrum alone and continued to fill in the boxes. On TV the soap had finished and a photograph flashed up on the screen. It was a close-up of a man taken at some function or other. He was sitting at a table with an array of empty glasses in front of him, smoking a cigarette and smiling cheekily at the camera. Whoever had been sitting next to him had been pixelated. It took a few moments for me to realise that the subject of the photo was a young Chic Kelly and I wondered how come he had made the early afternoon news. I turned up the volume.

'...Kelly who was sentenced to life imprisonment for the murder of Lord James Hewitt of Muthill, former Lord Justice Clerk, was found by prison staff hanging from a makeshift noose at six-thirty this morning...'

A screw with a lot of silver braid on his shoulder made a brief appearance, stoutly defending prison procedures.

Brendan, ever the economist, grunted. 'Been a lot bloody cheaper if they'd hanged him years ago.'

My concerns that Oskaras Salavejus might not fulfil his potential were unfounded. No sooner had he 'walked free', as the local newspaper would later refer to his acquittal, than after over-indulging in some liquid celebrations he'd been lifted again, this time for a breach of the peace on the train to Glasgow.

They'd huckled my client two stops down the line from Linlithgow at Falkirk High station where, after his now customary struggle with the cops, they'd carted him off. He'd been out of custody for less than four hours. With clients like him I'd be back on my feet in no time. I felt like pinning another medal to his chest and for such conduct above and beyond, I thought it only fitting that I should go pay him a visit. That and because I didn't want the local duty lawyer hoovering him up.

Two sets of automatic doors swung open for me as I swept into Falkirk Police office and a reception lobby of Orwellian proportions. The vaulted ceiling, marble floor and silk banners lining the sandstone walls brought to mind footage I'd seen of the Reichstag circa 1933. High on a wall, between torpedo-shaped plant holders, a plasma screen played a short information loop proclaiming the achievements of Central Scotland Police.

I rang the bell at reception and was told I'd have to wait to see my client. I sat down on one of the two metal benches that had been designed with no regard to comfort, the hard edge of the seat catching me just behind the knee cutting off the circulation. Parts of my lower anatomy grew numb. To ease the flow of blood I paced the lobby, reading crime protection leaflets. 'Look out There's a Thief About'; 'Lock It or Lose It'; all the old favourites were there and, pride of place, a new poster announcing yet another knife amnesty. Operation Cutting Edge: one month to hand in your unwanted chibs.

I was spared the tedium of perusing the Force's response-time statistics by a female member of the civilian staff who came around from behind the bullet proof glass and held the security door open for me. She was a large, friendly woman whom I recognised from the Sheriff Court, where until recently she had been a bar officer. Shona was her name, good with the punters as I recalled, had defused many a volatile situation with a wise-crack and a friendly warning. She'd swapped her crisp blue court uniform for a saggy black police tracksuit. The rear view was not flattering.

'We've had a bit of trouble with your client,' she said as I followed her wobbly buttocks along the corridor. 'I have to warn you, he's had a bucketful. He was shouting and threatening folk on the train.' Sounded like Salavejus's M.O. 'I doubt if you'll get much sense from him.'

'At least he remembered to ask for me.'

We came to another security door. Shona stopped. 'He didn't. We found your business card in his property.'

The door led to the top of a flight of stairs so steep that I didn't wonder why prisoners often fell down them. At the bottom was a barred gate through which was situated the custody suite or, as we lawyers prefer to call small rooms with locks on the doors: the cells.

'In here.' Shona let me into an interview room and I sat down on one of the bolted-down steel chairs either side of the equally bolted down steel table. 'Maybe you can talk some sense into him and get him to belt up for five minutes. He'll not stop rambling on about war and death and dying. The inspector's talking about having him sectioned. He'll be a custody at the Sheriff Court tomorrow, that's a certainty.'

Shona disappeared to return moments later carrying two plastic cups. She set one down in front of me. 'They'll bring him through in a minute. I thought you could both use some coffee,' she said, referring to the scummy brown liquid in the cup. Still, it was kind of her. I thanked her and was blowing on the drink to cool it down when Salavejus arrived under the escort of a uniformed officer. He looked in much the same condition as I remembered seeing him at our first meeting; although on this occasion he was dressed in a white-paper boiler-suit and was obviously less hung-over and much more drunk. He was ushered into the room and told to sit down. I waited for the cop to leave.

'We meet again,' I said and slid a legal aid form across the table at him; always important to get your priorities right.

Salavejus pushed the form back across the table. 'Get me out,' he slurred.

'I can't do that. Sign the form, go back to your cell, get your head down and I'll see you in the morning. Do you have a bail address yet?'

He saw the cup of coffee, took a mouthful and spat it out on the floor. I thought maybe I should come back when he'd dried out, but I was here now and he hadn't signed the legal aid form yet. 'You must know by now that you need an address – any address. No address, no bail. Is there somewhere you can go? You were on the train to Glasgow. Where were you going? Do you have any family, maybe a friend who'll take you in for a couple of weeks?' I remembered Dougie Fleming's evidence about Salavejus's antics in the Bombay Balti. 'Do you have a girlfriend?'

In answer to my question Salavejus drew an arm across the table sending the plastic cups across the room. Unfortunately, most of the burning hot contents stayed behind, splashed onto the table and all over me. I yelled and jumped to my feet. Shona burst in through the door, reached across me and slammed her hand against the panic button on the wall. In an instant the door crashed open and the uniformed cop came in, grabbed my client and dragged him backwards off the chair and onto the floor. Salavejus thrashed about, kicking his legs wildly and screaming. Even in his drunken state he was threatening to overpower the cop until a few more of the custody team arrived and quickly quelled his drunken struggles. Altogether it took four of them to carry him back to his cell.

'You okay?' asked Shona, as my client's shouts echoed down the corridor. 'Hope those stains will come off your suit. Been a bit of a waste of time for you, I'm afraid. Mr Sal.... your client. We're not keeping him. He can go.'

'What?'

She held up a slip of paper. 'Inspector's instructions. As soon as your man's sobered-up he's out of here. No charges. Free to go.'

Oh well. No doubt I'd see him again.

I followed her out, watching from the top landing as the cops tried to stuff Salavejus through the barred gate at the foot of the stairs while he flailed his arms and legs like a cat being put in the sink.

Drink: it was a terrible thing. Unless you happened to be a criminal defence lawyer: in which case it was your main source of business.

CHAPTER 34

The end of another long week. My landlord was out to evict me, I had a murder client whose only defence was, I never done it and an assistant with a crisis of conscience. Then, of course, there was the fact that one of my best friends had been murdered and his paramour found dead in a field. Bubbles billowed around my shoulders. Hot water lapped against my neck. I groped for my slippery glass of whisky and took a sip. I was going to relax if it killed me and, hey, they were talking football on the radio, tomorrow was Saturday and the next day Sunday. I leaned my head back against the edge of the bath and closed my eyes. When I opened them again the late news was on, the water cold and bubbles in short supply.

I stepped out of the bath and into a towelling robe. In the process I knocked the radio into the water. I was fishing it out when I heard a noise from the bedroom. I pulled the belt on my robe tight and opened the bathroom door but before I could set a foot outside, a black leather glove reached in, grabbed hold of my collar and wrenched me forward. I tripped and fell, knees burning on the carpet, head cracking off the wooden bedstead. Two hands reached down and pulled me upright. A fist slammed into the side of my face and I doubled up under a vicious blow to the ribs. I looked down at a pair of sturdy boots and then up at a familiar black ski mask. Deek Pudney - again?

'Where is it?' he growled.

It didn't sound like Deek. The voice was younger, somehow familiar. I remembered his spotty companion. 'Tell Jake I'll have his money next week.'

A gloved hand seized my wet hair, the grip tightened, jerking my head back. The blur of a fist. I only just managed to turn my head so that the blow didn't hit me full on the face. The taste of blood. The ski mask loomed over me. I sensed the fist drawing back again and raised my knee into my attacker's groin. The grip on my hair slackened. I lunged forward, my forehead meeting the nose under the mask full on. I had some more success with an uppercut and tried to keep the momentum going but my next punch was parried. Heavy boots squashed my bare feet. A blow to the side of my head knocked me off balance. Before I could recover I felt cold metal press into the flesh under my chin. A gun? He had to be kidding. His orders would be to rough me up, put the frighteners on me - so far he was doing a damn fine job - but kill me? No chance. Rule one of debt collecting had to be 'don't kill the debtor'.

'All right, All right.' I twisted my head to the side and pointed to the wardrobe. I had some rainy-day money stashed away. This was monsoon season.

The mask turned to look. I was shoved forward. The gun rammed into the small of my back. 'Get it.'

I sucked in a few fast breaths and holding my injured side limped towards the wardrobe. Another push in the back. I banged my leg against the wobbly bedpost. I pointed to the wardrobe again. 'Down the bottom. In a shoe box.'

The man in the mask opened the wardrobe door and crouched down. I saw the pistol for the first time; it was chunky, square and grey. He moved it to his left hand while he seized the handle of the drawer with his right, wrenched it open and shook out the contents, littering the floor with folding money.

'WHERE IS IT?'

What was he talking about? Okay, it wasn't all there, not nearly, but some cash had to be better than none. I backed off, bumping once more into the bedpost.

The man in the mask began to rise to his feet again, transferring the pistol from left hand to right. Now was my chance. I took hold of the bedpost. Half a metre of solid oak. I pulled it from its socket and brought it down, aiming for the intruder's head. He dodged and the blow struck him on the shoulder. As he recoiled in pain, I smashed the bedpost against one of his kneecaps. He dropped onto his good knee, trying to level the pistol. I struck again, catching him firmly across the right wrist. He fell back against the dressing table, dropping the gun.

I wanted some answers, but the pistol lay on the bedroom floor between us, a piece of unfinished business. My assailant's left arm tensed. His hand twitched.

I feinted with the bedpost. 'Try it and you'll be eating your next meal through a straw.'

The eyes staring up at me through the black ski mask showed mostly white. I shuffled forward and kicked the pistol under the bed, the bedpost still raised, ready to strike.

The intruder took stock of the situation, then, cradling his injured arm, hobbled out of the door.

CHAPTER 35

I didn't go to the police. What was the point? Undoubtedly, Jake would have a water-tight alibi and muscle like Deek Pudney and his young associate were ten a penny. Anyway, I couldn't afford to clipe on anyone, not even a psycho like Jake Turpie. If I did, any credibility I'd gained with the criminal fraternity locally would go down the toilet. Jake had a lot of serious contacts who wouldn't take it kindly if I involved the law over something which they, like Jake, would see as a matter of principle. After all I did owe him money and all's fair in love and debt-collecting.

So while I decided on the best way to deal with my landlord, I wasn't going to stay at home and wait for another visit. I'd spend the night at my dad's and formulate a plan of action. Naturally, the old man would want to know why I was turning up on his doorstep late at night with a black-eye, but excuses were my stock in trade. I'd come up with one on the drive over.

My car was a middle-aged, red hatch-back that Jake Turpie had saved from the crusher and given to me a few months back after my own car had died and when we were on friendlier terms. The vehicle was registered to some old guy who'd been about to emigrate and was sold for scrap with six months still on the tax disk. I hadn't cancelled the comprehensive insurance on my previous car, which covered me third-party for all other vehicles and having omitted to notify Swansea of the change in ownership, my driving licence remained unblemished and parking tickets weren't a worry.

Not sure what to do with it I took the pistol with me, shoving it in the glove-box out of the way. It was only a short drive to my dad's place and as I pulled up outside I was relieved to see that the lights were off. I had a key and could kip down in the spare room without waking him. I went around the back of the house. It was dark. I walked carefully trying not to make a sound. The crunch of glass underfoot told me something was not right - that and the fact that a panel in the back door was smashed and the door itself wide open.

I rushed in and switched on some lights. The place was trashed: every room a disaster scene, every item of furniture knocked over, every picture dislodged, every curtain torn down. Even Billy's cage had been ransacked and the evicted bird perched atop the mantelpiece. I charged upstairs. It was very much the same, with carpets ripped up, drawers pulled out and their contents scattered, but no sign of my dad. This wasn't happening. Jake Turpie could put the frighteners on me. To his own twisted way of thinking, I deserved it, but this was my dad. I ran downstairs. There was nothing for it but to call the police. I was hunting for the telephone when the back door slammed shut. I dived behind the couch and lay still.

'What the hell?'

The sound of that angry voice was music to my ears. I jumped up, causing my dad to take a backward step when he saw a figure leap from behind the couch.

'Where have you been?' I shouted at him.

He looked bemused, not surprisingly since he'd come home to find his house destroyed and his son playing hide and seek in the debris. 'Where have I been? What's happened here?'

'You've been broken into.'

'You don't say.' He shook his head trying to make some sense of the situation. 'What are you doing here? This place... your eye, your face... Robbie, what's going on? Are you all right? Look at you.'

'It's nothing. I just slipped getting out of the bath.'

He looked sceptical. 'Has this got anything to do with that man, McPhee?'

'I told you, I slipped.'

He found the phone. The cable had been ripped from the wall and it took him a while to re-connect it. After he'd made the call I waited with him for the police to arrive, wondering all the while if I should fill him in on a few details, like, for instance, the real reason I looked as though I'd gone twelve rounds with a threshing machine and why his house had been tanned; except, why would Jake Turpie want to break into my dad's house? For three months' rent arrears he seemed to be going to an awful lot of trouble and it didn't look like anything was missing.

There was no ice in the freezer, not even a bag of frozen peas. All I could find was a tin of beer in the fridge. I pressed it against my swollen cheekbone before downing the contents.

After a while a couple of uniforms showed up and took statements from us. They were about to leave when another police car drew up. Detective Chief Inspector Petra Lockhart alighted and, as the car drove off again, she walked up the path and into the house. Her hair was damp, she wore a navy-blue tracksuit over a white sports-top. A sweatshirt was slung over her arm. I suspected she'd come straight from the gym.

'I heard it over the radio,' she said. 'Mr Munro, are you and your father all right? You're injured—'

'It's nothing,' I assured her.

'Look at the state of this place.' She opened the hall door, peering into the livingroom and breathed a low whistle between her teeth.

'Careful ma'am,' said one of the uniforms. 'Scene of Crime can't make it 'til the morning.'

'So, what am I supposed to do?' my dad wanted to know. 'Stand here all night and not touch anything?'

The cop took a deep breath. 'Sorry, sir. We can't get it done any sooner. I think it would be a good idea if you spent the night somewhere else.' All eyes turned on me.

That was all I needed. The old man at my place, quizzing me over my injuries and how it was I'd managed to smash up my bedroom by slipping in the bath. He might have been an ex-cop but he wasn't completely stupid. I had another idea.

'Probably some junkie high on smack,' my dad told Lockhart as she escorted us on the short walk to Vince's house. 'Or one of Frankie McPhee's mob.'

I didn't know why I felt it necessary to stick up for Frankie, but I couldn't help myself; too many years spent tendering pleas in mitigation.

'Frankie doesn't have a mob,' I said. 'Not anymore.'

'Who's Frankie McPhee?' Lockhart asked.

My dad enlightened her. 'A crook!'

'A former client of mine,' I clarified. 'Now rehabilitated.'

But the old man was having none of it. 'He may have you fooled but not me. Frankie McPhee is a dangerous man. I don't care if he thinks he is a one-man Salvation Army. Him and his home for vagrants—'

'It's a soup kitchen,' I said.

'More like a front for drugs or something.'

Both Lockhart and I tried unsuccessfully to change the subject, but he kept up his rant until we arrived at Vince's. The porch light came on and the wee, stout man in the thick glasses trundled slowly into view like one of his slow-rolling bowling balls.

My dad turned to Lockhart. 'Are you a whisky drinker, ma'am?'

'Well...'

My dad pounced at the first sign of weakness. 'Come with me.' He took her by the arm. 'And you,' he said to me. 'Away and get your face seen to.'

Lockhart looked back over her shoulder as my dad towed her along. 'Are you not coming, Mr Munro?'

'No, he's not,' my dad informed her in a loud voice for my benefit, and with that the two of them set off up the path to where Vince was waiting at his front door for them with a bottle of something peaty.

CHAPTER 36

I'd had enough of Jake Turpie. Up until that night I had been on the back foot. Jake was my office landlord and I'd known what kind of man he was when we'd agreed the lease. There had been no paperwork, nothing signed, just a handshake and a promise of regular cash payments. I'd broken that agreement and he had a right to be a bit touchy about it. What he had no right to do was send a thug round to my house to stick a gun in my face – not for a measly six grand - and what he definitely should not have done is gone anywhere near my father. He needed sorting out. That was why I was on my way to Edinburgh and Frankie McPhee's soup kitchen, which I expected to be in full swing around that time of night. Of course, Chic's revelation that Frankie had killed Lord Hewitt was a concern, but surely that was just the ranting of a dying man. Anyway, Frankie owed me one. If I could persuade Frankie to have a serious word with Jake, then that should give me enough time to get in some money and pay the rent. According to Frankie, he was a new man. I hoped he'd kept enough of the old man to give it to Jake Turpie tight.

It was approaching midnight as I drove towards the city centre. My temper had cooled to a simmer and I started to think some more about my visit with Chic Kelly. If he was right about Frankie killing the judge and that the mysterious package contained the proof, then it stood to reason that Frankie would be extremely anxious to get his hands on it. For a moment it crossed my mind that the man in the ski-mask may not have been sent by Jake Turpie at all, and yet Chic had assured me Frankie McPhee didn't even know the contents of the package still existed. Had Chic not told me that, I would have seriously considered another possible reason for the attack on me. For if

Frankie thought I had the package it would be easy for him to send someone to collect. Even with Chic's assurance, I couldn't keep from wondering if there was any direct connection between the package, Frankie and Max's murder. I was almost at the old church when I decided that for the time being I'd leave Frankie out of it and find another method of dealing with my landlord. Simply paying him the cash would have been one rather obvious answer. If I paid up, Jake would back off. There was nothing personal. It was purely business. Trouble was, I didn't have enough cash at the moment. Maybe I could get a loan from somewhere.

I eased my foot off the accelerator pedal and looked for a quiet spot to do a U-turn. I still didn't fancy spending the night at home. I would find a cheap hotel and think about things in the morning when I had a clearer head.

Bright lights in the rear-view mirror. Police. I checked my speed: thirty-five. Blue lights swirled. They had to be kidding. A siren squealed. They weren't. I glanced in the mirror again and got a close-up of my face: hair everywhere, swollen cheek bone, black eye, fat lip and a scratch along the line of my jaw. I tried to remember - how much whisky had I drunk in the bath? And the tin of beer at my dad's? I remembered the pistol in the glove-box. Why on earth had I brought that with me?

I worked it out: speeding – possibly; drink-driving – probably; possession of a handgun – definitely. I had some explaining to do and although I was good – I wasn't that good. There was nothing for it. A section 163 contravention: failing to stop when signalled to do so, wasn't going to get me one more minute in jail. Not that attempting to outrun the police in an eight-year-old, one-litre hatchback was the best idea I'd ever had, but at that precise moment it was the only one that sprang immediately to mind.

I clenched the wheel with both hands and put the pedal to the metal. Very little happened. I shook the steering wheel, willing the car to go faster. The speedometer's little red arm swung in a lazy arc: forty, forty-five, fifty. The headlights in the mirror were still there and shining as brightly as ever. The blue lights swirled, the siren wailed.

I screeched the car to a halt at a T-junction. The police car rolled up behind me and stopped, waiting for me to make my next move. Traffic cops loved a chase; otherwise what was the point of sitting all those advanced drivers' tests and being given the keys to a souped-up Volvo V70?

Which way? Left? Right? Surrender? In front of me stood a tenement building. A woman in a pink nightgown and slippers came out of a close taking a carrier bag full of rubbish to one of the green wheelie-bins that were lined up at the side of the pavement.

I accelerated straight ahead, crossing the white lines in the middle of the road, bumping over the kerb, sending the woman diving for cover, her slippers taking flight in different directions; add dangerous driving to the list of offences. What was I doing? Too late to go back now. Bracing myself for the impact I ploughed the car into the close entrance. The seatbelt bit into my shoulder, jarring my chest. Tender ribs shrieked in agony.

I took a deep breath and fought back the pain. In the rear view mirror I could see the police car following, pulling up at the kerbside. The cops were in no rush. I was going nowhere. My car was jammed, wedged between narrow walls. The doors wouldn't open. I couldn't get out but more importantly for me, no-one could get into the close.

I unclipped myself, leaned back in the seat and kicked the windscreen. Nothing. I tried again. The rubber soles of my shoes merely skidded off the glass without making so much as a scratch. Shouts. Someone banged on the back of the car. I had to hurry. Eventually the cops would realise they couldn't get in, go around the end of the building and outflank me.

Scrabbling about in the dark, I found the glove compartment and wrenched it open. Inside there was a can of de-icer. At breaking windows it proved about as much use as my feet. The shouting and banging stopped. There was no time left. The pistol. I took it out of the glove-box. I didn't dare shoot the windscreen. For one thing I had never fired a gun before, for another it would only escalate matters. Right now there were two traffic cops dealing with a dangerous driver. One gunshot and in five minutes the armed response team would be swarming all over the place, eager to shoot someone and answer questions later.

I whacked the handle of the pistol against the windscreen and met with some success. Three or four blows and a spider-web fracture appeared. One more and the middle of the screen fell in. Small cubes of glass sprayed everywhere. I widened the hole with a few well-placed kicks, cleared what I could from the frame and clambered through, snatching the key from the ignition as I went.

In a moment, I was sliding down the bonnet, ripping my clothes as I did. I ran down the close and burst through the door at the rear into a back green that was an obstacle course lit by pools of lights from upstairs windows. I hurdled a heap of kids' toys, leapt over bikes, scooters, a plastic tractor complete with trailer, and side-stepped a partially demolished Wendy house. At the far side of the green all was dark. I could just make out the shape of a rolled-up carpet propped against the boundary wall and next to it the unkempt figure of a man lay slumped, his bed a mattress of flattened cardboard boxes surrounded by a massed ranks of empties.

I ran past him, lobbed the car keys over my shoulder into his lap and while he was still trying to focus on them I was scrambling up the carpet, over the wall and away.

CHAPTER 37

Andy lived in Marchmont. A second-floor property owned by the parents of one of his three flat-mates: a nice little investment situated in the centre of Edinburgh's studentland just a stone's throw from the Meadows. I knocked. No-one answered. I tried the door and it opened. The main room was in darkness. I switched on the light and took in a scene of devastation. Amidst the chaos, Andy was lying on the couch, fully clothed and unconscious. I was checking him for signs of life when he rolled onto his side and let rip a loud snort. I gave him a shake. He chomped a couple of times and squinted at me.

'Robbie?' He reached under a cushion and brought out his glasses. He put them on and looked at me again. 'Your face...'

'I'm all right. What happened here?'

Andy looked about. 'What happened where?'

'This place, look at it.'

More chomping. He rubbed his eyes. 'A few of the boys were round for a game of COD. Haven't quite made it to bed yet.' Andy swung his legs around and sat up, kicking over a half full can of beer that was on the floor. Some of the contents spilled into a large glass ashtray setting adrift a flotilla of cigarette butts in a frothy sea of ash and eighty shilling. 'Fancy a coffee?'

I'd said yes before realising it. Andy tottered through to the kitchen to put the kettle on.

A sleepy young man in a T-shirt and boxers walked into the room, tailed by a girl wearing an out-size football top. 'Everything all right Andy?' he mumbled.

'It's cool, Kev,' Andy called back to him. 'This is my boss. He's here to see me about err... work.'

'Sound.' Kev yawned widely and left with the female footballer.

I found the bathroom. There was plenty of deodorant spray around but not much in the way of soap. I cleaned myself up as best I could and went back through to the sitting room by which time the kettle had boiled.

Andy came from the kitchen carrying a mug of coffee. He swept aside what remained of a pepperoni pizza and placed the mug on the arm of the couch.

'Why are you here?' he asked. 'Are you all right?'

'I had a bit of an accident. I'm looking for somewhere to crash.' Perhaps not the best choice of words in the circumstances.

'No sweat, you can take my room.'

'The couch will be fine.'

Andy yawned and stretched. 'Away to your bed,' I said. 'You look knackered.'

'You sure?'

'On you go. Catch some zeds.' Did anyone still say that? Andy swayed his way across the room. 'Oh, and I'll be up and away early tomorrow - something important to do. Is it okay if I borrow your car?'

Andy reached for his bedroom door, stopped, turned and removed his glasses. He chipped off a piece of dried tomato paste that was spot-welded onto one of the lenses. 'What's going on, Robbie?' he asked once he'd replaced his specs.

'Had a bit of an accident. Need a car. Don't worry about it. Off you go to bed.'

He shrugged and disappeared into his room. The door closed, but only for a moment before it was thrown wide and Andy marched out again. I'd never seen him angry before.

'What's this all about?' he demanded. 'You come here in the middle of the night, torn clothes, face like a pound of mince, asking for a loan of my car and then pack me off to bed. When are you going to stop treating me like a child?'

'When you stop throwing tantrums.'

'Everything I know about throwing a wobbly I learned from you,' he said. 'Now, if you want my help, I need to know a few things first - like what the hell is going on?'

I drank, wincing less from the pain in my injured lip than at the taste of Andy's coffee.

'It's complicated. I don't want you involved.'

'I can handle myself.'

I forced myself to drink some more of his coffee.

'I've been about a bit,' he said.

'Andy, you think you know all about the mean streets because you saw a fight outside a chip shop once. This is a serious business, involving an extremely serious person. I didn't get this black-eye by looking through a trick telescope.'

'Tell me or you're on foot.'

He was either very brave or very drunk.

'You know Jake Turpie?' I asked.

'Of course.'

'Well I owe him some money and he seems fairly determined that I settle up.'

'Are you talking about the rent?' I nodded. Andy thought for a moment. 'And you say he did that to your face?' He looked sceptical. 'When? Tonight?'

'Yes, well not him personally. One of his boys.'

'I don't believe you.'

I was taken aback. 'Want me to take the oath?'

'Robbie, I think we've already established that you don't even have a nodding acquaintance with the truth.' For his sake I hoped it was the beer talking. Andy gazed at the ceiling. 'I mean, why would Jake Turpie do that to you?'

'Hmm, let me think... because I owe him six grand and because he's a vindictive little shite? That would be my guess.'

Andy walked to the door and held it open. 'I think you should leave.'

The boy was a P45 waiting to happen.

'You heard me.' There was a sideboard by the door. He lifted a chunky beer mug from it and emptied a set of car keys into his hand. He threw them at me. 'Now, go.'

I checked into a roadside hotel on the outskirts of Edinburgh, near to the airport. The room had a splendid view of a motorway flyover and a thermostat on a blast-furnace setting. I didn't care. I slept like a baby and woke at eight. By nine I'd showered and had breakfast, by ten a chunk of my rainy-day stash had been spent on some new clothes and by eleven I was pulling into the yard of Turpie (International) Salvage Ltd, a forty-acre piece of wilderness to the south of Linlithgow.

When I arrived that Saturday morning, I was met by vehicle transporters coming and going, a crusher squeezing former showroom specials into one-ton blocks and a grab hand crane swinging backwards and forward, loading a fleet of flatbed lorries.

I parked near the gates. Some of the water-filled potholes dotted around the red blaize surface looked big enough to swallow Andy's Fiat and I was slightly worried in case I came back to find my assistant's car gone and a small cube of squashed metal in its place. That's if I came back.

It was by no means my first visit to Jake's place and as always it confirmed my opinion that the man was as bent and twisted as one of his scrapped cars. There he was, the proprietor of a large slice of real estate, with a thriving business, and yet he didn't smoke, didn't drink, never went on holiday, his favoured mode of transport was the Ford Transit van and I'd never seen him wear anything smarter than oil-stained overalls. He had to be seriously minted and yet he was prepared to have me threatened, beaten up and my dad's house wrecked all for the sake of some back-rent.

In my new shoes, my fear neutralised by anger, I picked my way through the puddles and pot-holes to the headquarters of

Turpie (International) Salvage Ltd, a prefabricated hut with sagging roof and walls that looked incapable of standing up to a reasonably loud fart. I still had the pistol and had thought about sticking it in my belt so that I could pull it out and wave it around if things got a bit hairy. I'd had second thoughts about that. Even if I could have worked out how to take off the safety, I wasn't about to shoot anyone. Jake would know that. He'd have called my bluff, taken the gun and even if I didn't end up with a bullet in me, he'd have the pistol again and I was damn sure he wasn't getting it back.

As I climbed up the wooden steps to the door, the bad-tempered mongrel that was tethered to the flimsy handrail growled at me. I growled right back. I was all set for Jake Turpie. Maybe I wasn't going to shoot him, but verbally he was about to get both barrels. I'd take out a loan, borrow from my dad if need be; he'd get his rent money, somehow, but after that he could find another tenant for his run-down office premises, and find himself another lawyer. It made me furious to think of the number of times I'd acted for Jake and his associates. Jake wasn't such a great payer himself. I always had to demand money upfront and he'd never not quibbled over a legal fee. Well, he'd have to find a new brief after this. I was moving out. I'd worked from home before and could do it again.

At the top of the steps I threw open the door to reveal the younger of Jake's two minders, lounging around, picking the spots on his face and watching Saturday morning kids' TV. The steps behind me creaked.

I turned around to see Jake Turpie standing at the foot of the steps. He had a length of scaffolding pole in his hand. Maybe meeting Jake on his own turf was a bad idea. Why hadn't I brought the gun?

'Robbie, what the hell are you doing here?'

'I want a word.'

Jake grimaced. 'I'm trying to get the alloys off a write-off and get a set of steelies on it before the insurance engineer gets here.' He walked up the steps and right past me. 'Have a seat, I'll not

147

be long.' He gestured to an orange velour cushion running the length of the back window from which brown stuffing protruded through a number of split seams. 'Hey!' He tapped the top of the television with the length of scaffolding pole, making both the picture and his minder jump. 'Make Mr Munro a cup of tea.'

The young man made a face and dragged himself to his feet. He lifted a grimy looking kettle and followed Jake out of the door. I went after them.

Spotty went to a nearby standpipe and began to fill the kettle. A cigarette packet peeked out from under one of the sleeves of his short-sleeved T-Shirt. His arms were thick and white and hairy, his wrists both uninjured. Deek, Jake's other minder, was nowhere to be seen. Was his right arm similarly unscathed?

Jake crouched down beside the jacked-up rear end of a badly smashed Ford Mondeo. He attached the length of scaffolding tube to a wheel wrench to give it extra leverage and started to loosen the studs of the nearside rear wheel one by one.

'The rent.' I said, after he'd removed the wheel and rolled it to the side.

'S'alright,' Jake grunted. Deek's out on police bail, but don't leave it so late next time.' He fitted an old steel wheel onto the bolts where the alloy had been. 'I've other tenants. It doesn't look good if I have a favourite.'

Me? Jake Turpie's favourite tenant?

He quickly tightened the wheel nuts while I was trying absorbing that thought. 'Frankie McPhee?' he said, wheezing a laugh like a faulty ignition. He trundled the trolley jack around to the offside and pumped the handle of the jack hoisting the car up again. 'Hope you know what you're doing. I don't care where you get the money from to pay your rent but I heard the last man who bumped McPhee is still trying to swim the Forth in Blue Circle Speedos.'

What was he saying? Frankie had settled my debt? Standing there in that rutted wasteland of dead motor cars, my new shoes sinking into the mud, all set to haggle with my landlord over rent arrears that no longer existed - I suddenly felt a little bit silly. Jake looked up at me. 'Apology accepted. Now, if that's all you came for, d'ye mind? I'm busy'

Any feelings of relief over the settling of my rent arrears were quickly swamped by a dread realisation that someone other than Jake Turpie had been responsible for the attack on me. On a better the devil you know basis, when I'd believed my landlord to be behind it all at least there had been one obvious solution: keep on my toes, pay up and Jake would leave me alone.

Now that it was clear someone else was to blame, I had to work out who and why. Thinking things through logically, whoever it was who had attacked me and ransacked my dad's home had been after something; that much was clear. Unless they'd been particularly badly advised on the state of my finances, that more or less ruled out money as a motive. My thoughts came around once again to the package Chic Kelly had tried to send me; the bag allegedly containing evidence sufficient to convict Frankie McPhee of murdering Lord Hewitt. Chic's plan, or so he had told me, was for the package to be used as the means of negotiating a reward that would provide financial security for his next of kin.

On that count, regrettably, I'd had to put him right for he hadn't appreciated that no matter his offer of a generous commission or the fact that he believed the brand-new Frankie posed no threat to my safety, it wasn't possible for me to act if there was a potential conflict of interest with another client. As I'd explained to Chic, shortly before his next and even more dramatic seizure had aborted my visit, arranging to have one client sent to prison for life so that the other could benefit financially was about as extreme a conflict as I, or the Law Society, could imagine and one that if taken forward would see me struck off and render any evidence inadmissible. He hadn't been at all pleased. I'd left fully expecting some other lawyer to get the call. Two days later Chic had danced a Tyburn jig. Still, everything now led me to think that the package was the reason I'd been attacked and, more importantly, the reason for Max's murder. My friend had been shot the very same day that Sean Kelly had taken the package to his office, and I'd been attacked only days after I'd met with Sean Kelly and his father at their respective prisons, by which time it would have been reasonable for anyone interested in such matters to assume that I either had the package or knew where it was. Who could possibly want it so much that they'd be prepared to kill for it? What if Chic had been wrong? What if Frankie knew about the package of evidence? Had word of Chic's intentions reached Frankie? The one person who knew for certain that the package existed and of Chic's intention to have it delivered to me was Sean Kelly. Frankie and the boy had seemed quite friendly as I recalled from my first trip to Polmont. Sean trusted him. Who knew what had been said between them?

So deep in thought was I as I sped along the coast road to St Andrews, that the beautiful scenery of the East Neuk of Fife went past unappreciated. Andy's car was of reasonable spec and nippier than the one I'd rammed up the close. I wondered how he could afford it given what I paid him and the size of his student loan.

It was early afternoon as I neared the ancient burgh and I thought I'd stop off at The Barns: a pub, the only pub, in Kingsbarns. The beach there had been a popular day-trip destination for the Munro's and I held fond childhood memories of summer days spent paddling, building sandcastles and fishing in the rock pools for hermit crabs. My dad had always threatened to retire there. What better place? The beach but a gentle stroll away, world famous links courses right on your doorstep and some great fish and chip shops only a mile or two down the road in Anstruther. Then he'd discovered the price of property in the pretty wee village and decided to stay put.

I ordered a pint and a steak pastry and began to feel more like a holidaymaker and less like Victim Support's next customer. Pleasant thoughts, though, soon made way for more pressing matters, like the identity of my assailant. The ski-mask hadn't offered so much as a glimpse of his face; however, I could rule out Jake Turpie's boys and I knew it hadn't been Frankie McPhee, at least not him personally.

If I went to the police, what would they do? Not provide me with round the clock police protection that was for sure. As for proof that Frankie was behind the attack, I had nothing to give them other than the ramblings of a dead man. A convicted murderer who at the last had claimed to be innocent, and my own cobbled-together theory. Without something concrete I'd be wasting my time. I carried the drink and pastry to a table by the window. From there I could see Andy's car. The pistol was locked in the boot, hidden beneath the spare tyre.

Suddenly, I realised I had more to give the police than just Chic's story. The holiday feeling evaporated. If the person who attacked me was the same person who'd killed Max, was the gun in the boot of my car the one used to shoot my friend? Professor Bradley, my favourite pathologist, had thought a thirty-eight. The gun my attacker had left behind was a nine millimetre. The difference in slug size between the two was minimal.

I left half my pint, most of my pastry and walked back to the car, debating with myself. Should I go to the police with the gun, tell them what had happened? If I did, they'd want to know why I had waited to hand it in; especially, as I'd met with three cops, including a Detective Chief Inspector, on the very night I'd acquired it and said nothing. Possession of a handgun, even for a short space of time, was a mandatory five-year sentence. No ifs, no buts, just jail – Dunblane had happened, the tabloids had spoken, Parliament had written.

Of course, I could throw the gun away or leave it somewhere and make an anonymous call to the cops, neither of which would help in the search for Max's killer. If I was right about the gun, the murderer was still on the loose. Max had been killed by someone who thought he was in possession of the package. That person hadn't realised the package had been tossed out of the fire exit along with the young man who was trying to deliver it. If I actually did get my hands on what was in it, I'd not have to go looking for Max's killer. He'd come looking for me. I had to find it. Where would a nineteen-year-old hide something so important? Somewhere safe. Somewhere he knew intimately, but where no one else would think of looking. Somewhere close to home.

It took only ten minutes to drive the last few miles to St Andrews: a lovely town though one where a defence agent could easily starve; the only things criminal in the place being the house prices and the lack of parking spaces. After several circuits, I found a bay at the far end of Market Street, paid and displayed and from there walked down onto South Street and into Queens Gardens.

Strolling along the terrace, counting down the numbers on the door mantles of the period properties, I almost bumped into four boys running out of a doorway, pushing and shoving each other as they made their way along the pavement. They were twelve, thirteen years old: private schoolboys, who played rugger, steeped their conkers in balsamic vinegar and thought Buckie was a town further up the east coast and not a tonic wine. On approaching me they organised themselves into a semblance of orderliness and filed by. It was a nice, middle-class neighbourhood. Not where I had expected to find the widow of the man who'd blasted the Lord Justice Clerk.

I chapped the door, and it was answered by a tall angular woman in a pale blue twin set. Around her neck she wore a thin gold chain and crucifix. She was too hatchet-faced for a 'Betty', I thought, and younger than I'd expected. At first sight, she didn't look the sort of girl to whom most men would dream of bringing home a broken wage packet, and yet there was something vulnerable about her; it was the eyes. I guessed that nobody knew the trouble she'd seen. I took to her straight off.

'More tea, Mr Munro?' Betty asked, teapot poised over the porcelain cup that sat in a saucer on the small side table by my knee. Once I'd introduced myself as her son's lawyer, I'd been shown through to the best room and she'd insisted on providing afternoon refreshments.

'Please.' I sat back in the soft armchair watching as she calmly poured. I had to hand it to her: for someone whose man had hanged himself a few days before and whose only child was behind bars and odds on for a life sentence, she seemed to have her emotions well under control. Out of the corner of my eye I saw a strip of silver foil poking from behind a pigeon racing trophy on the sideboard. Dr Prozac I presumed.

'You've a fine house,' I said, stirring my tea and the coals of conversation.

'Not what you expected?'

A three-bedroom town house in one of the more desirable parts of Scotland's property hot spot? She could say that again. I smiled diplomatically. Betty didn't look like a captain of industry and whereas the late Charles Kelly may have been the nearest thing to Raffles that West Lothian had ever known, the man I remembered used to divvy up any ill-gotten gains between the bookies and the nearest boozer.

'I don't suppose house prices are cheap in this neck of the woods.'

'Chic always said he'd look after us.' Betty pulled a little embroidered handkerchief from the sleeve of her cardigan and dabbed the corners of her eyes in turn. 'He never let us down. His cheque comes in every month.'

'Cheque?' I asked as casually as I could.

Betty sniffed. 'Regular as clockwork from his trust fund. When Chic...' She blew her nose on the little hanky. 'When he went inside, I bought this place to get away from the wagging tongues. I love it here by the sea and the folk are so friendly.' She sniffed again and tucked the hanky away.

My mobile went off. It was Frankie McPhee.

'Would you like to take it in private?' Betty asked.

'No need.' I bumped the call. 'It's Frankie McPhee, I can speak to him later. Frankie's the reason I'm acting for Sean. Tells me you and him used to be quite friendly.'

'Did he?' A cold light flashed in Betty's eyes. She lifted a tray of biscuits from the coffee table and I helped myself to a piece of shortbread.

'He's been buzzing about my office, wanting to know about Sean's case,' I said. 'Tells me he's a friend of the family —'

Betty snorted and looked away.

'Betty. Do you know why Frankie is so interested in Sean? If there's anything you think I should know then, please, tell me.' I reached out, gently took the tray of biscuits from her and laid it down on the coffee table. 'Whatever you say will be in strict confidence. I'll not say a word.' I reclined into the comfortable armchair and bit the tip off a petticoat tail.

Betty thought about it for a moment or two and then asked, 'have you seen Sean lately?' Whatever she had on Frankie, it wasn't for my ears.

'I was out to see him in prison a few days ago,' I said, turning to the real reason for my visit. 'He said something about a package that his dad had asked him to give to me. I was thinking he might have had it the night... the night Mr Abercrombie died.'

Betty shook her head. 'The police have already been here asking about that. The night they came for him, Sean had hardly been in the house five minutes and he never had any package.'

'Could look in his room just to make sure?'

'Be my guest,' Betty said. 'But the police turned this place upside down. They lifted the carpets, made holes in the walls. One of them went up the loft and put a foot through the dining room ceiling. They even took the toilet apart.' Her laughter broke down into helpless sobbing. I waited. The tears stopped as quickly as they had started. She smiled at me, her face streaked, eyes puffy. 'I'm sorry,' she said. 'I'm fine now. Come on, I'll show you Sean's room.'

Betty was right. I needn't have bothered. The bedroom was not how I imagined it would have been on the night the police arrived. Now the bed was stripped, the carpet gone and there were clean square patches on the walls where posters had been removed. The walls were pretty thick, but the room must have been sub-divided at some time and a series of holes had been cut in the plasterboard of the partition for a look inside. The few items not taken away - one or two books, some CDs and other odds and ends - were inside a cardboard box on top of a chest of drawers on the far side of the room next to a curtainless window. There was nothing there to interest me.

'Is there anywhere else he might have hidden something important?'

Betty gave a dry little laugh. 'They were through here like a plague of locusts. They found an earring of mine that had been missing for years down the back of a radiator. Believe me. If there was ever any important package, the police have got it now.'

Betty wanted some fresh air and said she'd walk me back to my car. The trip had been a waste of time. To make matters worse, I had stayed longer than intended and was sure my parking ticket had expired. I could see from a distance that there was a small piece of paper under one of the windscreen-wipers of Andy's car. When we got to it, I was relieved to find it was only a flyer for a Chinese restaurant in Leuchars. I lifted the wiper, pulled out the piece of paper and was screwing it up when a splat of white landed on the bonnet, narrowly missing my hand. One of the problems with living on the coast – bloody seagulls.

'They say it's lucky,' Betty called to me.

The number of times I got shat on in the average year, I had to be the luckiest person alive. I stared into the sky, trying to fix the culprit with an evil eye, but there were no seagulls in sight, only a solitary pigeon sitting overhead on a lamppost.

CHAPTER 40

I still wasn't keen on going home. Rather than endanger my dad any further and not wanting to waste any more cash on a hotel, I decided to bunk down at the office.

I went into my room and flopped on the couch, worried and yet at the same time pleased with my day's work. I had the package at last. The pigeon may have missed me, but its inaccurate defecation had proved lucky nonetheless. It had reminded me of Sean Kelly's fondness for the birds and inspired me to take a look inside the pigeon loft I'd noticed situated in Betty Kelly's back garden. The boy was to be congratulated for an excellent choice of hiding place I thought as I placed on my lap a small canvas satchel.

I'd found the satchel lying in a corner, presumably where Sean had thrown it the night he came home from Max's office, but at some point in the past it must have been secured to the interior structure of the pigeon loft, the roof joists perhaps, for there was a row of puncture holes in the fabric, frayed and tinted orange with rust. Other than those perforations and some encrusted pigeon poop it showed little sign of wear and tear.

I undid the straps. My desk was a mess of files and papers, so I cleared a space on the couch and emptied the contents out on to it. The first things I saw were two clear plastic bags each sealed with sticky tape, one containing a ball of black leather. I poked at it with a finger. It fell apart into a pair of gloves, scrunched up and stiff. The other bag held a crushed-up white cotton shirt. It was stained with dark patches here and there. Blood. I put both items to the side and turned to the second object: a faded blue cardboard folder, tied with red legal tape.

I opened the folder carefully. Inside were several A4 size black and white photographs, individually wrapped in cellophane bags and, like the bags containing the clothes, sealed with sticky tape that was yellow and brittle with age. One of the bags didn't contain a photo; only a single sheet of good quality writing paper folded in half.

I took a paper tissue and used it to hold them up to the light one at a time, while I studied the photo inside each. The first showed two men standing outside a restaurant on a busy city street. The picture had been taken through a telescopic lens. There was a blur of traffic in the foreground, but the subjects were in sharp focus. I recognised only one of the two: an elderly man, tall with a slight stoop, his hawk-like profile more used to jutting from beneath a horse-hair wig than a skipped cap. He was dressed casually, no red and white silk smock on this occasion, his arm draped around the shoulder of the other, much younger male.

The remaining photographs had been taken in a hotel room and were of a more intimate nature. The quality was grainy, the shots taken in poor light with fast film but showed unmistakably the same two men from outside the restaurant one of whom was clearly Lord James Hewitt of Muthill, former Lord Justice Clerk.

Once more I thought back to my Glenochil trip and the conversation with Chic Kelly.

According to the dead housebreaker it had been an early August evening in two thousand and one when, fresh from a pigeon meet, he'd walked into his local to discover that Frankie McPhee had been looking for him all afternoon. No-one who enjoyed breathing kept Frankie waiting, so Chic had gone straight round to see him. Frankie was furious. He'd wanted Chic for an urgent job and been forced to make other arrangements. Chic wasn't told the details but gathered that things had not gone to plan. Frankie gave him a shotgun and a canvas bag and told him not to show face again until he'd got rid of the stuff.

Anxious to make amends Chic agreed but being something of a connoisseur in stolen goods couldn't fail to admire the rather interesting antique shotgun he'd been handed. Next day, the death of the Lord Justice Clerk was all over the news. The police were everywhere. When Frankie was pulled in for questioning, Chic got scared. He panicked and was caught trying to off-load the shotgun; there being honour amongst thieves but apparently not amongst fences.

Found in recent possession, his prints all over the murder weapon, a long history of housebreakings behind him, Chic's only defence to the charge of murder was to explain how he'd come by the gun. He'd have to impeach Frankie McPhee: he didn't; a life sentence being preferable to a death sentence. That was Chic's version of events. Chic, it had to be remembered, was mildly insane at the time he'd recounted it to me and now he was dead; however, one thing was clear in my mind: the satchel was the package Sean Kelly and Max had quarrelled about on the night of my friend's murder. I could understand a solicitor of Max's integrity wishing to have nothing to do with the stuff or for me to get involved. I couldn't think of any reason the young man would shoot Max because of that or why he would have gone to the office with a gun. It didn't make sense. What did make sense was that if Chic had been telling the truth, for once, and the package could prove Frankie McPhee had killed Lord Hewitt, then, surely, there was only one person prepared to kill for it. After all, who else would want some dirty photos of a dead judge? Blackmail was a little too late so far as Lord Hewitt was concerned.

Of course, there was the reward money to consider. After all, that had been Chic's reason for bringing the package to light after all these years: to leave behind a financial bequest for his family. Had someone else in prison got wind of Chic's plan and sent word to the outside? Had Max really been killed for the measly twenty-five grand reward put up by the Government all those years before? It was possible. People were killed for a lot less.

Carefully, I opened the final bag and removed the piece of paper. Holding it steady with the tissue, I gently unfolded it to reveal a few letters and numbers written in a precise, distinct

159

and perfectly legible hand: ED01011276. I recognised it straight away as a case reference: one from a prosecution initiated at the Procurator Fiscal's office in Edinburgh. The ED for the court district, 01 the year and it was case number 11276.

I put the photos and note back in the blue folder and the clothes and the folder back into the canvas bag which I then placed in the big bottom drawer of my desk. I couldn't see how the items in the canvas bag incriminated Frankie McPhee or anyone else for the murder of Lord Hewitt. I could easily have come to the conclusion that Chic was a sad demented man were it not for the fact that Max must have been murdered for a reason and the contents of the satchel were all I had to go on.

I lay back on the couch to think. My eye was drawn to the print-out of Max's diary lying on my desk. I began to thumb through. He had been a busy man. The print-out contained hundreds of entries: appointments, notes to himself, reminders, bring-backs, telephone numbers. I lay down on the couch and adjusted the lamp. It was going to take a while.

I awoke early next morning with my head lying at an awkward angle and my left arm dangling off the side of the couch. The diary print-out lay across my chest; I hadn't got past the first page. I rubbed the back of my neck and stood up slowly, stretching the seized muscles in my back. I needed caffeine.

Down at the café, I made Sandy's day by settling my tab with the remains of my rainy-day cash. The team from Jay Deez were gathered for a pow-wow at their usual corner table, discussing the future of the salon. By the sound of things Butch had completed the grieving process and was chairing the meeting. The Queen is dead, long live the Queen.

I placed my order, pulled up a seat and began to go through the print-out. I was engrossed in my work when Sandy materialised at my side and placed a mug of coffee and a bacon roll on the table.

I inspected the roll. Exterior: lightly toasted. Interior: melted butter, extra-crispy bacon, plenty of brown sauce.

'How come you've not been back to see us, Robbie?' Butch shouted over to me as I took a bite of roll.

'Been dead busy,' I said, amidst crunching shards of best Ayrshire and returned my attention to the print-out, searching for a clue that might lead me closer to Max Abercrombie's killer. I continued to scan the schedules until I came to the day of Max's death. My dad had been right: Sean Kelly's name was in the diary. He had a five o'clock appointment on the very the day Max was shot. The purpose of his visit, so Sean said, was to deliver a package to me. According to the Crown, his purpose was to gun down my friend in cold blood.

The coffee and roll were long scoffed by the time, working backwards from the date of Max's death, I reached November. The last entry for the thirtieth said simply, 'Boxing Night.' There were two phone numbers beside it: one a landline, the other a mobile. I was sure the former was the number of The Red Corner Bar. I called to confirm. The barman answered and I hung up. I turned my attention to the mobile number, recalling Brendan's comments about 'the girls' and having a good time.

If I dialled, I might get Brendan, who'd be packing his Lanzarote-bound suitcase, or, if my suspicions were correct, the female who'd accompanied Max that night. I was sure that person was not Irene Abercrombie.

I clicked the numbers into my phone. Faintly, I heard a ringtone I recognised: the Age of Aquarius, the theme from Hair. It grew louder then stopped.

'Hello?'

I heard the voice in stereo.

'Hello?'

I turned my head slowly in the direction of the voice and there at the next table saw Butch sitting with his ex-boss's pink mobile phone pressed to his ear.

CHAPTER **41**

Monday morning and it was business as usual. I was due in Glasgow Sheriff Court at ten and traffic on the M8 was nose to tail.

At a quarter to ten I abandoned Andy's car in a side street at the Gorbals, not far from The Citizens Theatre. I didn't even attempt the court car park. The chance of finding a space after nine-thirty was about the same as the Sheriff being sympathetic if I were ten seconds late - theoretically possible but not bleeding likely.

I pushed through the revolving door into the perpetual half-light of the Sheriff Court. Through the cold and cheerless lobby I went up the stairs to the agents' room where I dumped my coat. Gowned-up I descended to the basement where, outside court three, I was met by my client, John Calder, a young man from Falkirk, looking smart if uncomfortable in suit and tie and accompanied by most of his immediate family.

John's problems had started three months before when he'd gone for a night out in Glasgow with some friends from work. Sometime in the wee small hours, drunk and separated from his workmates, he'd found himself in a nightclub far from home and in the company of strangers. Had John not sunk enough lager to float a canoe he might have paid more heed to the growls of the locals. As it was, there'd been a shove, a spilled drink and before the bouncers could step in, one of John's attackers had a second smile, courtesy of a pint glass: the drinking man's sabre.

At his trial John pled self-defence. In Scots Law, self-defence requires the presence of three elements. Firstly, the accused must believe himself to be under threat. Secondly, he must do everything within reason to avoid the use of force, even if it means running away. Thirdly, the force used must not be excessive.

Persuading a jury to accept that those criteria existed in John's case would not have been a great problem. The average Glasgow juror is sufficiently street-wise to know that when one is eyeballed in a pub by three young men from Springburn, it's safe to assume that they're not admiring one's coiffure. As for the other two criteria, well, running away from a fight and using only moderate force simply don't compute.

The Crown hadn't fancied its chances with a jury and so had cut its losses by reducing the prosecution from solemn to summary procedure. In doing so they reduced the potential jail term from five years to twelve months but the prospects for conviction were much higher if the trial proceeded before a Sheriff alone. Sheriffs understood well the legal test for self-defence and seldom had any first-hand knowledge of hostile encounters with young men fuelled up on Stella and disco biscuits.

Three weeks after the trial I was back for John's sentencing. In mitigation I tried to persuade the Sheriff that there had been a degree of provocation and watched as my pleas bounced off him like machine gun bullets from Superman's vest. Shortly afterwards I was bidding my client adieu. With standard half remission he'd be out in six months. That news didn't cheer his mum who gave me pelters before being dragged off by the rest of the away support.

I felt like wrapping my head in a wet towel and lying down in a darkened room. What I did was go for a walk to try and collect my thoughts so that I could piece together a strategy for Sean Kelly's defence. I gave Grace-Mary a call as I was strolling back across Jamaica Bridge on my way to the car and asked her to book me an appointment at Polmont.

'No need,' she said. 'You're sacked.'

A letter had come in that morning written on thick-lined prison paper, accompanied by a mandate from Lorna Wylie ordering me to forward her the case papers.

'Oh, and that reporter phoned again,' Grace-Mary said. 'I told him you'd give him a call when you got back.'

I hung up, leaned against the railing and looked back at the big grey building erected on the banks of the Clyde like a tombstone to justice.

'Robbie Munro, how the hell are you?' Gordon Devine seemed to have developed the habit of sneaking up behind me.

'I'm fine. Just taking a moment to watch the salmon leap.'

He blinked several times in a row. 'And I'll bet if you fell in you'd come out with one in your pocket.'

'You think so? Tell that to my client who's just been launched for twelve moons.'

'Come off it. A not proven on that Heimlich manoeuvre defence? Pretty spawny even for you.'

Gorgeous Gordon had ears everywhere.

'It's not all luck,' I said. 'In fact sometimes I don't bother with bridges, I walk across the water.'

Devine glanced over his shoulder towards the bustling city centre where old stone buildings rubbed grimy shoulders with steel and glass structures that reflected the greyness of the sky. 'You worked here once. Don't you miss it? The history, the architecture, the people - so friendly, so—'

'Mental?'

'If there was no crime we'd be out of a job and this is where the action is.'

'I'm a small-town boy and right now I've pretty much got my hands full, thanks.'

'Tell me about it. The crime business – it's always booming. By the way...' Devine fired-off a volley of blinks. 'When's Max Abercrombie's murderer going to trial?'

'That's something you'd need to ask his new lawyer.' I didn't like admitting that I'd been given the heave-ho, but with his contacts he probably knew already and was just on the wind-up.

He fabricated a smile. 'All for the best, ay? I can understand how a case like that could be too much for you - emotionally I mean. Legal aid cash aside, you really should have passed your client to me when you had the chance.'

I would never have tired slapping his smug face, but he was right. Sean Kelly deserved a good defence and when Gordon Devine had offered to put the resources of his Firm into the defence, I'd been crazy to refuse. 'I wish I had.' I told him.

'Really?' Devine blinked rapidly. 'Do tell.'

'I have this horrible feeling he's innocent.'

'Innocent?' Devine laughed dryly. 'I don't do innocence. I do not guilty or, at a push, not proven, but innocence is something that doesn't concern me.'

'It might,' I said. 'If you thought you had evidence to prove it.'

'And you think you do?'

I'd said too much already.

'I've had an idea,' Devine's face had gone all extra bright and shiny.

'And that is?' I felt it only polite to enquire.

He paused to let loose a broadside of blinks. 'Let me tell you all about it over a cup of coffee.'

CHAPTER 42

The offices of Hewitt Kirkwood & Devine were part of Glasgow's Merchant City; an old established building for an old established law firm. Devine whisked me through the plush vestibule and, giving me no time to take in the works of art that adorned the walls, led me to his office. Outside the door hung an oil portrait of an Edwardian gentleman wearing a black frock coat and a very serious expression. He looked familiar: it was the flowing white hair, the high forehead and Roman nose.

'Sir Gilmour Hewitt. Our founding partner,' Devine said, door half open, realising I'd stopped to study the painting.

'Any relation to the late Lord Hewitt of Muthill?'

'Grandfather.' Devine pushed open the door to his office and guided me in.

'Be it so humble,' he said, one arm around my shoulder, the other held out in an expansive gesture. 'Make yourself at home.'

He collapsed into a red leather armchair and I pulled up a chair on the other side of his enormous desk.

'He ever visit?'

'Who?'

'Lord Hewitt.'

'Not recently.' Devine blinked a few times, laughed and then frowned. 'Sorry, that was tasteless. Jim Hewitt trained here. Before my time of course. He went to the Bar after that and, as they say, the rest is history. He did drop by very occasionally. The Firm handled his private affairs and he used to turf up for a sherry on special occasions or if we were trying to impress some big commercial client.'

'Do you know if... was he... you know... Lord Hewitt... gay?'

Devine stared at me unblinkingly. 'Very.'

I didn't know what to say after that. Eventually I came out with, 'nice place you have.' I looked around the office; it certainly was something special. I was admiring the arched ceiling with its intricate cornicing when there was a gentle knock at the door and a young woman came in carrying a tray. She was tall, slim and totally stunning.

'Ah, Valerie,' said Devine. 'This is Mr Munro.'

'Robbie,' I managed to splutter.

'Pleased to meet you,' the pretty young woman said, like she actually meant it and then laid the tray on the desk.

Devine pressed down on the cafetière. 'Thanks, Val, we'll take it from here.'

With a parting smile the young woman withdrew. Devine poured and I accepted not a chipped mug or a cardboard tumbler but a delicate white china cup. I sniffed and inhaled pure Arabica.

Devine pulled open a drawer and removed a heavy gold chain from which hung a deep blue enamel plaque. He put the chain around his neck. 'What do you think? Vice President of the Law Society this year, El Presidenti next.'

'Very nice and er... well done.'

Devine pointed to a large marble award on the edge of his desk. 'Scots Lawyer of the year, two-thousand and eight.'

'Belated congratulations. Now, what's your big idea?'

'Straight to the point. I've always liked that about you.' Devine leaned back in his chair and put his hands behind his head. 'Robbie, you know me and you know I can always pick a winner.' He blinked. 'Actually, that's not true, but if I back a loser I send someone else to the press conference.' He laughed uproariously, sending himself into a blinking fit. He waved a hand in front of his face. 'But before we talk business, there's something I'd like to show you. Something that will help you to understand what we at H. K. & D. are all about.'

He sprang to his feet, clearly expecting me to do likewise. I took a gulp of coffee, burnt my tongue in the process and followed his pinstripe suit out of the room at a trot, tailing him further into the building to where it opened up into an atrium with a glass ceiling. At this, the crossroads of the office, legal assistants, paralegals, clerks and secretaries, who had been scurrying about their business, scurried a wee bit faster when they saw the boss on the march.

We continued until Devine stopped and pushed open a great wooden door that led onto a cobblestone courtyard.

'This,' he said grandly, 'is what used to be the main entrance. And this…' he pointed down to the large sandstone doorstep on which we stood, 'is the original Attorney's Stone.' Devine bobbed his head, blinking enthusiastically, expecting, it seemed, some kind of equally eager response from me. I smiled politely. 'You have heard of the Attorney's Stone?' I hadn't. Devine was only too happy to cure my ignorance. He scuffed the sole of his shoe on the doorstep. 'See how the stone is bevelled, worn away with the passage of feet over many years? Well, sometime between the world wars, the then senior partner, Sinclair Kirkwood, decided to replace the stone with a new one. Peter Hewitt, Lord Hewitt's father as a matter of fact, was an apprentice at the time and had the bright idea that in order to save money they should simply dig up the existing stone, turn it over and put the worn surface on the underside. Mr Kirkwood agreed. He even told young Peter that if he did the job himself he could keep the sum the Firm would otherwise have spent on a stonemason. One Saturday morning, Peter got up early and set about the doorstep with hammer and crowbar. Eventually, after much blood, sweat and tears, he levered up the stone and flipped it over, only to discover that sometime in the past some bright spark had come up with the same idea – the stone was worn on both sides. The young law apprentice learned the hard way the importance of knowing the history of any situation before embarking on what is perceived to be a novel course of action.'

'It's a fine story,' I told Devine as we walked back to his room.

'It's history, Robbie. It's tradition. We at H. K. and D. have all the latest technology, yet we never forget who we are. I want you to be part of this.'

I wasn't sure I was hearing him properly. 'Did you just offer me a job?'

He blinked several times at me. 'It would be a great opportunity for you. All I'd ask in return is your full commitment.' I wondered if that included sharing the cash donations that I encouraged from grateful clients.

Devine offered his hand. 'We'd be a great team. We might even be able to wrest back that murder case of yours. In fact I'd make it my top priority.' It was all happening so fast. With Devine on my side I could surely solve the riddle of Max's death and while Sean Kelly no longer wanted me for his defence, surely he wouldn't turn down the great Gordon Devine.

'Send me the papers.' Devine was on fire. 'Whatever you've got, anything and everything you think might be relevant and leave the rest to me. I'll have this new lawyer ditched in two seconds and young master Kelly eating out of my hand in no time. It will be the first of many famous victories for us.'

I listened on a like an enraptured juror as Devine continued his pitch. Working for a Firm like his was certainly an attractive proposition. I thought about the glass-domed atrium, the courtyard, the worn sandstone doorstep and I remembered the dingy close that served my own office. I thought of the works of art that were strewn around the corridors of Hewitt Kirkwood & Devine and of my own mummified rubber plant and the piece of tinsel taped to the ceiling of my room that I hadn't managed to get down since Christmas. I thought of Valerie's beautiful smile and Andy's petted lip.

'What do you say?'

I stared at the compact little hand thrust out to me, the light falling through the big sash window catching the gemstone pinky ring.

I hesitated. Why? What was there to think about?

Devine's warm smile began to ice up. He retracted his hand.

169

'Tell you what,' he said. 'Take some time. Think it over.' He guided me to the door. 'You know, I'm sure I heard it said somewhere that you're a golfer.' He made it sound like an afterthought, but someone had done their homework. My dad was hugely keen, if ungifted, and his enthusiasm for the game, and, sadly, his swing, had rubbed off on me at an early age.

'I hack about.'

'Superb. Why don't we go out for a few holes next Sunday, talk things over some more and, if you like, you can let me have your decision at the nineteenth? How does that sound?'

It sounded great.

CHAPTER 43

Back at the ranch Grace-Mary was at the reception desk, manning the phones and reconciling the bank statement, wielding, I noticed, a lot of red pen. Andy was floating about trying to look busy.

I sat down at my desk. My office suddenly appeared so very shoddy. My clients, everything, seemed like a complete waste of time. Why did I bother? If I packed up and went to work for Devine, who'd care? One or two more toe-rags get banged up – so what? Most of my clients were junkies, never eating, always stealing, spending every penny their sticky little fingers could grab on smack. They needed the jail as much for nourishment as punishment.

Frankie McPhee walked past my door and caused me to jump. The man was the reason I'd slept the last two nights in my office and why I was in the process of having a new door installed and security locks put on all the windows at home. I went out into the corridor to see him standing on a chair in the waiting room, replacing a fluorescent strip. I stepped into reception.

'What's he doing here?' I whispered to Grace-Mary.

'He said something about Mohammed not answering the mountain's telephone calls. While he's been waiting he's fixed the cistern, bled all the radiators and now he's onto the electrics.'

'Doesn't he know about me being sacked from the Kelly case?'

Before my secretary could answer my question, Frankie came through wiping his hands on a green paper towel.

'Too bad about Sean,' he said. I thought he was taking the news very philosophically considering how much he'd wanted me to take on the case in the first place. 'The boy's his own worst enemy. Terrible business about his dad wasn't it? Poor old Chic.' Frankie threw the paper towel in the bin. 'I heard,' he said lightly, 'that you paid his mum a visit.'

I took him into my room and closed the door. 'About the rent…'

'For old time's sake.'

'Why didn't you tell me? And how did Andy know about it and I didn't?'

'Turpie, your landlord, dropped in one day when I was here trying to find you. He was making a fuss so I squared him up. Your assistant was there at the time but I asked him to keep quiet. I know you have a lot on your plate and I wasn't sure how you'd take it. I hope you don't mind.'

With a promise to repay him – sometime, I led him back out to the corridor where we were met by Andy. He needed his car back for the weekend. I could hardly say no, but it did leave me with a problem. I needed a car for my golf trip with Gordon Devine.

'You can have Big Jo-Jo's motor, if you like,' Frankie said. 'Really, I mean it. He hardly uses it during the week and we're always busy at the soup kitchen on a Saturday night and Sunday anyway.'

I didn't want to be any more beholden to Frankie than I already was, but I had places to go, people to see and Jo-Jo's motorised scrapheap was the only mode of vehicular transportation readily available to me.

'It's not a problem,' Frankie said. He slapped me on the back. 'I'll have the big man drop it off here on Saturday morning. He can get the train back to Edinburgh.'

Once Frankie had left, Grace-Mary appeared and dragged me through to her room where a ledger book lay open on her desk. She was about to start lecturing me on cash-flow or, rather, the lack of it when she seemed to sense something. She looked me in the eyes. 'What's going on?'

'What do you mean?'

'Something's going on and I want to know what it is.'

The woman was psychic. She would have made a fortune picking lottery numbers if she didn't think the whole thing was a tax on the statistically challenged.

'Do you like it here?' I asked.

'I suppose.'

'How'd you fancy a move?'

'How do I fancy a move?'

'You and me.'

'And Andy?'

'Andy's young. There will be other opportunities, better than this dump.'

Grace-Mary hitched her tartan skirt, revealing an inch of American-tan tight above the knee and sat on the edge of my desk.

'What is going on?' she asked. 'Exactly.'

'I'm being head-hunted.'

'Oh, I see.' She snapped the ledger shut, jumped down from the desk and walked to the door. 'Then you'd better be careful – it's a big target.'

I alighted from the train at Waverley station and set off for the High Court. The reason for my trip to the capital was to find out what I could about case reference ED01011276 and the link, if any, between it and Max's murder. Sean Kelly may have sacked me, but I was out to get justice for Max and not quite ready to end my involvement in the case. The Crown would continue to join their few dots to make a picture of young Sean as the killer, he was all they had, but I believed the killer was still at large and that I had the murder weapon and bruises to support my theory.

From the foot of Cockburn Street, I climbed the steps of Advocates Close, all one hundred and eighteen of them, and entered onto the High Street.

At the Lawnmarket, a bunch of Japanese tourists kitted-out in a rainbow of plastic waterproof ponchos, were studying the statue of David Hume, thumbing through guidebooks, trying to work out who exactly he was and what he was doing sitting on a plinth opposite St Giles Cathedral. I'd always wanted to meet the town planner who out of ignorance, mischief or as part of a crazy philosophical balancing act, took the decision to park a monument to Scotland's most famous atheist directly across the street from the High Kirk of Edinburgh.

I skirted the ponchos and entered the building which had formerly housed the Sheriff Court until a no-expense-spared refurbishment had transformed it into the High Court of Justiciary. The whole place was fitted throughout with plenty of glass and polished brass, contemporary tapestries hung on the wall of the mezzanine floor outside court three, rubber plants loitered in corners; all in all it was a bright and cheery place to start a prison sentence.

Two flights up in the Clerk's office there was no queue and only the counter separated me from four paper-shuffling civil servants.

I cleared my throat, drummed my fingers, rang the bell and while I was wondering if I'd accidentally donned a cloak of invisibility, I spied, to my right, beside the window, a fifth figure, that of a young man sitting at his desk. He was eating a bridie and reading a graphic novel; the kind where the women are all candidates for breast reduction surgery and apparently never seem to feel the cold.

'You busy?' I called to him.

He set down the comic, placed his pastry on top and came over to the counter. His shirtsleeves were rolled up, his collar button undone and his floral tie, either horribly out of fashion or cutting edge, was askew.

'Can I help?' he asked, concealing his enthusiasm behind a yawn.

'Hope so. I'm looking for some information about a case from a few years back.'

I could almost see the spirit try to depart his body.

'We're terribly busy.'

'It's terribly important.'

The clerk sighed, went to the nearest computer terminal and tapped a few keys.

'Name?'

'Munro.'

He looked about, possibly for a weapon.

'Not your name. The name of the accused.'

'I've got a PF's reference number if that's any good.'

'Might be - if this was the PF's office. I need a name and a date of birth.'

He needed a slap. 'I think it was one of Lord Hewitt's last cases if that's any help.'

'Hewitt?'

'James Hewitt - of Muthill – he used to be Lord Justice Clerk.'

'Never heard of him.'

'He died.'

'When?'

'Two thousand and one...ish.'

The young clerk rapped the fingers of both hands on the keyboard with an air of finality.

'The computer only goes back five years. We'll need to get the books out.'

I checked my watch.

'How long will that take?'

'I dunno,' said the clerk. 'Two... three... weeks.'

'What?'

The clerk gave me a condescending look and I only just refrained from jumping the counter.

'And,' he continued, 'I can't get the books out unless I have a request in writing specifying the precise information you require and why it's needed. It's a big job and we're snowed under.' He gestured to the still life of humanity behind him. 'Sorry.' He didn't look it. He turned his back on me and skulked off to his snack and reading material.

I was on the point of leaving when an older clerk wandered over. He was a friendly wee man with a bright, cheery face and a toupee that was fooling no-one. I recognised him, but for the life of me couldn't remember his name.

'Problem, Mr Munro?'

'Could say. I'm doing some research on a case —'

'And want someone to dig through the Books of Adjournal for you?'

'Would you?'

'No.'

'Come on. It's not like I'm asking you to journey through the mists of time.'

'Might as well be. All the records are archived. They're not even stored in this building.'

'Then it looks like I've had a wasted journey.'

He thought about that for a while then held up a finger. It was clearly a eureka moment, minus only a small illuminated light bulb hovering over his head. 'I think maybe I can help,' he said. 'Do you fancy a small refreshment?'

Not as much, I suspected by the look of his tomato of a nose, as he did. 'Come on,' he said. 'I've time for a swift one.' The civil service shuffle had disappeared and he moved much more freely now. Unhooking his jacket from the back of a chair, he lifted a flap in the counter and came through to my side. Two minutes later we were sitting at the bar in Deacon Brodie's.

'What'll it be?' I asked.

'Rum,' said my new-found friend, gesturing to the barman with thumb and forefinger alarmingly wide apart.

The barman poured a double. The clerk knocked it back in one and nodded to the barman who hadn't moved, the hand holding the bottle poised at the ready. I had the distinct impression the two had met before. His glass recharged, the man in the dodgy syrup seemed to remember why it was we were there. 'What's so interesting about a dead judge?'

'Let's say I'm following a lead.'

He fuelled his grey cells with another swig of rum. 'Not an awful lot I can do, really.' He reached for his glass. I grabbed his wrist.

'Do you know Bob Coulsfield?' he asked quickly.

I racked my brains. 'The Macer?'

Monarchs have footmen. Army officers have batmen. High Court judges have macers.

'Aye, the very man. He worked with Jim Hewitt for years, right up until he was bumped off. He might be able to help.'

He made a try for the glass again, but I still had a hold on his wrist.

'Aye, well,' he looked longingly at the drink just out of reach. 'Bob's retired now and hasn't been well. He stays out your way somewhere and...' He rescued his arm, put the glass to his eager lips and poured the contents down his throat. 'I think...' he rattled the empty tumbler on the countertop. 'I think I could possibly dig out an address for you.'

CHAPTER 45

'It seems like only yesterday.' Bob Coulsfield knelt in his back garden, weeding a rose bed. I leaned against a dilapidated bird table watching him. He ran the back of a hand across his forehead, leaving streaks of dirt across his wrinkly brow. 'You were just a boy back then. Dodging about Parliament House, always running late and looking for counsel to instruct on some last-minute job.' The cigarette adhered to Bob's bottom lip, waggled up and down as he spoke. Although he'd lived in Scotland for many years, he was originally from Newcastle and his Geordie accent remained intact.

He paused to stuff a handful of weeds into a black bin liner. 'The judge was late that morning. Must have been nearly ten when he got in, which wasn't like him at all. I had a cup of tea ready and usually we'd talk football first thing on a Monday. He was a great man for the Jam Tarts and seeing as how they'd lost the Edinburgh derby at the weekend, I wasn't expecting him to be in a right good mood but he were as grumpy as Old Nick and started firing questions at me all about the trial that was due to start that morning. I didn't know what to say. In all my years as his macer we'd never discussed a case.'

'What did you tell him?'

'Only what I knew: that it was fraud or something and that the advocate-depute reckoned it would go on for at least six weeks.' He dug into the soil, severing the roots of a particularly stubborn dandelion with the blade of his trowel. 'I used to hate those white-collar crimes, dead boring. Always hundreds of paper productions to lay out. Used to take me ages. Give me a rape or a robbery any day.'

It had started to spit. Bob looked up to the darkening heavens from which he deduced he had a minute or two weeding left before it came on heavy.

'Go, on,' I encouraged him.

'Hewitt wanted to know more, so I was sent out to speak to the Clerk, Jock Morrison it was, remember him? Mind the way his long hair used to poke out from under his wig? I think he was a veggie an' all. Anyway, he tells me it's tax evasion. I asked him if there was a lot of money involved and he comes back with, 'best part of a CRUISE missile'; just the sort of sarky remark you'd expect from a lefty like him.' Bob was in full flow, punctuating his sentences with stabs of his trowel. 'Anyway, his lordship empanels the jury and then discovers he's left his pen in chambers. He looks at me like it's my fault and sends me off to get it. I mean, I've a bloody four-foot solid silver mace to carry, you'd think he could manage a four-inch gold fountain pen.'

Bob stood up. He tied a knot in the black bin bag and put it on a pile of similar bags at the side of his hut. Touching the cigarette in his mouth with his hand for the first time since we'd started our conversation, he threw it down and ground the butt into the earth with the heel of his boot. 'Come away in,' he said. 'I'll put the kettle on.'

Bob lived alone in a house to the south of Falkirk, not far from the monument to the second Battle of Falkirk where in 1746 the Jacobites scored a victory over the royal troops of King George II. Through the kitchen window there was a fine view down the valley, across the smoking stacks of Grangemouth and over the Firth of Forth to the Kingdom of Fife.

He took off his gardening jacket, hung it on a nail on the back door, went to the big white sink and rubbed a large green bar of soap in his dirt-blackened fingers. After carefully washing and drying his hands he went over and filled the kettle. It was a museum piece, huge, with a flame-blackened base. It even had a whistle. He put it on the hob and lit the gas. He seemed to do everything in slow motion as though he'd got all day to do it, which he probably had. It came to me that he might be making the most of my visit. I didn't suppose many folk came to see him. I sat down at the kitchen table.

'You were saying?' I asked, wishing the old man had a fast forward button. 'About Lord Hewitt?'

'Oh aye, well, I assumed his pen would be lying next to his newspaper - he liked the crossword - but it wasn't there. He'd been in such a black mood that morning he hadn't even opened the Scotsman. I didn't want to go back without it. I looked everywhere, even in his briefcase. Eventually, I found it in the top drawer of his desk. That's when I saw a big brown envelope and a folder inside. I could see it contained photographs – well I could after I'd had a look inside, like – and right away I knew what was going on. I also knew that Jim Hewitt would never let himself be blackmailed.'

From my briefcase I took the blue folder containing the photos and laid them out on the table.

'Look anything like this?'

'Aye,' said Bob. He lifted the flap and removed one or two of the photos, holding them at arm's length and squinting. 'Disgusting.' He laid them down again, reached into one of the kitchen units and brought out a pair of mugs. 'Would have been a bloody scandal if word of them had got out.'

'But word didn't get out.'

'No,' he said. 'No, it never did.'

Bob took a large brown teapot down from a shelf.

'Never mind the tea,' I said. 'I want to know what happened.'

Bob sighed. 'Well, the judge always took a break mid-morning. He said it was to let the jury have a coffee, but personally I think it was more to do with his bladder. There's me all set to nick off for a cuppa but Hewitt insists I call everyone into chambers: the Advocate-depute, defence counsel, solicitors… It was standing room only. Once everyone's gathered, he takes the folder from his drawer, doesn't open it but lays it down in full view. He asks if anyone knows about an unusual package he has received that morning and, of course, no-one does. 'Good,' says Hewitt, 'then no-one will mind if I hand it over to the proper authorities.' Next morning he was dead. I never saw those photos again – until now.'

The kettle whistled and Bob rinsed the inside of the teapot with a splash of boiling water.

'What happened to the trial?'

'Collapsed.' He poured us each a mug of tea. 'That same day, right after lunch. The Crown had spent the morning with one or two formal witnesses, I wasn't really listening, and then at two o'clock they put in this D.I. He's hardly got warmed up when the A.D. says, 'I wonder if you would kindly look at Crown production number fourteen.' So, I goes off to fetch it from the production table but it's not there. 'Is there a problem Mr Coulsfield?' the judge asks. All eyes are on me. What can I say? I tell him production fourteen is missing and he glowers at me over the top of his half-moons. 'What is production fourteen?' he asks and the A.D. tells him it's a search warrant. He's got the look of a man who's found shit on his shoe.' Bob pushed a carton of milk across the table to me. 'They searched the court room for hours looking for that warrant.' He laughed. 'Quite amusing really, a bunch of cops searching for a search warrant. They never found it. Didn't surprise me, mind. You know what security was like back then. Be the same now, I expect, even with all them rag-heads blowing themselves up and flying planes through windows. There's always counsel, solicitors, clerks, cops, journalists, court runners, coming and going.'

'And there was you too.'

Bob snorted in derision. 'Me? Never. Completely trustworthy me. Fair enough, the productions were my responsibility and the court manager did have a go at me later about keeping vigilant but anyone could have done it if they knew what to look for and were prepared to take a risk. It's a wonder it doesn't happen more often.'

I helped myself to sugar. 'And the photographs? Did you tell the police about them?'

Bob lit another cigarette.

'No chance. Too many awkward questions. At least the old bastard died with his reputation intact.'

'He was gay, Bob. He wasn't a child killer.'

From the look on the old man's face he didn't seem to appreciate the difference.

'Don't suppose you remember the name of the accused.' I crossed my fingers.

'Oh, yes,' he said. 'I remember his name all right.'

'Care to enlighten me?'

Bob took his mug over to the window and stared out at his garden deep in thought.

'I left court the back of four on the afternoon of the trial. By half-past I'm waiting for a train to the High Station, when who should come along but the accused. He's got a few gadgies with him. Rough lot. He walks over to me smiling, friendly like, shakes my hand. Then he gives me an envelope, about an inch thick, and tells me he wants me to go back to the court and fetch that.' Bob nodded at the blue folder lying on the kitchen table. 'Now I'm worried. He's maybe got a friendly face but there are a lot of unfriendly faces with him and they're all looking at me. I had to tell him there was no way I could do it 'cause I'd seen Lord Hewitt put the folder in his briefcase before he went home that night. I tried to give him back the envelope, but he wouldn't take it. Put that towards a holiday, he says, or if you feel you want to tell anyone about our conversation you'll have enough for a really nice coffin.' Bob flicked the ash off his cigarette into one of the numerous ash trays; most of them were full. 'That night and the next day I made a few telephone calls, asked some questions about the accused and realised I had a serious choice to make. I chose a fortnight in Majorca.'

'And the name of the accused?' I said, repeating my original question. 'Do you remember it?'

'McPhee. Killed some bloke a few years later, I heard.'

I sipped at my tea. I couldn't say I was greatly surprised by Bob Coulsfield's disclosure, but it was progress. I'd come hoping to learn the significance of the photographs and the note and if there was any link to Frankie McPhee. It was clear to me now that Frankie had been behind an attempted blackmailing of Lord Hewitt and, with the judge threatening to go to the police, I could understand why he'd want the photos back.

I joined Bob at the window. The rain had stopped and the dandelions in his rose beds would be sprouting. He'd be off out again soon to get half an hour's weeding done before sunset. I suppose gardening helped keep his mind off things. He drew hard on his cigarette, coughed and spat blood into the sink. Lung cancer. Inoperable. Maybe he'd still be around in the spring. If not, there'd be flowers for his grave.

CHAPTER **46**

The King's Course Gleneagles: a seriously good golf course for seriously wealthy people. My very own wealthy person was waiting for me on the first tee. Gordon Devine was clad in a salmon pink cashmere sweater and a pair of sky-blue slacks. The stump of a cigar was clenched firmly between his teeth. It was cold but dry and bright for the time of year and a peaked sun-visor that matched his trousers protected his blinking eyes from the weak winter rays.

It had been quite a while since I'd swung a club in anger but somehow, I felt Devine would be nothing to worry about. We agreed to play off scratch.

Devine gestured to the tee. 'Shall we say five a hole, just to keep it interesting?'

The pro shop at Gleneagles offered free wooden tee pegs, a generous gesture of which I'd taken full advantage, and, placing the best ball I could find on one of the recently acquired pegs, cracked a nice drive that couldn't have been far short of two hundred yards. Not bad for me. It came to rest just off the fairway in some light rough. I felt good and made a mental note to get out more.

Devine grunted faint approval and flipped his cigar behind him where it lay smouldering on the closely mown grass. After a few stretches he strode onto the tee and stared down the fairway, visualising the line of his drive. His caddie, a wee man with a walnut of a face, put a driver in his outstretched hand. The gleaming new club had to have cost more than all my gear put together. After a couple of practice swishes, Devine tee'd up, heaved the club at the ball and sent it careering off to the right, deep into a sea of gorse. Playing three of the tee, his next attempt found an even more impenetrable patch of rough. He stooped, picked up his cigar and took a puff, blinking furiously.

'Your hole,' he said, pointing the way to the next tee with the handle of his driver.

As we walked on, it was hard keeping my mind on golf and off Bob Coulsfield's revelation about Frankie and Lord Hewitt and how it all might relate to Max's murder. Even although I was no longer instructed by Sean Kelly, in a way, knowing what I did, I felt responsible for his defence. I couldn't help thinking that by refusing to tell me where the blackmail package was, and now by my dismissal, he was trying to protect me – but from whom?

My second drive was almost as good as my first. Devine stepped up and nobbed his blow fifty yards straight left into the undergrowth. He hurled the driver to the ground.

'I don't know what's wrong with me today,' he complained. 'I don't normally play this badly.'

The caddie picked up the club and he muttered in my ear as he went off in search of Devine's golf ball, 'he has played before then?'

While Devine was swinging like an axe-murderer, I couldn't believe how well I was playing. It should have been a battle of the hackers but I was striking the ball like a dream and was six up after six. I lost the seventh, after my playing partner fluked a chip in from the rough, and the eighth when my wayward drive found a bunker with a side like the north face of the Eiger. The ninth was halved so at the turn I was four up and despite minor signs of a deterioration in my game, the ease with which I was winning was such that I thought I might have to deliberately misread a few putts on the back nine, just to be sociable.

As we made our way to the tenth I unwrapped my half-time chocolate bar as Devine checked the scorecard.

'If I'd known you were this good I'd have asked for some strokes – or bet less money,' he laughed.

Somehow I didn't think four holes at a fiver a hole was going to trouble a man who must have lost more than that in golf balls so far.

'Two grand,' he said. 'What's that in Legal Aid terms? Four fixed fee cases?'

The chocolate turned to dust in my mouth. Five hundred a hole?

It was Devine's honour, but he waved me onto the tee: less to do with good manners than the fact he'd produced a banana from somewhere and was now munching away at it.

I sucked chocolate off my fingers. My hands were shaking as I pulled the driver from my bag. Five hundred a hole? The state my finances were in, I'd thought a five spot was a risky enough wager. I bent to tee up the ball and could hardly get it to balance on the peg. I peered into the distance and found a red flag fluttering far off on the horizon. The fairway seemed awfully narrow, the gorse creeping in from either side. I took three deep breaths, steadied myself and swung.

'Unlucky. First bad one today,' Devine said, cheerily, as my golf ball scuttled off at an acute angle and buried itself in the long grass.

His caddy sidled up to me as Devine stepped onto the tee. 'Nae worries, son. This clown couldnae hit a coo's arse wi' a banjo.'

Devine wound up his swing and released. There was a horribly satisfying ping as titanium met Titleist and the little white ball rose into the air as though setting off on a mission for NASA. It soared for a mile or two before falling to earth, splitting the fairway. It was the kind of drive Bing Crosby used to sing about.

'That's more like it,' Devine said. 'Now you're in for a game

I drove back down the A9 flushed with success. After eventually winning by three holes, I hadn't felt so bad about buying Gordon Devine dinner, even at Gleneagles prices. We spent the evening eating and talking over his job offer and sometime after the pistachio crusted sea bass with artichoke foam, and shortly before the carpaccio of pineapple, I'd agreed in principle to join Hewitt Kirkwood & Devine as a senior associate with partnership prospects.

The more I thought about the move, the more it seemed like the answer to my problems. True, I'd no longer be my own boss, and I'd have to churn out the billable hours, but I'd be working on high profile cases with properly funded defences and have a steady income. My first salary cheque might even arrive before the man from VISA with his scissors.

That said, my feelings about going to work with Devine were mixed. He was opinionated, greedy, vain and professionally unethical, which was fine by me. The problem was, I knew there was no way he'd let Andy tag along. Grace-Mary, yes; experienced criminal law secretaries were worth their weight in legal aid certificates, not so inexperienced Stirling Uni law graduates. I only hoped that where one door closed, another would open for the boy - and that it wasn't the door to a Local Authority job or, heaven forbid, the Public Defence Solicitor's Office.

We left things on the basis that Devine would take the news to his partners for their consent; a formality he assured me; and all going well we'd get together later in the week and hammer out the fine detail.

As I neared home my feelings of exhilaration after playing the King's and eating a meal fit for one, began to wane at the thought of another restless night. I kept my eyes fixed on the white lines and centre studs as the car sped on down the dark road, my mind racing along with it.

What was I going to do about Max's murderer? Would Sean agree to Gordon Devine taking up his defence? I recalled Devine's story about the attorney's stone and how important it was to know the history of any situation before embarking on a course of action. If Max's death was linked to Chic Kelly's blackmail package, then I felt pretty sure I now knew most of the history to that.

Many years ago, Frankie McPhee had tried to blackmail the Lord Justice Clerk. When Lord Hewitt threatened to go to the authorities, Frankie needed to act quickly to retrieve the blackmail material. Not so much the photos, I was sure, unless his fingerprints were on them, but the note; it was handwritten – how stupid was that?

To break into the judge's home Frankie would have needed expert help and who better than his old pal, Chic Kelly? But, according to Chic, he'd been unavailable. Obviously, Frankie had tried to do it himself, been rumbled and ended up killing the judge. Chic's attempts to clear up the mess by disposing of the murder weapon, had only made things worse and ended up with him being convicted of the murder. Then, after years in jail and with not long to live, he'd looked to cash in on the reward by revealing the true killer's identity.

The history was clear in my mind. What about the present? Other than the part where Sean Kelly made an appointment to see Max, everything else was extremely hazy.

Back home again I was heating milk in the microwave and listening to the re-assuring stutter of the espresso machine, when there was a loud clatter as my dad came in the back door, tripped over my golf bag and nearly gave me a heart attack.

'What are you doing here?' I asked.

'I'll be pushing up daisies if you keep laying traps for me. I nearly set my neck there.' He stood the bag up, leaned it against a chair and sat down at the table. He was quick to eyeball the cheque that was lying in the fruit bowl.

'My golf winnings,' I said.

'Turned pro have you?' He picked the cheque up and whistled. 'Fifteen hundred? That'll come in handy.'

I shoved a mug of coffee at him. He ignored it and studied the cheque that had been signed with a flourish of Devine's Michel Perchin fountain pen. 'That's some signature. Pity it's illegible. Who'd you hustle?'

'Gordon Devine.'

'Don't say. What were you playing golf with that flannel merchant for? He's a bigger crook than most of his clients.' He looked at the cheque again. 'What's he like at golf? Any good?'

'Evidently not,' I said, retrieving the cheque, 'but he can afford to be bad.' I folded the cheque and placed it back in the fruit bowl beside a hand of squishy bananas and a couple of shrivelled-up tangerines.

My dad decided it was too late for coffee and started raking in the cupboard under the sink until he found what he was looking for. He brought forth a bottle and gave the pale liquid inside a little swirl. 'Rosebank? Nice. A wee bit girly for me but if you've nothing from the sacred isle —'

I relieved him of the bottle and replaced it under the sink. 'They make whisky other places than Islay. Now leave my booze alone and tell me why you're here. It's way past your bed-time.'

'If you're going to be like that...'

'Out with it. And if you've come to rant on about Frankie McPhee, you needn't bother.'

'Seen through him have you?'

'Like a double-glazed window.'

'Good because if I get the chance to nail that bas —'

'I know how you feel about him, thanks.'

'And anyone who sides with him.'

'Flies with the crows, you mean?' I felt we'd had this conversation already.

'Exactly.'

189

'You've retired,' I reminded him.

'Once a cop—'

'Dad, why are you here?'

'I've something to tell you. 'He rubbed his throat, a painful expression on his face. 'I think you'll want to hear it,' he croaked, pathetically.

I fetched the bottle of Lowland malt and poured us each a small measure. He took a sip, smacked his lips and cleared his throat noisily as though his vocal chords were now sufficiently lubricated for him to pass on the important news he'd come to deliver. 'The dead hairdresser—'

'Jacqui Dillon?'

My dad nodded gravely. 'The gun... the one that killed her. There's nothing certain yet...'

'It was the same one that killed Max, wasn't it?'

'They're pretty sure.' My dad sighed. 'Look, this is all still hush-hush. The details haven't been officially released.'

'So how come you're in the know?'

He finished his drink and helped himself to another. 'I was talking to Dougie Fleming. Good man, known him since he was a blue band. Hates you of course.'

'So maybe he is innocent.'

'Who?'

'Sean Kelly – you know my former client – the one who's on remand for Max's murder.'

'Not necessarily.'

'Come off it. Max was killed on the Friday night. Sean Kelly was arrested in St Andrews late Saturday. I was at the police station early on the Sunday morning when they were bringing him in.'

'So?'

'So, according to Butch—'

'Who's he?'

'The salon manager at Jay Deez. He said that Jacqui was at work until closing time on the Friday Max died. So, Sean would have had to have shot Max and then shot Jacqui within twenty-four hours, otherwise he would have been in police custody at the time of her death. That's what I call an alibi.'

My dad wasn't so easily persuaded. 'Or maybe he killed them at the same time. Maybe she was in his office.'

'What else has Dougie Fleming been saying?'

'What do you mean?'

'I mean did Fleming say something to you about Max and Jacqui?'

'No. Should he have?'

For a girly whisky, my dad didn't seem to mind drinking it.

'You know they don't make Rosebank anymore,' I said, pulling the bottle out of his reach after he'd replenished his glass, leaving behind only an inch in the bottom.

'My dad frowned. 'Oh, I see. Like that is it? I tell you what I know but you keeping everything to yourself?'

'It's not like that?'

'No? What's it like then?'

'Petra Lockhart has this theory about Max and Jacqui being an item.'

My dad laughed. 'No danger. Not Max.'

That's what I'd thought until Brendan's revelation about his night out with Max and the girls and then there was Jacqui's mobile number on Max's diary print-out.

'And anyway, if Jacqui was with Max in his office the Kelly boy would have killed her there and then and left her. Why cart her off to the Bathgate Hills?'

In his efforts to protect Max's honour my dad was inadvertently making a good point for Sean Kelly's defence. After all, Sean had travelled by bus from St Andrews to Linlithgow. It wouldn't be easy transporting a corpse by public transport. 'Then you've got to admit, as reasonable doubts go it's a belter,' I put to him.

'Maybe.' My dad rubbed his moustache contemplatively with a finger. Sean Kelly wasn't off the hook yet. 'Unless the wee bastard had an accomplice.'

The gun was in a drawer in my bedroom. If it was found, I knew how it might look.

'Dad. There's something I want to show you.'

I left to fetch the bright blue folder. I thought about showing him the gun as well and then remembered the old man's blood pressure. When I returned, the level of the whisky bottle was even lower. I dropped the folder on the kitchen table. He pulled it towards him. 'What's this?'

I opened the folder and laid out the photos. My dad donned his reading glasses and didn't say anything until he had carefully studied each one.

'Where'd you get them?' he asked, replacing the photos inside the folder.

'Sean Kelly had them stashed in a pigeon loft, or I should say his father, Chic Kelly, did.'

'Why?'

I removed the note, still in its plastic bag, from the folder. 'See the numbers on this?'

'A PF crime reference number isn't it?'

'I think it was Lord Hewitt's last case. These photos were sent to the judge before the trial.'

'What trial? Wait, don't tell me – Frankie McPhee?'

'Correct. And I think we'll find the note was written by him as well.'

My dad took the note and held it to the light. A familiar look of triumph spread across his face that meant he knew something I didn't. 'No, I don't think we will.' He set the note down on the table, then reached over, took the cheque from the fruit bowl, unfolded it and laid it alongside. He removed his glasses and sat back in his chair. 'It was written by his lawyer,' he said, smugly.

I studied the cheque and the note. The digits written on each were in a similar hand, no, not similar, identical.

Frankie McPhee and Gordon Devine; it was quite a team.

CHAPTER **48**

Wednesday morning, I wasn't far from Sandy's and breakfast when a car pulled up at the kerb. It was Detective Chief Inspector Lockhart, in civvies and looking as good as ever.

'Mr Munro, can you spare a moment?'

'Business or pleasure?'

'I'm afraid I'm never off duty,' she said. Sounded ominous. Sounded like me. 'Know anything about a Vauxhall Corsa, registered to one Arthur Ramsay, now of Queensland, Australia, found rammed into a close entrance in Fountainhall and subject of a number of unpaid fixed penalties and parking tickets?'

'Clearly, officer,' I said, 'you're mistaking me for someone who doesn't know of his right to remain silent.'

She smiled thinly and pulled out into a gap in the traffic. We headed west along the High Street. It was only after a mile or so, once we'd crossed Linlithgow Bridge, leaving the Lothians and entering Central Region, that she spoke again.

'All right, I'm officially no longer in Lothian & Borders jurisdiction. Off the record, tell me - what the hell is going on?'

Her directness surprised me almost as much as her apparent naivety.

'Please. Do you know how many of my clients are in the jail for speaking to cops, off the record? Your colleague, Dougie Fleming, being responsible for most them.'

From somewhere in the deepest regions of my jacket pocket I felt faint vibrations. I dug out my phone. It was Gordon Devine. I hadn't expected him to get back to me this quickly. I apologised to Lockhart and took the call. Devine wanted us to meet up at his place in the country the next day to talk terms over lunch. I agreed, wondering if I should take the chance to ask him about his role in Frankie McPhee's attempted blackmailing of Lord Hewitt. Was it possible to get sacked before actually starting work?

'Inspector Fleming has his policing methods, I have mine,' Lockhart said after I'd put my phone away. By this time we had sped on to the Lathallan roundabout and down the hill past the artificial ski slope at Polmont and into Grangemouth. 'I don't know how many of your clients he's verballed. What I do know is that you've a client awaiting trial for a murder that he didn't commit.'

'What makes you so certain?'

'Because I interviewed him. I've seen enough killers to make me a good judge and my gut says Sean Kelly's not got it in him. I suppose he could have been involved in some way or other but I'll guarantee he never pulled the trigger.'

'Sounds like you'd be an excellent character witness. Any actual evidence to go on?'

'Have you read the lab reports? There wasn't a trace of gunshot residue on Kelly - his skin, his hair, his clothes - nothing. These days they can locate and identify a single microscopic particle. The stuff hangs around in the air for hours in enclosed spaces, sometimes days. I wouldn't be surprised if the cleaner who found Abercrombie, even the cops who attended the scene, were covered in it. You ask me? Sean Kelly wasn't there when the shots were fired.'

The lack of gunshot residue was definitely one chink in the prosecution armour. There was also the fact that the gun that killed Max was probably the same one that killed Jacqui. I assumed that piece of evidence would be disclosed to the defence at some stage but I didn't want to mention it in case I landed my dad in trouble for leaking information. A bit of work on both those lines of defence and they might very well evolve into a reasonable doubt.

'Why don't you tell the Crown about your concerns?' I said. With Lorna Wylie as his lawyer, having the Lord Advocate drop the case was definitely Sean Kelly's best chance.

Lockhart glanced right and left as she slowed for the junction at the foot of the hill. 'I have and it's made no difference. The plain fact is that Sean Kelly is the only show in town. Let's not forget the eye witnesses and the fact that he was in Mr Abercrombie's diary as his last appointment on the evening in question. Then there's the forensics indicating he was involved in a violent struggle with Mr Abercrombie shortly before his death.'

'What about Jacqui Dillon?' I asked. Lockhart's source seemed to have been right about her and Max having an affair.

'She's a puzzler. I don't know what to think. You'll be aware that traces of her blood were found in Mr Abercrombie's office,' Lockhart said. 'Actually, not traces - quite a lot. It looks like she was shot there and her body dumped.'

That more or less answered the point my dad and me had discussed the night before. What other important new information was I missing out on? But why would the killer get rid of Jacqui's body and not Max's? Had Irene Abercrombie discovered her husband's infidelity, shot them both and got rid of her rival to save face? Or had she employed a hitman?

'Whoever did it would have needed a vehicle,' I said. 'As far as I'm aware Sean Kelly came to Linlithgow by bus. He doesn't drive far less own a car.'

'No,' Lockhart said, 'but Frankie McPhee does, and I understand you've been driving around in it lately.' Lockhart took her eyes off the road and looked at me instead. 'This discussion between us is unofficial. Now is your chance to tell me anything important you think I should know. My rank allows me to exercise a certain amount of discretion.'

I didn't reply.

She continued. 'I don't believe Sean Kelly killed Max and I think you can help me find out who did.'

I shifted slightly in my seat. Finding the real killer was precisely what I wanted. How much could I tell her? About the attack at my home, the one I'd failed to report? About the gun I'd held onto for the past week and a half? I knew the way so-called informal discussions with the police could go. If I came clean and handed over the gun, it might help catch Max's killer, but even if it didn't, there would always be the consolation of nailing a defence agent for being in possession of a firearm. I might even be in the frame for Max's murder on the basis of fingerprints and DNA on the murder weapon. Whatever Lockhart might say about her discretion, she didn't decide who to prosecute and possession of a handgun was a zero-tolerance offence. Whether I'd be prosecuted was down to the Crown Office and unfortunately I couldn't count the Lord Advocate amongst my close personal friends.

'What do you think I can do?' I asked. 'Did you not hear? I don't act for Sean Kelly anymore. If you want the real killer, you're going to have to do your job.'

Lockhart made a right turn opposite Grangemouth Stadium, past the enormous BP settlement tanks and in the direction of Bo'ness on the south bank of the Forth. In summer, close your eyes and the aroma of sweet garlic growing wild on the embankment of the Bo'ness & Kinneil Railway line was more reminiscent of Provence than the outskirts of Scotland's main petrochemical plant.

'I'm trying to do my job,' she said. 'Encouraging witnesses who may have valuable information to come forward is all part of it.'

I couldn't argue with that, but I tried. 'What makes you so sure I can help catch Max's killer?'

'I believe that Abercrombie's death is somehow linked to Chic Kelly and I think it's more than coincidence that the person charged with the murder is Chic Kelly's son.'

It was so tempting to tell her everything. Could I take the chance? 'What's that got to do with me?' I asked, stalling.

'I know that you visited Chic Kelly in prison. I also know that Frankie McPhee, a former associate of Kelly, has been seen around your office lately. I'm sure you must know that Mr McPhee is on licence for murder —'

'Culpable homicide.'

'And is suspected in several unsolved killings spanning three decades.'

'He's an old client, concerned for his friend's son.' There I went, defending Frankie again. Force of habit.

'Is it his money? Is that why you let him hang around your office?' Clearly, Frankie was under surveillance. How much did Lockhart know? Had she found out about Frankie paying my rent arrears? 'What have you told him about the case?' she asked.

I had told Frankie very little about the case, and what I told or didn't tell clients, even former clients, was nothing to do with any cop, no matter how pretty.

'Frankie's a charity worker now. He runs a soup kitchen.'

'As well as owning the actual Church building and a portfolio of other properties throughout Edinburgh.'

We didn't enter Bo'ness town centre, instead Lockhart took the right fork onto Dean Road, past the cemetery and then over the Flints in the direction of Linlithgow. Such was the rivalry between the two towns that when I was young the folk used to say that the only good thing to come out of Bo'ness was the road to Linlithgow.

There was no further talk until we reached the brow of the hill at the entrance to West Lothian Golf Club and from there into a tight S bend. It was a stretch of road I knew well. A stretch of road that always caused the hairs on the back of my neck to prickle. I felt a lump in my throat as we approached the very tree where my mother had died so many before, on the way to the police station to bail out her favourite pupil.

'What's Frankie McPhee ever done for you?' Lockhart said, breaking the silence with timing that was too perfect. She was some machine. 'Tell me what you know and I promise to keep whatever you say strictly between us. I guarantee your name will not be mentioned.'

It was tempting, so very tempting. We entered Linlithgow. On our left, a pen swan and her cygnets waddled down to the reeds at the edge of the loch. In the distance, the open crown spire atop St Michael's Church shone in the winter sunshine. I'd liked Lockhart from the moment I'd first met her. I had no doubt she'd be as good as her word.

'Okay,' Lockhart said. She must have sensed that I was beginning to wilt. 'Maybe it would help if I told you that I was one of the officers who interviewed Chic Kelly after Lord Hewitt's death. It was my first major assignment after returning to the force with my law degree. I was a Detective Sergeant. Chic confessed. I made Inspector.'

There was no note of pride in her voice. Did Lockhart know about Chic's theory on the death of Lord Hewitt? Did she now believe she may have got the wrong man?

Lockhart pulled the car over. 'Mr Munro... can I call you Robbie?' I consented. She continued. 'Robbie, at the turn of the year, Chic wrote to me from prison. He told me he was terminally ill and wanted to put the record straight. He also wanted to know if there was still a reward on offer for information leading to the conviction of Lord Hewitt's killer. I thought it was a joke and though I did go to see him, I have to say, I didn't take what he had to say very seriously. I do now.' Lockhart reached into her jacket pocket and removed a turquoise-covered police notebook.

'I can't help noticing that we're back on your patch,' I said.

'I'll give you a formal caution if you like, but I don't want you to say anything. I just want you to read this.' She handed me the notebook. There was a rubber band around it from top to bottom marking the place.

I'm always wary about the contents of police notebooks, but I felt sure I already knew what was in this one. I looked at Detective Chief Inspector Lockhart and her serenely beautiful, yet earnest face and began to wade through page after page of

Chic Kelly's statement. It was just as Chic had told me. And yet the housebreaker hadn't known the whole story. He didn't know why Frankie had wanted so badly to retrieve the stuff from Lord Hewitt's house. I did and could easily imagine Gordon Devine in a state of panic contacting Frankie after the aborted fraud trial. Probably out of arrogance more than ignorance he'd written the blackmail note in his own hand. Now he had to get it back. He would be willing to pay anything and Frankie would do anything for money. What to do? A break-in artist like Chic could have been in and out in no time at all. Frankie on the other hand lacked his friend's expertise as Lord Hewitt had discovered to his cost.

I turned to the last page.

'It's signed,' Lockhart said.

I'd expected nothing less. I knew where this conversation was going.

She stared hard at me. 'What does it matter if Sean Kelly doesn't want you as his lawyer? He's still entitled to justice like everyone else and so is Max Abercrombie.' I looked straight ahead out of the windscreen. She moved nearer. I could feel the breath from her lips against my cheek, smell the light fresh fragrance of her perfume. 'Robbie, you owe Frankie McPhee nothing. He's scum.'

She was keen, I'd give her that. Then again you didn't get to be Detective Chief Inspector at Lockhart's relatively tender age without some fairly dramatic results. Nailing the true killer of Lord Hewitt of Muthill, Scotland's former Lord Justice Clerk would be another rung on her ever-extending career ladder. I was sure that her superiors could overlook the small fact that all those years ago, Lockhart and her colleague had extracted a confession from an innocent man.

I gave her back the notebook. She didn't have to tell me how important Chic Kelly's statement had become. While Chic had been alive, the statement in Lockhart's notebook had been interesting but of no evidential value. It was hearsay and inadmissible. For it to stand up in court, Chic would have had to go into the witness box, adopt the statement as his own and testify to its accuracy. Prisons weren't safe places for rats. But people's attitudes changed as death beckoned. When Chic called Lockhart had he been aware that upon his death his statement would become admissible; courtesy of section 259 of the Criminal Procedure (Scotland) Act 1995. If Chic hadn't been prepared to grass Frankie in life, he could do so from beyond the grave him and it might mean leaving his family a financial legacy.

'What do you think?' asked Lockhart.

What I thought was that Chic's statement was a decent piece of evidence, but it was only one source. To seek a conviction, the Crown would need a second and Lockhart was looking to me for that corroboration. I realised now that the photos and blackmail note were not the important things. It was the clothes: the gloves and shirt, splattered with judicial blood on the outside, smeared with the killer's DNA on the inside. Was that why Max had been killed? So Frankie could make sure the package, kept safe by Chic all those years, never saw the light of day? It was so difficult to make sense of it all. Why would Chic think that I would use the package against one of my old client's? What was in it for me? Any skim I could have taken from the reward could easily have been matched by Frankie and without any retribution. No, I had to be certain of my facts before I opened up to the police.

'Sorry,' I said. 'I can't help you.'

'Can't, Mr Munro, or won't?' Lockhart slipped smoothly from good into bad cop mode. 'I think I should warn you that I'm going to get to the bottom of this case with or without your help. If you choose not to assist my enquiries, then should I discover any illegalities involving yourself I will not turn a blind eye.'

She sounded like my dad.

I undid my seat-belt and made to open the car door. Lockhart reached across me and held it shut.

'If nothing else, heed your father's warning,' she said. 'Frankie McPhee is a dangerous man.' She let go of the door handle and thrust a police calling card at me. 'My mobile number's on the back. You can call me anytime, day or night.' I took the card from her. She smiled. Good cop again. 'I mean it,' she said. 'Any time.'

CHAPTER 49

Following hard on the heels of the lecture from Chief Inspector Lockhart, next morning I received another; this time from Grace-Mary, on the subject of Munro & Co.'s finances. I tried my best to pay attention though at that time I had more things to worry about than the size of my overdraft; like an imminent face-to-face with Frankie McPhee.

I'd been up all night thinking about Frankie's possible involvement in Max's death. I was certain that Max, and, for some reason, Jacqui, had been murdered by a person attempting to recover Chic's blackmail package. Frankie McPhee clearly had a motive, as did, I now realised, Gordon Devine.

At a corner table in Sandy's that morning, over a coffee and bacon roll, I was still mulling things over, trying to come to a verdict on who had killed my friend. On any rational view of the available evidence it had to be Frankie, and yet although my dad would undoubtedly disagree, I believed that Frankie McPhee was most certainly… well almost certainly, a changed man. Anyone who knew Frankie's track record from way back would not have been unduly astonished at the suggestion that he was responsible for Lord Hewitt's murder, but I was sure he hadn't killed Max. For one thing my childhood friend had been shot by an amateur. Frankie was a pro. For another, if Frankie was after Chic's blackmail package then he'd have it by now and myself, Sean Kelly and anyone else who'd set eyes on it would be an integral part of Britain's motorway network. Of course, I might be horribly wrong, which was why I intended to return Big Jo-Jo's car personally. I wanted to test Frankie's reaction to a few questions and asking them in broad daylight, with plenty of witnesses around, seemed to me the best way to go about it.

So, after keeping my secretary at bay with some wholly unjustifiable profit forecasts and dropping into Sandy's for a coffee to go, I set off for Edinburgh and Frankie McPhee's soup kitchen.

It was the back of eleven when I arrived and found to my alarm that the place was empty. Obviously, they didn't do lunch. I heard noises coming from the back hall and I went through to the kitchen where I came across Frankie standing at a large wooden table, chopping vegetables with the sort of knife familiar to slasher-movie aficionados. His disciple, Big Jo-Jo Johnstone, was standing at the sink in apron and pink Marigolds, scrubbing at a soup pot with an orange scouring pad.

When Frankie saw me enter he put the knife down on the chopping board. 'Robbie. Good to see you. Didn't hear you come in. As you can see we're a bit short-handed. Me and Jo-Jo have been here all morning and there's still a mountain of spuds to peel.'

If that was a hint for me to grab an apron and tattie-peeler, I didn't take it. Instead I took the faded blue folder from my coat. Inside it were the photos of Lord Hewitt and Gordon Devine's handwritten note.

I breathed in deeply and handed the folder to Frankie. He wiped his hands on the tea cloth that was tucked into his belt before opening the folder and flicking through the photos.

'What do you know about these?' he asked, his expression giving nothing away.

'That Gordon Devine used them to try and blackmail the judge at your trial back in two thousand and one. And that you stole them, or, rather, reclaimed them on Gordon's behalf.'

'Where did you find them?'

'Chic had them stashed. I think he's been blackmailing Devine for years. Betty says she gets money from a trust fund. When he knew he was dying, he wanted the truth to be told.'

'The truth? Really? Who, Chic?'

'Okay, he mainly wanted his family to claim the reward money when it was proved who the real killer was. He needed somebody to carry out the necessary negotiations. He asked his son to deliver the evidence to me.'

Frankie nodded. 'Makes sense. Chic would know you'd do anything so long as there was a few quid in it.'

'Yeah? Well judge not,' I said. 'Remember you're the one on licence.'

Frankie shrugged. 'Anyway, what's all this got to do with me? Lord Hewitt's dead and buried and so is the man convicted of his murder.'

Skilfully put, I thought. I took the folder from him and waved it in front of his face. 'Sean couldn't find me. He went to see Max Abercrombie. These photos and the note are the reason Sean Kelly is looking at a life sentence for a murder he didn't commit.'

Frankie picked up the knife and started chopping again. 'That's something you don't have to worry about, seeing as how you're off the case.'

I put my hand on his, pressing it down against the wooden chopping board. 'I'll decide when I'm off the case, not some nineteen-year-old who doesn't know any better.'

Frankie pulled his hand away. Still holding the knife, he took a step back. 'What's this? Robbie Munro emotionally attached to a client - and one who can't pay a fee at that? You must be getting soft. Face it, there's nothing in this for you anymore. You're out. Is that not what you wanted from the start?'

'I'm doing this for Max. If Sean Kelly is acquitted that's a bonus.'

Frankie dumped a few double handfuls of diced turnip into a large cooking pot. 'Why are you here?'

'To ask for your help.'

'What kind of help?'

'Your speciality - protection.'

Frankie went to the sink and filled the pot with water. 'Have you thought of going to the police?'

'No, but the police have thought of coming to see me. They think that you were responsible for killing the Lord Justice Clerk.' Frankie's face remained expressionless. 'I don't care if you were. For what it's worth I do believe that you're a changed man and I want your help to find out who's chasing these photos because I believe that's who murdered Max.'

He put the pot on the stove and lit the gas. Throughout our conversation I never mentioned the gloves and shirt. I wanted to see if Frankie would mention them. Did he know they still existed? If so, why wait until now to try and recover the contents of the canvas satchel? Chic had spent years in prison, an easy target for someone with Frankie's connections.

Frankie began to wash a stack of bowls. 'What are you going to do with the folder?'

I picked up a tea towel. 'One person who has to be keen to recover it is the man who wrote the note. I'm having lunch with Gordon Devine at his place in a couple of hours. I don't see him as the hitman, but I'll bet he knows who pulled the trigger. Plan A is to confront him with what I know. If he gives me Max's murderer, I'll give him back his photos and the note he so stupidly wrote.'

'Got it all worked out, haven't you?'

'I like to think so.'

He rinsed a bowl and handed it to me. 'You took a risk telling me all this. I could be working with Devine.'

It had crossed my mind more than once. 'What can I say? I'm a good judge of character.' I dried the bowl and put it on the draining board. 'Well? Can I count on you?'

Frankie was giving the next dirty bowl his full attention. 'Robbie, I told you before. I can't. I'm on licence. If I so much as drop a toffee wrapper on the pavement, I'm back inside. I've put a lot into this place. I've too much at stake...'

'The old Frankie McPhee would have helped me.'

He took the dish towel from me. 'The old Frankie McPhee is dead.'

I'd been half expecting a refusal, but when I thought of all the strokes I'd pulled for him in years gone by I was still hurt.

'Be seeing you, Jo-Jo,' I said, as I walked past the big man on my way to the door. Out of the corner of my eye I could see something protruding from underneath one of his rolled-up shirt sleeves and into a pink rubber glove. As far as I could make out it was some kind of bandage. My blood ran cold. The bed-post: it was half a metre of solid oak.

'See ya Mr Munro.'

I knew I shouldn't but I had to ask. 'What happened to you?' I went up to him and rapped his arm with a knuckle.

'Repetitive strain injury,' he said, proudly. 'Peeling tatties.' He rolled the rubber glove down to partially reveal a light blue plastic splint. He held out his injured arm to me. 'It's not exactly a stookie but you can sign it if you want.'

I ran my eye down the splint. There were only one or two scrawled signatures. Given Jo-Jo's contacts, if he'd been wearing it for any length of time I'd have expected it to read like the custody sheet for Monday morning at the Sheriff Court.

'How long you had it?' I asked.

'Not long. When did I get it, Frankie?' Frankie stirred the pot and said nothing. I studied the scribbles, trying to decipher them. Jo-Jo sighed enormously. 'Are you gonna sign it or no?'

'I'm a lawyer,' I said. 'I don't sign anything without reading it first.'

'Suit yourself,' Jo-Jo said. He pulled his arm away, rolled the rubber glove back over the splint and plunged his arms once more into the soapy water.

CHAPTER 50

I drew off the A9, drove through the small Perthshire town of Braco and onto a single track road for several winding miles. The countryside around was beautiful: green rolling hills and clutches of woodland. I remembered reading that James the Sixth used to have hunting lodges all about the area. Apparently, after a day's boar-spearing he liked to round up some witches, tie them to posts and set fire to them, like giant candles. A medieval form of patio heating I supposed.

I rounded yet another corner and the Hewitt ancestral pile hoved into view. I knew the lawyers at Hewitt Kirkwood & Devine charged like wounded rhinos, but the Firm must have been doing even better than I imagined for Gordon Devine to have been able to buy the stylish courtyard mansion from the dead judge's estate.

Having gone through to Edinburgh to meet with Frankie McPhee, I was well behind schedule even though the journey had taken less time than I'd expected; partly due to me having borrowed my assistant's nippy wee hatchback again and also because the property was not as far away as the village of Muthill and a lot closer to Blackford. Then again, Lord Hewitt of Blackford hadn't quite the same ring - too many council houses.

It was nearly two o'clock as I swung the car through the big black gates and onto a gravel driveway, the tyres on Andy's car crunching like a hippo wallowing in a river of cornflakes. Taking the blue folder with me I jumped out of the car, pulled the brass bell at the front door and waited. A place like that, there had to be a butler or a maid. I waited some more. Still no response. I rang the bell again and then tried the door. It was open. I walked inside.

The hallway was the size of my flat. An enormous rug ran the length of the hardwood floor. The ceiling was high and there were hunting trophies everywhere. A huge set of antlers, a stuffed boar's head, the preserved remains of a couple of unlucky otters and what I could only guess was very possibly a polecat, hung along the walls. Atop a massive sideboard, next to a vase of fresh-cut flowers, a brace of cock pheasants stood frozen in time. It all gave me the creeps. I ventured on searching for a sign of life, poking my head into various rooms including what I took to be the very drawing room where Lord Hewitt had been murdered.

'Gordon!' I shouted, my voice echoing around the hall but eliciting no response.

Upstairs, the first room I came to was a study, spacious and well lit by a picture window looking onto the rear of the house and giving a splendid view of the fields beyond. In the near distance, I could make out a figure, bundled up against the cold and striding through the heather. Gordon out killing more of God's creatures, I presumed. The clock on the wall chimed to confirm that I was exactly one hour late. My prospective employer had given up on me and in a way I was glad. Now that I was actually here in the study of his splendid house, the scenario I intended to put to Devine seemed more and more like the ravings of a conspiracy theorist and less and less like hard evidence. Did I really want to throw away my future career prospects on some half-baked notion that Devine was involved in Max's death? Even if I confronted him with what evidence I had, wouldn't Scotland's most famous criminal lawyer simply discount the note as a forgery, a hoax? I could almost see him blinking back the tears of laughter. 'Handwrite a blackmail note? Give me some credit. If I managed a first at Edinburgh, don't you think I could pass blackmail 101?' I needed something more to go on. Fortunately, my tardiness had presented me with a chance to snoop around, to see what else I could dig up. Where better to start than the man's private study?

I glanced around. Pride of place on the mantelpiece stood the bronze figurine of a man aiming a shotgun and on a small plaque along the base the words, 'Winner - Perthshire Amateur

Clay Pigeon Open 2002'. That and some other less significant trophies set the tone for the rest of the room. Framed letters of thanks, newspaper clippings and photographs of Devine shaking hands with various luminaries, criminals and politicians - some were all three - covered the walls.

Where to begin? The most substantial piece of furniture was a mahogany bureau that took up most of one side of the room. It was an impressive piece, the dark wood warm and waxy to the touch. I started there, pulling open the drawers one by one and carefully sifting through the contents, my search hindered by the fact I had very little idea what I was looking for. After the drawers I checked the end cupboards that turned out to be filled mainly with sporting magazines, legal journals and old newspapers.

A few raindrops tapped against the windowpane. The change in weather might curtail the shooting trip and lessen the time available to me. I'd have to be quick.

I moved onto the desk and then a chest of drawers. There was nothing remotely useful.

Besides a nest of tables the only other items of furniture in the room were a gun cabinet near the window and a small safe that was bolted to the floor and secured to the wall. Surprisingly, both were unlocked. The cabinet housed a number of shotguns and the safe was empty save for Devine's passport, a set of keys, and miscellaneous papers that were of no interest.

I was thinking I should leave, when I noticed a tapestry hanging from a rail on brass hoops. I pulled it to the side to reveal a second door. I turned the handle. It was either stiff or locked. I put my shoulder to the door and gave a firm shove. It didn't budge. I tried again, harder. It flew open and I stumbled into the next room, falling and skidding on the polished parquet flooring. I pushed myself up on the arm of a chesterfield sofa and dusted my legs. They were covered in something sticky. I checked the palms of my hands. Blood. Why? I wasn't injured.

In front of me I saw a pair of shiny black shoes and above them a pair of pin-striped trousers. I gasped, straightened and took a step back. It was Gordon Devine, or, rather, from the clothes, I assumed it was Devine, for he sure wasn't blinking any more. In fact he wasn't doing anything anymore; except sitting on the sofa with most of his head missing.

CHAPTER **51**

D.I. Dougie Fleming laid the shotgun on the table between us. It was wrapped in a heavy duty polythene bag, a brown cardboard police production label attached to the cable-tie that bound the top. We were in Linlithgow police station; not the muster room on this occasion, but a much smaller room, along with Detective Chief Inspector Petra Lockhart and a tape-recorder.

Immediately after I'd discovered Gordon Devine's body I'd called Petra Lockhart. Not only was she the highest-ranking officer I knew, she was about the only cop with whom I was on relatively friendly terms and, after all, she had kindly given me her card only the day before. I gave a brief statement to Central Scotland Police at the scene and Lockhart had arranged for me to provide more details the next day at Linlithgow.

The chance to interrogate a defence lawyer must rank high on every cop's professional wish-list; revenge for hours spent cross-examined in the witness box on the subject of notebook irregularities and the like, and, even though I was there on a voluntary basis, Fleming was making the most of his opportunity.

'They usually destroy murder weapons but not this one,' he said. Through the thick polythene production bag I could see the intricate carving on the weapon's stock and silver ribs. 'It's a Boss & Co. over and under, thirty thousand quids' worth of firepower. Lovely isn't it? Even your pal Frankie McPhee wouldn't saw down those barrels.'

'Is that the gun that killed Devine?' I ventured, feeling ever so slightly off the pace.

'And Lord Hewitt,' Fleming said. Lockhart was taking a back seat. 'Gordon Devine bought it along with the rest of Lord Hewitt's estate.

'Gordon's death,' I asked. 'Suicide?'

Fleming rubbed his chin and frowned. 'Possibly, but only if he shot himself from the other side of the room.'

'That's enough, Inspector,' Lockhart said. 'Robbie... Mr Munro, we think Mr Devine's wound...' she made it sound like a grazed knee and not the loss of a head. 'There is only a slight possibility that it was self-inflicted. His safe was found open and we don't know yet what, if anything, was taken.'

Fleming dived in again. 'A bit strange, don't you think?' He jabbed a finger at me. 'One lawyer friend of yours shot dead, another, you just happen to be visiting, also shot dead. You seem to be the common denominator when it comes to murdered briefs.'

I leaned forward across the table, my hands clasped tightly, wishing they were around my interrogator's fat neck. 'Am I a suspect?' I stood up. 'Because if I am we can stop this interview right now.'

'The interviewee is now standing,' Fleming said for the benefit of the tape.

'Well he can sit down again.' Lockhart tugged my sleeve. 'No, Mr Munro, you are not a suspect, you are a witness, and if Inspector Fleming can bear that in mind perhaps we can proceed.'

'Seems a bit strange to me, that's all,' Fleming muttered under his breath.

'What's a bit strange?' I asked. 'That if I were the killer, I'd bother phoning you lot to tell you about it? Or that I'd blow the head off the man who was about to offer me a job with one of the country's top law firms?'

'Oh, yes,' said Fleming, 'the job offer. I've had someone make a call. Why is it, you think, that none of Devine's partners seem to know about it?'

'It was early days,' I said. 'That's why we were meeting - to talk things over.' I looked to Lockhart. 'I was in your car the other morning when I took the call, remember?'

Lockhart grimaced. 'Not sure if I do actually. I mean, I recollect you took a call but my mind was on other things.'

Fleming held out a hand. 'I'll have the hi-tech unit check over your mobile phone. I take it you've no objection?'

That would be shining. I was sure Fleming's ability to fabricate evidence wasn't limited to police notebooks.

'Not without a warrant,' I said. 'Now if that's everything, I think I'll leave.'

Fleming leaned back in his chair, hands behind his head. 'Before you do, I'd like you to tell me again about the mystery man you say you saw walking through the Perthshire countryside.'

I went over it all again but when he asked me to go through my entire movements that day in reverse order - a classic police interview tactic based on the premise that it's much harder to tell lies working backwards – I declined.

'I'm finished,' I said, 'If you want to ask me any more questions, you'll have to detain me.'

Fleming leaned forward, pushing his face at me. 'Don't think I won't. I'm the one who decides when we're finished.'

I said nothing and that's how I planned the rest of the interview going. Fleming could detain me at the police station for the purpose of his investigations and ask all the daft questions he wanted, but I was under no obligation to answer any and in due course he'd either have to charge me or let me go.

'Actually, Inspector Fleming,' Lockhart said, 'I'm the one who decides when we're finished and we are.' She switched off the tape. I politely declined to sign Fleming's infamous notebook and was free to go.

I walked to the door accompanied by the two detectives. Lockhart held the door open for me, her friendly smile in stark contrast to Fleming's dark scowl. 'Better not skip town.'

CHAPTER 52

Back at the office, Grace-Mary was waiting for me with a face like a half-chewed toffee. There are only two things in the world that really frighten me: the Scottish Parliament's criminal justice reforms and the sight of my secretary as the month-end looms with the Firm account in overdraft.

'Do I take it we're staying put?' she asked.

'For the moment.'

'Good. I don't like the city. Too many crooks.'

I was about to explain, not for the first time, that crooks paid her wages, when Frankie strolled into the office and went straight to the toilet. He came into my room brushing hair trimmings from his shoulders. 'Just back from the barber's. What do you think? It's the new me.' He went to the mirror and ran his fingers over his short stubbly hair.

I'd seen enough new Frankie McPhees. 'Get out.'

'What?'

'You heard. I want you to leave - get out.'

'Robbie, are you okay?'

I took the blue folder from my desk drawer and laid it on the desk. 'You never really cared about Sean, did you?' You came here looking for me so you could get your hands on the evidence that links you to the murder of Lord Hewitt.'

Frankie hesitated, but only for a second. He moved closer and picked up the folder.

'Chic Kelly gave the cops a signed statement,' I said. 'All they need now is corroboration.'

'Robbie, you're making a mistake.'

I lifted a brass letter-opener off the desk; the handle was shaped like a golf club. I levelled the pointy end at him. 'The only mistake I made was in believing that you'd changed. My dad was right. People like you don't change.'

'Your dad hates me. He's got every right to. But, Robbie,' he implored, moving even closer, 'trust me, I don't care about the photos or the note.'

'Give me them back then.'

Frankie puffed out his cheeks and blew a sigh. 'No. While you have them you're in danger.'

'Did you kill Max?'

He laughed. 'Are you being serious?'

'What about Hewitt?'

'No.'

'That's not what Chic says in his statement.'

'Chic didn't know the full story. He was never the brightest. Getting caught with the gun was proof of that. He knew he was never going to walk from the murder charge and asked me to do something about his wife and wean. He was in a terrible state. The police had already questioned me about the judge. I couldn't trust him.' Frankie shuffled his feet and looked embarrassed. 'I could have lifted the phone and Chic wouldn't have been a problem any longer, but we were mates. I told him that if he confessed, kept my name out of it, then for as long as he was in prison I'd see that Betty and Sean were never short of cash.'

It was plausible, almost, and yet people were dead because of those photos and I had no intention of joining them.

Frankie moved closer still. 'Robbie, I came to you looking for help for Sean, nothing else.' He leaned the palm of a hand on my desk.

I gripped the letter-opener. 'I'm not wearing it, Frankie.'

'Well you should. You see Sean's my son.'

I lowered the letter-opener.

Frankie pushed himself away, turned and paced the room. 'Years ago Chic got himself a new bird, young and a bit of a looker. I sent him away on a job and took her out for the night. I told her we'd meet up with Chic later, though I don't think she

215

believed that line for a minute. We had a good time. She'd never tasted champagne before. We ended up staying the night at a hotel.'

I could just about imagine a young Betty, late teens early twenties, being given the full five-star treatment by Frankie McPhee in his prime. It would have been like a night out with Royalty, swanning around all the best clubs, money no object.

Frankie stopped pacing and stared down at his shoes. 'After that she wouldn't stop calling me. She seemed to think it had all meant something. I didn't. She was Chic's bird and there were plenty of fish, you know?'

'And Chic? Did Betty never tell him about you and her? About Sean?'

'No way. He was just daft enough to do something rash. Betty wasn't stupid. She married Chic and told him the wean was his. Better a wife than a widow. Chic's trust fund isn't the proceeds of blackmailing Gordon Devine. It's from me. Money for my son. I pay it through Devine's firm, not even Betty knows where it comes from.'

Frankie's revelation certainly explained Betty's reaction when I'd mentioned his name and, of course, Frankie's interest in Sean's case. That is if what he was telling me now was the truth.

'Whatever you may think about these.' He held the folder aloft. 'Think again. The photos and the note prove nothing against anyone other than Gordon Devine. Have you ever thought that Chic might have talked while inside? That someone else has worked out that the blackmail note is in Gordon's handwriting and wants to put the squeeze on him?'

'This no longer concerns Gordon Devine,' I said. 'He's dead.'

If Frankie had already heard the news then he was one hell of an actor.

'When?'

'Yesterday. Shot by someone not long after I'd told you I was going to see him.'

Frankie shook his head sadly. 'I didn't know. I swear, I had nothing to do with it and there's a soup kitchen full of witnesses who'll testify in my defence.' I only remembered Jo-Jo Johnstone being in Frankie's company around the relevant time. He waved the folder at me. 'If I wanted these so bad, I could have taken them from you yesterday. I didn't need to kill Gordon Devine.'

Who said he hadn't tried to take them? Not yesterday perhaps, but I remembered Jo-Jo's shiny new plastic stookie. He used to be a bare-knuckle boxer. These days he got injured peeling spuds? I lifted the phone with my free hand. 'Get out or I'm calling the cops.'

'Don't do this, Robbie. Keep the photos. Show them to whoever you want. I don't care.'

I opened the bottom drawer of my desk and pulled out the crunched-up leather gloves wrapped in their plastic bag; they'd been the first things to fall out of Chic Kelly's canvas satchel, and, next, the bag containing the white shirt. The bloodstains were clearly visible even through the yellowing polythene bag. The type of bloodstains that come from blasting someone at point blank range with a shotgun. DNA testing would tell exactly whose blood it was. It would also tell who'd been wearing the gloves and the shirt when the trigger was pulled.

I laid the items on the desk in full view. 'Come near me or my office again and it's going to be case re-opened.'

In all the years I had known Frankie McPhee, that moment was the first time I had ever seen fear on his face.

'Robbie…' Frankie's voice was suddenly very hoarse. 'You don't know what you're doing.'

'Out,' I said.

He tried to speak. The words wouldn't come.

'I'm counting to three.'

I had reached two when he turned and walked out, taking the folder and photos with him.

I don't know how long I sat there in a daze, my heart pounding.

'Hello?'

217

I didn't recognise the voice. I put the letter-opener down and went to the door of my office to see who it was.

'Robbie Munro?'

The man in the hallway was wearing a hounds-tooth sports jacket. Around the neck of his lemon shirt was a candy-striped silk tie. His brown corduroy trousers were faded at the knees, his ox-blood brogues gleamed. Anyone who dressed that badly had to be a journalist. The only thing missing was a trilby hat with a ticket sticking out of the band.

'Samuel Reynard. Please, call me Sam.' His voice was as rich and fruity as a slice of clooty-dumpling. For a moment I thought he might bow. 'We meet at last.'

CHAPTER 53

Sam Reynard was a former Fleet Street feature-editor, now freelance. He'd been so keen to meet me I thought the least he could do was take me to lunch.

I suggested the Champany Inn, arguably Scotland's top eating place, a mile out of town on the road to Blackness. I'd had a minor disagreement with the management previously, but not sufficient to prevent my mouth watering at the prospect of a medium rare porterhouse steak washed down with something from St. Emillion old enough for a bus pass. Instead, we adjourned to a pub by Linlithgow Cross for a passable, if under-heated, steak pie and a pint of ale with bits in it. Was there a real ale anywhere that hadn't been awarded a gold medal by some organisation or other? Not one to grumble, my plan was to scoff lunch and get rid of the journalist right after pudding.

'So, what story are you after,' I asked. 'Doing an article on Scotland's top lawyers?' I laughed. He didn't.

'Mr Munro...' He dipped a hand into his pocket and produced a wildly vibrating mobile phone. 'Do pardon.' He looked at the display, grunted and put the phone on the table. 'You were saying?' he asked, once the phone had ceased buzzing.

'I was saying—'

The mobile phone lit up again and started to jump about the table. Reynard glanced down at the number flashed up on the screen and then ignored it.

'I was asking why you'd come all this way to see me.'

'Why? Chic Kelly, of course,' he said, in a ripe, plummy tone of surprise. 'He called me - from prison – a few weeks back. You'll understand that I receive a lot of calls from prisoners. I suppose they've little else to do. Mercifully their phonecards tend to run out so I don't have to be rude and hang up. One can never be too careful about how one speaks to the criminal classes, what with early release and such like.'

'You've been trying for weeks to speak to me about Chic Kelly - why?'

Over apple pie and ice cream, I learned that the journalist had chucked Chic a rubber ear until, on a slow news day, he'd had a researcher check out his credentials. It was then he'd realised he was dealing with something of a celebrity criminal and set off hot-foot for Glenochil Prison to meet the prisoner whose health was so rapidly deteriorating.

'I came all the way up to the frozen north only to find the chap was practically ga-ga and prattling on about the blackmail of a judge and a rather predictable tale of his own wrongful conviction.' He yawned, revealing a portion of half-chewed apple pie before covering his mouth with a paper napkin. 'You'll know better than I, Robbie, that our jails are simply crammed with innocent people.' His stiff upper lip twitched. 'Anyhoo, Mr Kelly said he had photos. Not Lord Lucan stacking shelves at Sainsbury's, I'll grant you, but I have to say I was quite interested. Sex and the judiciary - it always sells newspapers. I think it's something to do with the wigs and silk stockings and if there's a hint of blackmail to boot, so much the better.'

'Chic Kelly was trying to sell you photographs?'

'Wanted fortunes for them. How I laughed. Told him I'd need to see the stuff before he saw a penny.'

'And he told you to contact me?'

'Precisely. Said I should get in touch with you and, as I've now discovered, you are a very busy man.'

'The photos - I can't give you them.' No point beating about the bush.

'Has someone else approached you?'

'No,' I said.

'Then if it's about your commission, I'm sure we can work something out.'

I would have loved to have worked out something, but I feared my commission and Reynard's feature-spread were both lost.

'I'm sorry,' I said. 'I don't have them. I mean I did - but I don't now - and I don't think I can get them back.'

At this news, Reynard put down the spoon with which he'd been prodding a concrete piece of pie crust and sat back in his chair. He looked like a vulture digesting a glass eye. He pulled out a cigarette packet. 'You Jocks and your smoking ban. It started up here and now it's everywhere. Bloody nuisance. My old boy didn't fight Hitler just for me to end up choking for a smoke.' He pushed his chair back. 'You'll excuse me, won't you?'

In the chrome rims of the cruet set I saw the waitress hove into view carrying a saucer with a folded piece of paper weighed down by a couple of sweeties.

'What it is to be a nicotine addict,' Reynard said, getting up from his seat.

'Sam,' I called out once he was near the exit. He turned and I held up his mobile phone.

He came back to the table and took the offered phone. He studied the dead screen and gave the phone a little shake. 'No-one there.'

'Yes,' I said, 'the reception can be a bit iffy up here in the frozen north.'

He made to leave again but not before he'd bumped into the saucer carrying waitress.

'Thanks for lunch,' I said. 'I'll walk you to the train.'

CHAPTER 54

I left Reynard at the station and headed up the brae to the Union Canal. As a boy I'd gone there often with Max. Armed with jelly jars and fishing nets made from his mum's tights, we'd spent many a happy hour catching tadpoles and minnows. Back then it had always been blue skies and sun. Today it was cold, the sky heavy with rain clouds.

At the canal basin there was a bench. It was a peaceful spot and that was precisely what I needed: peace, time to think, take stock. I sat back and watched the coots dart in and out of the reeds. Soon it would be spring. Until then there wasn't much food for the birds apart from the occasional school kid prepared to share a packed lunch.

I tried to concentrate. Chic Kelly. What a man. He'd obviously expected that when he died the trust fund money from Frankie would die with him. Not only had he been after the reward money, he'd also tried to punt the story, complete with photos of Lord Hewitt and his lover to the Sunday papers as a legacy for his son and soon to be widow.

Surely that couldn't be the link between Max's death and the photos? Surely he hadn't been murdered to stop the News of the World or some rag getting its inky hands on some pictures of a dead judge and a rent boy: front page one day, fish supper wrapping-paper the next. There had to be something more. I recalled the look on Frankie's face when I'd showed him the blood-stained clothes.

Frankie McPhee is a dangerous man. The opinion of former Police Sergeant Alex Munro and Detective Chief Inspector Petra Lockhart. If Frankie had killed Max he would kill me too if he didn't get what he wanted. He had the photos and blackmail note that linked him to Devine. Now he'd want the rest of the stuff. I had left myself two obvious options.

Option one: give the clothes and pistol to Frankie. Max's killer would go free and Sean Kelly would probably do life.

Option two: go to the police, tell them everything and hope that the Crown would grant immunity to me for my possession of the pistol in exchange for testimony at Frankie's trial. Chic's statement to Lockhart and the clothes that were now locked in my office safe should be enough to see him convicted of murdering Lord Hewitt.

Option one was a non-starter and there were serious problems with option two. Grass on Frankie and I'd have to watch my back for the rest of my life whether he went to jail or not, and it still wouldn't guarantee the release of Sean Kelly for there was not one shred of evidence pointing to Frankie having murdered Max.

I was considering whether there might be a third option when behind me, across the other side of the huge 16th century sandstone doocot in Learmonth Gardens, the Glasgow to Edinburgh ScotRail express sped by shattering the tranquillity of my surroundings. The sounding of its horn as the train rattled through the station must have drowned out the noise of a dilapidated motor coming over the canal bridge and parking at the side of the road.

A crunch of gravel. The gloomy sky seemed to darken even more and I gazed up to see Big Jo-Jo Johnstone standing on the towpath looming over me.

'Frankie wants to see you,' he said. He took me by the upper arm and hauled me from the bench. 'Don't struggle.'

But struggling was exactly what I intended to do. I twisted and then dropped suddenly, trying to use the weight of my body to break free and scramble to safety. Big Jo-Jo's iron grip on my bicep did not lessen one degree. He wrenched me to my feet and pulled me close. 'Don't struggle,' he repeated and into my face pointed one of the fingers that protruded from his light-blue splint. It was the size of one of TESCO's posh sausages and he

223

placed it on my right eye, the pressure of it causing the eyelid to shut. One prod and... squish.

Spinning me around as though I were a doll, he dragged me from the canal bank down a short flight of stone steps to the roadway and his parked car where Frankie was sitting in the front passenger seat. Jo-Jo opened the back door, placed me inside and slammed it shut. Once behind the wheel, using his uninjured hand, he adjusted the rear-view mirror until it was just so. Without rushing, he started the engine and flicked the indicator on.

It was now or never. I reached for the door handle. Jo-Jo glanced at both side-mirrors then looked over his shoulder to check the deserted road for traffic prior to moving off. He saw what I was doing and pawed at me over the back of his seat, the seat belt and his bulky frame making it difficult for him to get at me.

The door was stuck. I flung myself at it and it flew open. Jo-Jo accelerated. Slowly the car began to move off. I rolled out onto the road and was at the top of the steps and onto the towpath before the car had come to a halt again.

Jo-Jo and Frankie jumped out of the car.

'Robbie,' Frankie called to me, 'I only want to talk. There's things I need to explain.'

I knew all about the ways Frankie McPhee and his pals explained things to people. I'd seen the photos of their victims when I'd defended them in court.

'You want to explain?' I shouted to him. 'Call me.'

Frankie glanced at Jo-Jo and the big man started to walk up the steps. I looked around for help. The problem with peaceful beauty spots is that they are peaceful and beautiful because there are so few people around.

I had gone there to mull things over, consider my options. Now I had another choice to make: I could run left or right along the towpath. Left it was seven miles to the Falkirk Wheel, right it was seventeen miles to Edinburgh. Jo-Jo reached the top step.

I feinted left, he moved left. I feinted right, he moved right. He came straight for me. I turned around and jumped into the canal.

Ice-cold water stripped the air from my lungs. Reeds wrapped around my legs. Mud sucked at my feet. I managed to push myself off from the side and into the middle, scattering the family of coots, the birds squawking, fluttering in all directions. The basin was the area where the barges turned and so was much wider than the canal itself and a lot deeper. Although I could feel the creepy caress of under-water weeds on my ankles, I was able to swim and as I splashed my way to the far side I heard a car engine rev.

I hauled myself out of the water and looked back. Frankie and Jo-Jo were gone. There was nobody there. Nobody except an old man in a tweed bunnet walking quickly along the side of the canal, dragging a small white dog along on a leash behind him and keeping a wary eye on the crazy man who sat soaking wet and bedraggled on the far away bank.

CHAPTER 55

My mobile phone was water-proof, I discovered, and so one short taxi ride and one surprised and slightly miffed taxi driver later, I was slopping my way up my dad's front path.

'You fell in the canal?'

'That's right,' I confirmed for the umpteenth time. I sat down on a kitchen chair and pulled off my wet socks. 'I went for a walk, tripped over something and the next thing I knew I was doing duck impersonations.'

The old man came over and stuck his nose in my face. 'You always seem to be slipping or tripping. Are you drinking?'

'I'm naturally clumsy – you know that.'

Former police-sergeant Alex Munro was clearly not satisfied at the suspect's replies to questioning but terminated the interview. He put on his coat.

'Well, I'm away round to Vince's.' He took a bottle of whisky from a cupboard and stuffed it in his coat pocket. 'We're going to watch some football: the sixty-seven game. The one you got me off the internet. You seen it?'

I hadn't. Only the clips they occasionally played on the telly to raise Scots' spirits in times of impending sporting adversity.

'Me and Vince were at the game, did you know?' I did. He'd reminded me frequently over the years. 'I went down with some of the boys from the station. You didn't need a ticket back then. Not if you were polis. A flash of the warrant card and you were right in there no questions asked. Vince was home on leave from Belize or somewhere. We arranged to meet at Piccadilly Circus.' My dad laughed at the memory. 'Took us an hour and a half to find each other. We went for a dook in the fountains at Trafalgar Square and then off to the pub – or it might have been the other way around. Anyway, by the time we got to the game we were too bladdered to know what was going on.' He made a selection from the row of football DVD's lined up on a glass shelf below the TV and inserted it into the coat pocket not otherwise occupied by a bottle of Islay single malt. He walked past me to the door, pinching my cheek as he went. 'Jim Baxter, digitally re-mastered – pure magic.'

Once he was gone I bolted the front and back doors, chucked my wet clothes in the spin-dryer and ran a bath.

Before I lowered myself into the foaming waters, I put on the latest Ojos de Brujo album; quite possibly it was their only album. Apparently, Andy liked to play the CD in the office when I was out at court and Grace-Mary, not a big fan of the flamenco/hip-hop scene, had confiscated it. When I found it in my desk drawer I wrapped it up and gave it to my dad as part of his birthday. I'd never heard him play it, but I liked the sound.

Sometime between 'Color' and 'Tanguillos Marineros' the phone rang and I let it. I closed my eyes and put all thoughts of Frankie McPhee and Max Abercrombie out of my head.

The phone rang again later when, armed with a bottle of cheap wine, I was sprawled on the sofa watching TV. Once more I ignored it. There was a horror movie on. Three teenagers stumble upon an ancient tomb in the basement of a ruined castle and instead of informing the National Trust, prise open the lid. It doesn't come as a complete surprise when one of the hapless three cuts his finger in the process and carelessly lets a drop of blood fall on the desiccated corpse of Count Dracula. Mayhem follows and everyone ends up at Dracula's place to find him entertaining some highly promiscuous and scantily-clad young vampire ladies. It made me wonder whether that sort of thing, orgies and the like, would still be as much fun if one were immortal. All that blood-letting and sex every night. Surely sometimes you'd just want to have a night in and crack open a thousand piece jig-saw.

The movie flew by in a lorry load of dry ice, buckets of ketchup and lots of dodgy Eastern European accents, before one well-placed tent peg rendered the man in the tuxedo no longer

227

a threat to nubiles in diaphanous nighties. It was a tired plot, poorly acted and just what I needed: two hours of brain inactivity.

The titles rolled. I went through to the kitchen to make a coffee, catching sight of my reflection in the hall mirror. Robbie Munro after half a bottle of Sicilian red and no sleep for a week - never mind the curse of the undead - that really was scary.

A noise in the street made me jump. Headlight beams shone in through the curtains, shredding the blinds and casting strips of light across the room for a second or two. I went to the window, pulled back the curtain a fraction and peeked out. One of my dad's neighbours was struggling from a taxi. He steadied himself, one hand on the roof of the cab the other digging deep in a pocket. At least someone had been away enjoying themselves. He chucked some cash at the driver and laid an uncertain path to his front door. I left him fumbling for his keys, went through to the kitchen and decided against making coffee. Caffeine was one drug I didn't need. I was edgy enough already.

I was drinking a glass of water, when from the pocket of my coat, slung over a radiator and dripping into a basin, I heard my phone play a drunken ring-tone. The number was withheld; that usually meant the police.

'Mr Munro?' Sure enough, it was the custody sergeant. 'I have one Richard Milligan, date of birth twenty-two, four, ninety-three, here on a fines warrant for two hundred pounds. He wanted you to know.'

I didn't recognise the name. He must have been a new boy otherwise he wouldn't be letting himself be arrested on a Friday night for an unpaid fine and he wouldn't have wasted his phone call having me informed – it wasn't like I was going to rush down to the station with the dosh. He'd be taken to court on Monday and given more time to pay or ordered to perform unpaid work in the community. The jails were too full to be clogged-up by fine-defaulters.

When the phone rang again a short time later, I answered expecting the custody sergeant to say that the fine-defaulter's mum had been in and paid the fine, but it wasn't the police; it was Frankie.

'Robbie, we need to talk.'

I hung up and peered through the window again. Though the street was lined both sides with parked cars there was no sign of life. Suddenly - brake lights. At the end of the road, a familiar beat-up motor carried out a laborious three-point turn and came rolling down the road towards me. It stopped, straddling the white lines. In the amber glow of a streetlight I thought I could just make out Jo-Jo Johnstone's bulky silhouette in the driver's seat.

There was a loud bang on the front door. I knew it was Frankie before I heard his voice.

'Robbie! Let me in!'

Through the spy hole I could see him standing there, a bulge in the chest of his jacket and a determined look on his face.

'Robbie!'

Another thump at the door. Frankie was taking a chance. He might have guessed I'd hole up here, but he couldn't afford to be arrested; even a breach of the peace allegation would see his licence recalled and he must have known that my dad wouldn't hesitate to call the police. He was clearly desperate.

Frankie McPhee is a dangerous man.

I should have called the cops but I hated the very idea. A defence agent can be many things: dishonest, greedy, opportunistic - come to think of it some of those were downright advantageous in my line of work - but not a grass. If word got out that I was a police informer, I might as well forget criminal law, leave town and start selling houses for a living.

After a while, Frankie grew fed up hitting the door. I watched him return to the car and even as I saw shadow hands reach up, adjust the rear-view mirror and the vehicle drive slowly off down the street, indicator flashing, I didn't feel greatly relieved. He knew I was onto him. He might not come back that night but return he would and when I least expected it. There was no way I could allow Frankie to choose his moment, and I definitely wasn't going to try and catch some sleep with him and Big Jo-Jo anywhere in the close vicinity. Detective Chief Inspector Lockhart, I recalled, had a reputation for not disclosing her sources. It was the choice my dad would have made for me if he'd been there. That is, if he hadn't gone out and tried to tackle Frankie McPhee himself. Lockhart's slightly soggy card was in the top pocket of my damp suit jacket. I made the call and five minutes later, in my almost dry clothes, was sneaking out of the back door.

CHAPTER 56

Lockhart was waiting for me in a wynd off the High Street. She drove me to my office where I collected the canvas bag containing the gloves and shirt from my safe, and then to my flat where I added to the bag the pistol and the clip of bullets. From there we went to her place: a cottage along a dirt track off the old Edinburgh Road, not far from the House of the Binns, where Tam Dalyell's ancestor had played the Devil at cards and won. I only hoped I had his luck.

'It's a former canal worker's cottage,' Lockhart told me, as we walked up the garden path leading through a manicured front garden and in the front door to the main room. 'Wasn't much more than a but and ben before I got my hands on it. Been something of a money pit – but I'm pleased with the finished result.' She flicked a switch and a dozen spotlights blazed down on the astringent furnishings, spotless walls and floor. Someone had turned housework into an extreme sport. The effect was startlingly clinical and the opposite of homely.

'It's all on one level.' She gestured to an arch leading off the main room and into a hallway. 'Bedroom, study, loo, down there, and...' she indicated a stripped pine door a few feet away, 'kitchen through there.'

From the outside I'd imagined the interior would be something straight out of Country Living: subdued lighting, rugs on the walls, chenille carpeting, perhaps a few chunky knit cushions scattered here and there. The reality was white-washed walls, scrubbed limestone floor and some uncomfortable looking furniture. It was cold and extremely clean and tidy. As Grace-Mary might have said, 'a place for everything and everything in its place.'

'What do you think?' Lockhart asked.

I rounded one of the pieces of sculpture that were dotted at regular intervals and parked myself on a firm but surprisingly ergonomic two-seater sofa to the left of the fireplace. My dad would have called the place 'trendy'. I was concerned there might be pop-art in the toilet.

'Very nice, but you're a bit out of the way aren't you?'

'That's what I like about it.' She went over to one of the small windows and looked out at the darkness. 'The Forth and Clyde Canal is practically on the doorstep. Sometimes if I'm feeling athletic I cycle along the towpath to Edinburgh.' She closed the curtains. 'I've never tried to go for a swim in it though,' she laughed. I was glad someone found it funny.

My hostess coaxed the coals in the fireplace back to life using a wrought-iron poker and without spilling so much as a thimbleful of soot onto the white-marble hearth. 'Yes, we saw the place and couldn't resist it.'

'We?' Was that a pang of jealousy I felt?

Lockhart looked at me. I thought I detected a slight smile at the corners of her mouth. 'Did I say we? Ancient history,' she said and leaned her back against the mantelpiece. 'What I'm interested in is the future and I'm glad you've seen sense at last.' She nodded her head at the canvas bag. 'So, what have you got? Or, first of all, should I caution you that you have the right to remain silent?'

There was a small glass table to the side of the sofa. I emptied the pistol on to it followed by the plastic bags containing the shirt and scrunched-up leather gloves.

'What have we here?' Lockhart gently prodded the pistol with her index finger. 'If I'm not mistaken, one Browning Hi-Power nine millimetre. Standard British Army issue and, incidentally, the late, not so great, Sadaam Hussein's side-arm of choice.'

'It's not loaded,' I told her. 'I took the clip out of the gun. It's in the bag.'

'So are you going to tell me how you came by all this stuff?'

'I was attacked in my home a few nights back.'

'Ah, the old Scots crime of Hamesucken,' she said as though forgetting I was a lawyer. 'Used to be a capital offence. Any idea who it was?'

Jo-Jo Johnstone was the name foremost in my mind and yet, deep down, I found it hard to believe. There was his connection with Frankie McPhee, not to mention the injured arm, but could I really have held big Jo-Jo at bay? I might as well have given NATO a square-go.

'I'm not sure,' I said, 'but whoever it was left the gun behind. I think it's the same one that killed Max Abercrombie.'

Lockhart studied the gun with renewed interest. 'What are the chances of finding fingerprints?'

'Other than yours? Pretty slim I'd say.'

I trusted Lockhart more than I could bring myself to trust any cop; nonetheless, I'd taken the precaution of thoroughly wiping down the pistol and clip.

She hefted the gun. The thing to remember when disarming one of these is to make sure you haven't left a round in the breech.' She slid back the barrel to reveal a brass casing. 'See what I mean? Can't be too careful.' She put the gun on the mantelpiece out of the way and began to pace up and down, her hands steepled, index fingers pressed against her lips. 'And why was it, do you think, that you were attacked?'

'Someone thought I had these.' I gestured to the items in the plastic bags.'

'And the photographs of Lord Hewitt? The one's Chic Kelly talks about in his statement…?'

'I did have them.'

'Did?'

'And the blackmail note. What Chic didn't know was that it wasn't Frankie who wanted the photos back, it was Gordon Devine. He'd handwritten the blackmail note.'

Lockhart looked at me, admiringly. 'Really? That was careless of him. Then again, there were rumours of Gordon Devine blackmailing certain judges doing the rounds way back in the late nineties.'

'And nothing was done?'

'It was all hearsay, I expect, and no-one would take on a man like Gordon Devine without a steel-reinforced case. Not unless they fancied a career as a traffic warden.'

I told her what I'd gleaned from my chat with Bob Coulsfield, the macer.

'I can see how it all ties in.' Lockhart examined the plastic bags on the table. 'The judge was ready to blow the whistle. Devine had messed up, knew he could be linked to the blackmail attempt and had to get the stuff back.'

I had been slightly sceptical of Chic's statement at first. Now I was sure there was hard evidence to back it up. 'I believe Chic. I don't think he did kill Lord Hewitt.'

Lockhart said nothing.

I picked up the bags containing the gloves and shirt, one in each hand and held them up to her. 'I think the real killer was wearing these. If I'm right they'll be spattered with Hewitt's blood. There's probably enough of the killer's DNA inside it to make a pot of soup.

She took the bags from me then let them drop onto the table. 'Your client, Frankie McPhee, I hear he likes to make soup. Did I not tell you he was a dangerous man?'

I felt stupid at having waited so long to come clean. My old man had been right about Frankie: once scum always scum. He'd gunned down the judge in cold blood and would stop at nothing to destroy the evidence that could put him back inside.

Lockhart returned to the fireplace and rested an elbow on the mantelpiece above which hung a picture in an ornate gold frame. It portrayed a medieval battle with waving banners, armoured knights and axe-wielding infantrymen very much in evidence. Such a violent scene seemed out of place in that sterile little room.

'It's by Kossak: The Battle of Grunwald,' Lockhart said, otherwise I wouldn't have known. 'It depicts the Grand Duchy of Lithuania's victory over the Teutonic knights. It's a print of course.' She smiled her beautiful smile. 'I should take it down. Not really my idea of art.'

'Ancient history?' I asked.

She smiled.

At the foot of the picture, embedded in the mount, was a medal: a cross, about one and a half inches wide, an enamel crown on a gold wreath of laurel in the centre. It was suspended from a ribbon, white with blue edges with a red middle stripe. I recalled my client. The one who'd attacked Dougie Fleming in the curry house. He had a medal. Hadn't the drunken soldier been of Lithuanian descent?

I gazed around at that soulless operating theatre of a room, up at the medal again and down at the pistol. It hit me – like I'd stood on the end of a rake. The gun that had killed Max: not the gun of a professional assassin but the gun of a professional soldier.

'Oskaras Salavejus.' His name tumbled out of my mouth before I could stop it.

The smile decayed on Lockhart's lips.

Salavejus had lived here. He was the we, the ancient history. He was the reason Lockhart had taken an interest in the case. Time to leave. I picked up the canvas bag and was ready to fill it again. Lockhart pushed me with surprising power, the flat of her hand on my breast bone. I fell back onto the sofa, the bag in my lap. 'It's not like that,' she said.

I jumped up from the couch. 'No? What is it like?' My mouth was a desert, my tongue a piece of stick.

'Let me explain.' Lockhart kneaded her brow with her fingertips. 'I hadn't heard Chic Kelly's name mentioned for years, then some newspaper man phoned HQ asking questions about him and photographs of Lord Hewitt. He was extremely persistent and was eventually referred onto me as I'd worked on the Hewitt murder. Next thing I knew Kelly himself was on the phone from prison asking about reward money for the true identity of the judge's killer. I went to see him. He gave me the statement and told me he'd been in touch with a journalist and was sending all the evidence to you.'

'And you didn't come and see me?'

'Why? Would you have given it to me?'

I took that as a rhetorical question. I'd hand nothing a client had given me over to the police without a warrant. Lockhart obviously knew that.

'I couldn't ask for a warrant unless I had grounds to believe a crime was or had been committed. The murder case of Lord Hewitt was long solved and, as far as the authorities were concerned, the culprit was in prison. There were no grounds for a warrant, so I tried to intercept the delivery. I knew Chic wouldn't trust just anyone to deliver it and he certainly wouldn't want Frankie McPhee getting his hands on the stuff. I went to see his wife and son but they said they knew nothing about any package and so I staked-out your place for a few days. Nothing happened. I'd almost given up when who comes wandering up Linlithgow High Street but young Sean carrying a bag. He'd lied to me. When I saw him going through the front door of Abercrombie's office I was confused. All I knew was that if Chic's story was true and made public, it would end my career. I'd extracted an admission from an innocent man - the real killer was still at large. I wanted to put things right and I needed what was in the bag.'

'So you went to see Max?'

'I called him. He refused to talk about it over the phone so I said I'd come to his office. He wasn't keen and said he'd get back to me.'

Max had called me that same day. To warn me? Ask my advice? If I'd taken that call could it have saved his life?'

Lockhart kicked the stone lip of the hearth. 'I thought I'd lost my chance. I didn't know how much he knew, who he'd told. I went home and let Oskaras know everything. He insisted on going and getting the stuff for me, by force if necessary. I wasn't happy, but he said if there were any problems I could have it all brushed under the carpet. He told me later he'd taken the gun to frighten him, how a female had jumped him from behind. He managed to throw her aside. By that time Abercrombie was feet away and closing.' Her voice faltered. 'Mr Abercrombie was a big powerful man... It was an accident more than anything else... I'm sure.'

'And when he killed Jacqui Dillon - was that an accident as well?'

Lockhart sat down in a chair at the fireplace opposite the sofa and put her head in her hands for a moment. 'She was screaming. Hysterical.'

The mist in my mind was slowly clearing but there were still wisps of uncertainty. Why had Salavejus assaulted Dougie Fleming on the night of the murder? To create a nice little alibi - locked up in the cells on an unrelated police assault before Max's murder had even been reported?

'It's all very interesting,' I told her, 'but I'm calling the police.' I reached into my pocket for my mobile. It was dead. Either the battery had run out or the phone had finally drowned.

'I am the police,' Lockhart said. 'Can you not leave this to me to sort out?'

'It's been left to you for weeks now and as far as I can see all you've done is attempt to defeat the ends of justice by covering over your boyfriend's tracks.'

There was a telephone on the wall by the archway leading to the bedroom. I got up from my seat and marched over to it. I could no longer trust Lockhart. Max's killer was her former partner. Salavejus had to be found and the sooner the better.

I should have been more careful what I wished for. As I reached for the receiver, through the arch and into the room right beside me, strode the tall figure of Oskaras Salavejus. He bore the fading remains of two black eyes and a cut on the bridge of his nose where I'd planted my forehead. From beneath one of the partially rolled-up sleeves of his green flannel shirt I noticed a cream-coloured crepe bandage peeking out. I stepped back, looking around for a means of escape. Lockhart was on her feet, blocking the way to the front door. I eyed the wrought iron

237

poker in the fireplace. It wasn't an oak bed-post but it would do. I lunged for it but only managed to knock the poker off the stand and clattering into the hearth before Salavejus was on me, a hand around my throat. He shoved me backwards onto the sofa. My neck jerked and my head cracked off the metal framework.

Salavejus towered over me.

Lockhart sat down again as though nothing had happened. 'For completeness sake I'd like the photos and the note. Where are they?'

I swallowed hard.

'Where are they?' her voice was raised now.

'I don't have them.'

Salavejus lifted the poker. 'WHERE ARE THEY?'

Before I could reply, there was a loud bang as the lock and associated woodwork on the back door disintegrated. The kitchen door burst open and Frankie McPhee materialised in the doorway looking along the stubby barrel of a sawn-off shotgun. It was the only the second time in my life I'd had a firearm pointed in my general direction. The first time I'd been scared. This time I was hugely relieved. Frankie hadn't killed Max. He'd told me the truth earlier that day in my office.

The merest glance from Lockhart and Salavejus had his forearm across my throat again, wrenching me to my feet and skilfully manoeuvring me between himself and the shotgun.

Holding the sawn-off with one hand, I supposed over the years practice had made perfect, Frankie reached inside his jacket, took out the by now familiar faded blue folder and tossed it at us. Photographs fluttered out and floated down to the floor by the hearth, two or three landing face up on the bleached flagstones.

'Let him go,' Frankie said. 'You've got everything you want.'

Salavejus's throttle hold on me weakened. 'Put down the gun,' he said.

Frankie lowered his weapon.

'On the floor.'

Again Frankie did as he was told. Salavejus looked to Lockhart who gave him a curt little nod of confirmation and a push in the back sent me staggering towards Frankie. I was free to go, and why not? Even supposing I went to the cops, they'd make sure the pistol, gloves, shirt, photos and note were all long gone and who in their right mind would take the word of a bucket shop legal aid lawyer and his criminal client over that of Lothian & Borders' great white hope and the winner of a war medal for gallantry?

Frankie nudged me. 'Let's go.'

I wanted nothing more than to leave. There was only one problem. 'What about Max?'

'He's dead,' Frankie said. 'Nothing's going to bring him back.'

'Then what about Sean?'

Frankie didn't answer. He took my arm and pulled me towards the kitchen door.

'He's your son,' I reminded him.

'And you're Robbie Munro. You'll get the boy off somehow, now come on.'

I made to leave, then stopped. I couldn't go. I wouldn't go. I dipped and picked up the shotgun. Even with cut-down barrels it was heavier than I'd imagined. The stock had also been shortened making the weapon poorly balanced and difficult to hold. Side-stepping away from Frankie, I did my best to point it at Lockhart.

'I'm taking all the stuff with me,' I said. 'Including the pistol.'

'I don't think so,' Lockhart said, quite casually. She picked up the plastic bag containing the white shirt from the small side-table and chucked it on the fire.

'What are you doing?'

'Destroying the evidence,' Frankie said. 'The evidence implicating Lord Hewitt's killer.'

Now I was really confused.

Frankie enlightened me. 'Miss Lockhart did me a favour many years ago. It stopped me going to jail, temporarily at any rate.'

'Your trial - she stole the search warrant from the court?'

'I had evidence that her father was on the take. If I went down, he was coming with me.'

'It wasn't enough of a favour for you, though was it Mr McPhee?' Lockhart said.

Frankie continued. 'Little did I know Gordon Devine had made his own, less effective, arrangements to abort the trial. He wanted me to get back some blackmail material. Time was running out and he was going mental, promising me fortunes. Trouble was, I'm no housebreaker. Chic would have been in and out in no time, but he was completely off radar. It was Devine's ideas to have another dash at Lockhart. I'd been acquitted at the trial and couldn't be done for the same thing twice. I was bomb-proof whereas Lockhart's old man was still a prosecution waiting to happen and you know how the polis feel about prison – they don't like it.'

I prodded the shotgun at Lockhart. 'You sent her?'

Lockhart confirmed. 'McPhee said it was the last time he'd ask me to do anything. I didn't know whether to believe him but, again, what choice did I have? It seemed simple enough. I'd pretend to be visiting the judge on official business, have him give me the folder to assist my enquiries and then make it disappear. There would be some explaining to do later, but it wouldn't have been the first item to go missing from a police production room.'

She lifted the bag containing the gloves from the small table. I realised then that they were police issue black leather gloves just as the shirt had been a police officer's white shirt.

'I had my story off pat,' Lockhart said. 'Then when I arrived at Lord Hewitt's place, I couldn't find any sign of him. I didn't know what to do until in the drawing room, lying on a coffee table right in front of me, I saw the folder McPhee had described. It was too good to be true. I was leaving with it when Lord

Hewitt came in. He'd been shooting. I tried to blag my way out. Said I'd see that the attempted blackmail was thoroughly investigated, but he was having none of it. Looking back I don't think he ever meant to report the matter because there was no way he was going to let me leave with that folder.' She sighed.' If only he'd let me go. Silly old fool pointed the shotgun at me. There was a struggle. I knocked the gun from his hand. It fell, discharged...' Lockhart stared through the plastic at the gloves. 'I should have made it look like a suicide.' She struck a fist against the side of her head. 'All I had to do was leave the shotgun and blackmail photos behind. Instead I panicked. I stuffed the folder into the judge's game-bag and ran out taking the shotgun with me. I was in such a state, I don't remember much of what happened afterwards.'

'I do,' said Frankie. 'It was chaos. I had Gordon Devine on the phone, screaming at me,' he pointed accusingly at Lockhart, 'her turfing up at my place in a state of shock and covered in blood. Next thing, Chic's at the door as well. I'd rung round every boozer and bookie in West Lothian trying to find him earlier and he shows up after the damage has been done. I was so angry I never even let him in the house. Just got Lockhart to strip off her blood-stained clothes, shoved everything into the bag and gave it and the gun to Chic with orders to get rid of everything fast.'

Lockhart lifted the bag with the gloves in it and strolled over to the fireplace again.

'Don't move,' I told her. 'Put the bag down.'

'Why? You heard McPhee. Chic was supposed to destroy the folder and my clothes; I'm just doing what he should have done all those years ago.'

'Stop,' I said. 'I mean it.'

'No you don't. You're not going to shoot.'

She was right. I'd never shot anyone before, never fired a weapon before, far less the sawn-off shotgun I held in my shaking hands. Was it even loaded?

241

'Do what he tells you, Petra,' Salavejus said. Gently, he took the plastic bag from Lockhart's hand. At his request she sat down again. 'Good,' he said. 'Now perhaps we can talk this through calmly.' He raised the plastic bag high. 'You want it?' He lobbed the bag through the air. It fell at my feet.

'I want the gun as well,' I told him. He turned to the mantelpiece. 'Put it in the bag, carefully, no funny moves.' Completely out of my depth I was resorting to lines from the movies.

He raised his hands, palms outwards. 'Whatever you say.' He reached out to where the pistol was lying with exaggerated slowness and then suddenly his hand was a blur. Ducking and spinning around, he brought the gun to bear. I hesitated and all was lost. Frankie barged into me, knocking me sideways. I felt the shotgun leap in my hands, the butt thump into my ribs. Thunder roared through the small room. I landed heavily on the hard limestone floor and found myself looking up at bare timber joists through a recently created hole in the lowered ceiling.

The shotgun still in my hand. I rose unsteadily to my feet, my heel bumping against something solid. It was Frankie. He was sprawled on the ground, jacket open, a red stain on the front of his white shirt growing larger by the second.

I knelt by his side and ripped the shirt wide to reveal a small blue hole in the centre of his chest. A steady flow of bright-red arterial blood seeped from under him and spread over the white flagstones. His Bible fell out of his inside jacket pocket. It was totally unscathed. Frankie peered up at me. He tried to speak and instead, coughed up blood. Salavejus walked over. The pistol pointed down at my head. Without a word, he pulled the trigger. Click. He checked the pistol. No clip.

I raised the shotgun, levelled it at him and stood up. 'Drop it.' Behind him I could see Lockhart rummaging in the canvas bag for the bullets. 'Drop the gun,' I repeated in a voice I hadn't heard before. Salavejus was paying attention now, reading my face. He must have seen something there because, smiling grimly, he set the pistol on the floor. 'Now, both of you sit down.'

Salavejus took a step back, hands raised, a look of pained amusement etched across his chiselled features.

'Do it!' I yelled. Salavejus looked at Lockhart. She nodded. He went over to her and they both sat down.

I sidled to the telephone. The weight of the shotgun, even in its shortened form would make it difficult for me to keep it trained on the two of them while I phoned.

'Calling it in? 'Lockhart said. 'Good idea. Saves me the bother.'

From her seated position on the sofa, she stooped, collected two or three of the photographs that were scattered about and fed them one by one to the flames. Each burned brightly for a moment and then was gone forever. Like the lives of Max Abercrombie and Jacqui Dillon. Frankie twitched and lay still.

'Tell you what,' Lockhart said. 'You put down the gun and when the police get here we'll say that McPhee came to kill us and Oskaras shot him in self-defence. The big man looked a tad uncertain until Lockhart placed a reassuring hand on his thigh and squeezed. There's nothing to worry about, Oskar. It's a perfectly credible story and we're reliable people. Credibility and reliability - that's what the court looks for in a witness. You know that, don't you Robbie?' She was so confident, so self-assured. I began to feel like I was the one with the ten-gauge pointing at me.

The fire in the grate glowed softly. The shirt and the photographs were nothing but a heap of ash.

I pressed the 9 button.

'People have died. I know and I regret it,' Lockhart said. 'But it was all McPhee's fault, right from the beginning. Surely you can see that? Why should we all suffer because of him? We're not scum like Frankie McPhee. Oskar is a war hero. I'll make Chief Super by the time I'm forty. I can go all the way to the top, make a difference, make sure that those who didn't deserve to die, didn't die in vain.'

I pressed 9 again.

Salavejus stood up. I let the phone hang by the cord and put both hands on the shotgun.

'Stay where you are.'

He froze. My hand moved to the phone again.

'I've fifty thousand in cash,' Lockhart said, still seated, still so relaxed. 'Devine's money. You can have it.'

I'd almost forgotten about Gordon Devine. I'd been as sceptical as Dougie Fleming about Lockhart's suicide theory. Gorgeous Gordon shoot himself in the face? Not likely. Someone had assumed, correctly as it happened, that I'd go to see him with the blackmail package. Fortunately for me I'd been late; late for my own death. Gordon hadn't been so lucky. The fifty grand was from his safe no doubt. Why? Like Jacqui's disappearance: to muddy the water? Leave the cops with a puzzle - suicide or robbery? The money would be untraceable; the contents of brown envelopes. With it I'd be right back on my feet. Max and Frankie were dead. Nothing I could do would bring them back and if I called the police I had a fairly good idea who it was who'd end up in the back of a meat-wagon.

I replaced the receiver. 'I want a signed confession from each of you to the murders of Max Abercrombie, Jacqui Dillon, Gordon Devine and Frankie McPhee.'

There was a notepad and pen on the telephone table. I threw them over. Salavejus caught the notepad, but fumbled, dropping the pen.

'We'll write whatever you like,' Lockhart said. 'Of course, we'll deny it later as having been coerced. I think you'll agree that pointing a shotgun at someone is coercion. Not even Dougie Fleming would go that far to extract an admission.'

'Just write it down,' I said. 'Everything.'

Lockhart sighed. 'Do as he says, Oskar.'

Salavejus bent over to pick up the pen from the hearth. Suddenly, the iron poker was in his hand. He spun, arm whipping around, hurling the poker at me. Instinctively, I twisted my body, squeezing the trigger. The clang of the poker

244

striking the wall behind me was drowned by the roar of the shotgun. The blast tore into the ex-soldier like a swarm of angry lead hornets, hurling him backwards. His shredded torso crashed against the mantelpiece and he collapsed in the hearth, injured arm landing in the grate where the hot coals barbecued the sleeve of his shirt and the crepe bandage. Soon the smell of scorched flesh filled the room.

In a daze, I stood and watched him die. It didn't take long; not surprising given the amount of blood and body tissue that was splattered up the wall and across the picture in the heavy gilt frame.

'We've got to get our stories right,' I thought I heard Lockhart say above the ringing in my ears. She picked up the remaining photographs from the floor and chucked them onto the fire. Then she strode over to me through the smoke and plaster-dust that clouded the room and slapped me across the face. 'Come on. We can make this look like a shoot-out between those two.'

I threw down the shotgun. She tried to slap me again. I caught her wrist and pushed her away. 'He killed Max and Frankie.'

'And now he's dead!' she screamed in my face. 'Don't you think that makes things even?'

'I'm calling the police. You can explain it to them.'

She ripped the cord from the wall. 'We don't get the cops involved until we've agreed what we're going to say. Look, I'm sorry about Max. I'm not particularly sorry about Frankie McPhee. You've got to try and see the big picture here. Sometimes things go badly. You just have to pick yourself up and keep going.' The woman was an ice-berg. She picked up the shotgun and wiped it with a handkerchief. 'To get out of this mess we need each other. Keep it simple. We say you came here to tell me Frankie McPhee had confessed to killing Max Abercrombie – got that? McPhee turned up with this sawn-off and would have killed us all if brave Oskar hadn't stepped in.' She placed the shotgun across Frankie's body. 'With me backing

245

you up it will be easy. No need to remember any details. You know what witnesses are like – everything always happens so terribly fast.' Lifting Frankie's arm using the cuff of his shirt sleeve, she dabbed his dead hand all over the shotgun before resting it on the shortened wooden stock. 'So what you spend another couple of hours being grilled by Dougie Fleming? Afterwards everything will be back to normal.'

I showed her my back and walked towards the front door.

The icy exterior vaporised. 'Stay where you are!' she shrieked.

I heard a click as I reached for the door handle. I was no firearms expert but could tell the sound of an ammunition clip being locked into place.

I wanted to get as far from the little cottage by the Forth & Clyde canal as I could, but not feet first and in a box. I turned to face her. 'Why don't you tell the truth?'

'I'm not throwing my career away when there's no need.'

'No need? Max Abercrombie's dead. I don't care about you or your precious career. '

'Oskar killed Abercrombie and you killed Oskar. Can't you see? What's done is done. We get our story right we can both walk away from this.'

'I don't think so.'

Lockhart's grip on the pistol tightened, her aim unwavering. There was something about her expression, the grim look of determination. Samuel Johnson said that the prospects of hanging helped concentrate the mind: well, so did having the muzzle of a nine millimetre semi-automatic pointed straight in the face. What if Lockhart's boyfriend hadn't shot Max. What if he'd found out that Lockhart had taken his gun. Was that why he'd been shouting gibberish at Dougie Fleming? Drunk, he'd gone looking for Lockhart, couldn't find her and as he'd staggered by the Bombay Balti on his way to the police station, had caught sight of Fleming's uniform through the window.

'Was it you?' I asked. 'Did you shoot Max?'

"Life or death,' Lockhart said. 'It's a simple choice. I like you Robbie. I'm offering you a way out. One that lets us both continue as though nothing has happened.'

But something had happened. Max was dead. A lot of people were dead. I wondered how good a shot she was and what chance I had of escaping without being hit. There was only one way to find out. I hadn't opened the door more than a crack when there was a loud bang and the frame above my head splintered.

'Last chance,' she said.

'How many more people have to die to save your career?'

She extended the pistol, straight arms, one hand supporting the other. 'Just one.'

She'd have to shoot me in the back. I turned, wrenched open the door and had scarcely moved when the gun exploded again. I froze; every muscle in my body seized rigid. Behind me the soft clump of a body falling, metal clattering on stone. I opened the door, walked outside and breathed deeply of the cold night air.

CHAPTER 57

Jo-Jo Johnstone was waiting patiently in the driver's seat of his battered motor car, parked neatly behind a row of hawthorn bushes at the road end. I gave him the news and the big man broke down and cried. There wouldn't be many tears shed over Frankie McPhee. When my dad heard, he'd be straight up the attic, looking out the bunting. I told Jo-Jo to go away and that, with his record, scaring up an alibi wouldn't be such a bad idea.

Considering my close encounter with death I felt strangely calm as I set off on foot for Linlithgow. Maybe I was numb with shock, but I did feel that a weight had been lifted. Max was avenged and as for Sean Kelly, I no longer feared for his liberty. The case against him was sufficiently weak that it had no chance of withstanding the aftermath of the night's events. The eventual discovery of the three bodies and the pistol that shot Max covered in Chief Inspector Lockhart's prints: even Lorna Wylie could conjure up a reasonable doubt from that little lot.

I made the three-mile walk in just under an hour, arriving at the east end of town shortly after midnight. Linlithgow police station was closed but there was a phone outside for emergency calls. My dad's house was not far. I could call the cops from there and in any case I wanted to break the news to him before I informed the authorities of my involvement.

I walked on. A growing part of me rebelling at the idea of going to the police. If I was one of my clients my advice would be simple: do nothing and say even less and yet I had this desperate need to talk to someone, to share the horror of what had happened. I'd killed a man. Yes, he'd attacked me, yes, I'd acted instinctively, but I had killed him. If I went to the police what would happen? I'd be tried. I could just imagine my cross-examination by some stuck-up Advocate-depute. Mr Munro -

about your defence of self-defence. As I understand it, your evidence is that Mr Salavejus was armed with a poker. You're a lawyer, wouldn't you agree that shooting him at close range with a sawn-off shotgun might be considered a tad disproportionate?'

I was at the corner of the street, not far from my dad's house when I saw the old man ahead of me making his way home from watching football at Vince's place. I caught up with him as he let himself in the front door.

He turned and looked at me, taking my chin in his hand and inspecting my bruises in the dim glow of the porch light.

'You look like how I'll feel in the morning,' he said when he'd let go of my face. 'What have you been tripping over now?' I didn't reply, just followed him down the small hallway and into the kitchen. 'Cup of tea?' he asked, hanging his coat on the back of the door.

I put the kettle on while he found some mugs and took the milk out of the fridge. 'Dad, I need to tell you something.'

I sat down at the table where over the years we'd talked about many things and argued about even more. 'Something happened tonight. Something serious.'

My dad looked down at me. 'I knew it.' His moustache curled downward at the edges. 'McPhee?'

I nodded.

'I warned you about him. If you've got yourself into some kind of bother then hell mend you.' The old man narrowed his eyes and thumped the table with a fist. The carton of milk jumped and would have toppled over if I hadn't caught it. 'When I get my hands on that b—'

'Frankie's dead,' I said. With my foot I pushed a chair out from the opposite side of the table. 'I think it might be best if you sat down.'

He did and I told him everything. The kettle boiled and the water in it had cooled by the time I'd finished my story.

'What are you going to do?' my dad wanted to know.

'Go to the police. Tell them the same as I've told you.'

249

'You want my advice?' He didn't wait for my answer, but then he never did. 'Don't. You go to the cops with that story and Dougie Fleming will stitch you up faster than a casualty surgeon. He's a good cop – but he hates you.' He left the table, went over to a cupboard and returned with two glasses and an unopened bottle of whisky; his birthday present.

'Been saving it,' he said. 'You don't crack open a bottle of eighteen-year-old Bruichladdich without cause to celebrate.'

'And that would be?'

He grabbed me in a headlock and kissed the top of my head. 'You're still alive aren't you?' He pulled out the cork and poured us both a measure of the amber liquid.

'Dad. When the shit meets the fan—'

'They'll find three bodies, one a suicide, and the weapons that killed them. Then they'll find a bundle of readies and realise no-one would have left there without taking the cash with them. No-one's going to go looking for anyone else. Trust me.'

'And if they do?'

'You were with me and Vince tonight. He took the DVD from his coat pocket and tossed it onto the kitchen table as though determined to knock over the milk one way or another. 'England two, Scotland three and Jim Baxter doing keepy-uppies.' He lifted his glass to his nose and inhaled the warm comforting fumes.

I downed my drink without the ceremony. 'That's really your advice?' I asked, as the smooth whisky warmed my insides. What happened to if you flee wi' the craws? Whatever happened to once a cop?'

My dad tilted his tumbler, let the expensive whisky trickle slowly into his mouth. Eyes closed, he savoured it and then set his glass down on the table again. 'I've retired,' he said, pouring us both another. 'I'm learning to live with it – so should you.'

MORE IN THE BEST DEFENCE SERIES

#1 RELATIVELY GUILTY

Follow the trials of Scots criminal lawyer Robbie Munro as he joins battle in the fight for truth and justice - hoping truth and justice don't win too often because it's terribly bad for business.

A policeman with a caved-in skull, his young wife found clutching the blood-stained murder weapon; it all looks pretty open and shut until Robbie detects the faint whiff of a defence and closes in on a witness who might cast a precious doubt on proceedings.

So why is it, the nearer he gets to the truth and a possible acquittal, that Robbie's murder client becomes more and more eager to opt for a life sentence?

Short-Listed for the Dundee International Book Prize

#3 SHARP PRACTICE

Scotland's favourite criminal defence lawyer, Robbie Munro, is back and under pressure to find a missing child, defend a murdering drug-dealer and save the career of a child-pornography-possessing local doctor.

Add to that the antics of his badly-behaving ex-cop dad, the re-kindling of an old flame and a run-in with Scotland's Justice Secretary and you'll discover why it is that, sometimes, a lawyer has to resort to Sharp Practice.

#4 KILLER CONTRACT

It's the trial of the millennium: Larry Kirkslap, Scotland's most flamboyant entrepreneur, charged with the murder of good-time gal Violet Hepburn. He needs a lawyer and there's only one man for the job – unfortunately it's not Robbie Munro. That's about to change; however, more pressing is the contract out on the lives of Robbie and his client, Danny Boyd, who is awaiting trial for violating a sepulchre.

Who would anyone want to kill Robbie and his teenage client?

While Robbie tries to work things out, there are a couple of domestic issues that also need his urgent attention, like his father's surprise birthday party and the small matter of a marriage proposal.

#5 CRIME FICTION
Desperate for cash, Robbie finds himself ensnared in a web of deceit spun by master conman Victor Devlin. What is Devlin's connection with the case of two St Andrew's students charged with the murder of a local waitress?

Enter Suzie Lake, a former-university chum of Robbie, now bestselling crime fiction author, who regards Robbie as her muse. Lois has writer's block and turns to Robbie for inspiration. She's especially interested in the St Andrew's murder and wants some inside information. How can Robbie refuse the advances of the gorgeous Suzie, even if they threaten to scupper his pending nuptials? And yet, the more Robbie reveals to her, the more he finds himself in a murky world of bribery, corruption and crime fiction publishing.

#6 LAST WILL
The trial of Robbie Munro's life; one month to prove he's fit to be a father.

No problem. Apart, that is, from the small matter of a double-murder in which Robbie's landlord, Jake Turpie, is implicated. Psycho-Jake demands Robbie's undivided attention and is prepared to throw money at the defence - along with some decidedly dodgy evidence.

Robbie has a choice, look after his daughter or look after his client. Can the two be combined to give the best of both worlds?

Robbie aims to find out, and his attempts lead him into the alien worlds of high-fashion, drug-dealing and civil-litigation.

It's what being a father/lawyer is all about. Isn't it?

#7 PRESENT TENSE
Robbie Munro's back home, living with his dad and his new-found daughter. Life as a criminal lawyer isn't going well, and neither is his love life. While he's preparing to defend the accused in a rape case, it all becomes suddenly more complicated when one of his more dubious clients leaves a mysterious box for him to look after. What's in the box is going to change Robbie's life – forever.

#8 GOOD NEWS BAD NEWS
Life's full of good news and bad news for defence lawyer Robbie Munro. Good news is he's in work, representing Antonia Brechin on a drugs charge – unfortunately she's the granddaughter of notorious Sheriff Brechin. His old client Ellen has won the lottery and she's asked Robbie to find her husband Freddy who's disappeared after swindling Jake Turpie, but he's not willing to bury the hatchet – unless it's in Freddy's head. Robbie juggles cases and private life with his usual dexterity, but the more he tries to fix things the more trouble everyone's in.

#9 STITCH UP
Everything is coming up roses for Robbie Munro, newly married and living in the country with wife and child. That is until his wife takes up employment abroad just as old flame, Jill Green, asks him to investigate the unexplained death of her partner. Suspecting foul play, Jill insists Robbie turns poacher to gamekeeper and does whatever it takes to find the killer – with no expense spared. Another killer on the loose is child-murderer Ricky Hertz, whose twenty-year-old conviction is under scrutiny. Was the evidence at his trial fabricated? Suspicion falls on Robbie's father who now faces a criminal prosecution. The

only way to prove ex-Police Sergeant Alex Munro's innocence is for Robbie to show there was no miscarriage of justice.

#10 FIXED ODDS

On the home front, defence lawyer Robbie Munro is looking forward to the birth of his second child, while at work he's called to defend George 'Genghis' McCann on a charge of burglary, and Oscar 'the Showman' Bowman, snooker champion, on one of betting fraud. Genghis has stolen – and lost – a priceless masterpiece, while Oscar doesn't seem to have a defence of any kind. With another mouth to feed and promises of great rewards if he finds both painting and defence, Robbie has never been more tempted to fix the legal odds in his favour.

#11 BAD DEBT

Defence Lawyer Robbie Munro's wife has been stalked by a witness in a trial she is prosecuting. When the stalker is killed and Robbie is charged with murder his friends are only too willing to come up with schemes to prove his innocence. In the end though, will it be his enemies who make the difference?

#12 BEST DEFENCE

Honesty is the best policy, but it's not always the best defence

When football legend Dario's estranged wife is charged with murder, Robbie Munro finds himself instructed for the defence, but what exactly is the defence? As his client's version of events keeps chopping and changing Robbie is left trying to choose the best, while all the time trying to save his brother whose media career seems certain to be a victim of cancel culture.

#13 HOW COME?

How come Robbie Munro's clients keep landing him in trouble?

How come he's let himself be talked into a hopeless drugs trial?
How come his dad has a new girlfriend?
How come a corporate raider thinks Robbie can find his daughter's killer?
And how come it all seems to relate to a witch trial in 1679?

www.bestdefence.biz

Printed in Great Britain
by Amazon

27514796R00148